THE B..KKACKS

John McGahern was born in Dublin in 1934 and brought up in the Republic of Ireland. He trained to be a primary-school teacher before becoming a full-time writer, and later taught and travelled extensively. He lived in County Leitrim. The author of six highly acclaimed novels and four collections of short stories, he was the recipient of numerous awards and honours, including a Society of Authors Travelling Scholarship, the American-Irish Award, the Prix Etrangère Ecureuil and the Chevalier de l'Ordre des Arts et des Lettres. *Amongst Women*, which won both the GPA and the *Irish Times* Award, was shortlisted for the Booker Prize and made into a four-part BBC television series. His work appeared in numerous anthologies and has been translated into many languages. In 2005, his autobiography, *Memoir*, won the South Bank Literature Award. John McGahern died in 2006.

JOHN McGAHERN

The Barracks

faber and faber

First published in Great Britain in 1963
by Faber and Faber Limited
3 Queen Square London WC1N 3AU
First published in paperback in 1983
This paperback edition first published in 2008

Printed and bound in Great Britain by
CPI Bookmarque, Croydon, CR0 4TD

John McGahern is hereby identified as author of this work
in accordance with Section 77 of the Copyright,
Designs and Patents Act 1988.

A CIP record for this book is
available from the British Library

ISBN 978-0-571-22565-1

2 4 6 8 10 9 7 5 3 1

To
JAMES SWIFT

1

Mrs Reegan darned an old woollen sock as the February night came on, her head bent, catching the threads on the needle by the light of the fire, the daylight gone without her noticing. A boy of twelve and two dark-haired girls were close about her at the fire. They'd grown uneasy, in the way children can indoors in the failing light. The bright golds and scarlets of the religious pictures on the walls had faded, their glass glittered now in the sudden flashes of firelight, and as it deepened the dusk turned reddish from the Sacred Heart lamp that burned before the small wickerwork crib of Bethlehem on the mantelpiece. Only the cups and saucers laid ready on the table for their father's tea were white and brilliant. The wind and rain rattling at the window-panes seemed to grow part of the spell of silence and increasing darkness, the spell of the long darning-needle flashing in the woman's hand, and it was with a visible strain that the boy managed at last to break their fear of the coming night.

"Is it time to light the lamp yet, Elizabeth?" he asked.

He was overgrown for his age, with a pale face that had bright blue eyes and a fall of chestnut hair on the forehead. His tensed voice startled her.

"O Willie! You gave me a fright," she cried. She'd been sitting absorbed for too long. Her eyes were tired from darning in the poor light. She let the needle and sock fall into her lap and drew her hand wearily across her forehead, as if she would draw the pain that had started to throb there.

"I never felt the night come," she said and asked, "Can you read what time it is, Willie?"

He couldn't see the hands distinctly from the fire-place.

7

So he went quickly towards the green clock on the sideboard and lifted it to his face. It was ten past six.

The pair of girls came to themselves and suddenly the house was busy and full with life. The head was unscrewed off the lamp, the charred wicks trimmed, the tin of paraffin and the wide funnel got from the scullery, Elizabeth shone the smoked globe with twisted brown paper, Willie ran with a blazing roll of newspaper from the fire to touch the turned-up wicks into flame.

"Watch! Watch! Outa me way," he cried, his features lit up with love of this nightly lighting. Hardly had Elizabeth pressed down the globe inside the steel prongs of the lamp when the girls were racing for the windows.

"My blind was down the first!" they shouted.

"No! My blind was down the first!"

"Wasn't my blind down the first, Elizabeth?" they began to appeal. She had adjusted the wicks down to a steady yellow flame and fixed the lamp in its place—one side of the delf on the small tablecloth. She had never felt pain in her breasts but the pulse in the side of her head beat like a rocking clock. She knew that the aspirin box in the black medicine press with its drawn curtains was empty. She couldn't send to the shop for more. And the girls' shouts tore at her patience.

"What does it matter what blind was down or not down? —only give me a little peace for once," was on her lips when her name, her Christian name—Elizabeth—struck at her out of the child's appeal. She was nothing to these children. She had hoped when she first came into the house that they would look up to her as a second mother, but they had not. Then in her late thirties, she had believed that she could yet have a child of her own, and that, too, had come to nothing. At least, she thought, these children were not afraid of her, they did not hate her. So she gripped herself together and spoke pleasantly to them: they were soon quiet, laughing together on the shiny leatherette of the sofa, struggling for the torn rug that lay there.

Una was eleven, two years older than Sheila, almost

8

beautiful, with black hair and great dark eyes. Sheila was like her only in their dark hair. She was far frailer, her features narrow and sensitive, changeable, capable of looking wretched when she suffered.

They were still playing with the rug when Elizabeth took clothes out of a press that stood on top of a flour bin in the corner and draped them across the back of a plain wooden chair she turned to the fire. They stopped their struggling to watch her from the sofa, listening at the same time to find there was no easing in the squalls of rain that beat on the slates and blinded windows.

"Daddy'll be late tonight?" Sheila asked with the child's insatiable and obvious curiosity.

"What do you think I'm airin' the clothes for, Sheila? Do you hear what it's like outside?"

"He might shelter and come home when it fairs?"

"It has no sound of fairin' to me—only getting heavier and heavier. . . ."

They listened to the rain beat and wind rattle, and shivered at how lucky they were to be inside and not outside. It was wonderful to feel the warm rug on the sofa with their hands, the lamplight so soft and yellow on the things of the kitchen, the ash branches crackling and blazing up through the turf on the fire; and the lulls of silence were full of the hissing of the sap that frothed white on their sawed ends.

Elizabeth lowered the roughly made clothes-horse, a ladder with only a single rung at each end, hanging high over the fire, between the long black mantelpiece and the ceiling.

"Will you hold the rope for me?" she asked the boy and he held the rope that raised and lowered the horse while she lifted off a collarless shirt and felt it for dampness. She spread it on the back of a separate chair, the sleeves trailing on the hearth. He pulled up the horse again, hand over hand, and fastened the loop of the rope on its iron hook in the wall.

"Do you think will he be late tonight?" he asked.

"He's late already. You can never tell what hold-up he

9

might have. Or he might have just taken shelter in some house. I don't know why he should have to go out at all on a night like this. It makes no sense at all! O never join the guards when you grow up, Willie!"

"I'll not," he answered with such decision that she laughed.

"And what'll you be?"

"I'll not join the guards!"

They looked at each other. She knew he never trusted her, he'd never even confide his smallest dream in her. She seemed old to him, with her hair gone grey and the skin dried to her face. Not like the rich chestnut hair of his mother who had died, and the lovely face and hands that freckled in summer.

"It's time you all started your homework," Elizabeth ordered. "If your father sees a last rush at night there'll be trouble."

They got their schoolbags and stood up the card-table close to the lamp on the laid table. There was the usual squabbling and sharpening of pencils before they gave themselves to the hated homework, envious of their stepmother's apparent freedom, aware of all the noises of the barracks. They heard Casey, the barrack orderly, open the dayroom and porch doors, and the rattle of his bucket as he rushed out for another bucket of turf: the draughts banging doors all over the house as he came in and the flapping of his raincoat as he shook it dry like a dog in the hallway, then his tongs or poker thudding at the fire after the door had closed.

"Will I be goin' up to sleep with Mrs Casey tonight?" Una lifted her head to ask.

"I don't know—your nightdress is ready in the press if you are," she was answered.

"Guard Casey said this evenin' that I would," the child pursued.

"You'll likely have to go up so. You'll not know for certain till your father comes home," she was abruptly told. Elizabeth was tired to death, she could not bear more questions.

10

Casey's wife was childless and when barrack orderly fell to his turn and he had to sleep nights in the dayroom, on the official iron bed between the phone and the wall of the lock-up, Una would often have to go to sleep with her, for she couldn't be got to stay alone in the house on these nights. Una would get sweets or pennies, the slice of fruit cake and the glass of orange if she went and she didn't care whether Sheila had to sleep alone in their cold room or not, even when the smaller girl began to sob.

"What's wrong, Sheila?" Elizabeth was quick to notice.

"I'm afraid. I don't want to sleep on me own."

"Oh, you're a small girl no longer, Sheila. Una mightn't be going yet at all. And even if she is we can leave the lamp lit! Shure you'll not be afraid then, Sheila?"

Elizabeth coaxed and she was quietened. They turned to work again at their exercises, Elizabeth kneading dough in a tin basin on the table beside them, her arms bare to the elbows and a white dusting of flour on the back of her hands and wrists.

It was their father's tyres they first heard going past on the loose gravel and, "Daddy's home", they said to Elizabeth. He'd leave his high policeman's bicycle in the shed at the back and come in through the scullery.

His black cycling cape and pull-ups were shiny with wet when he came, his face chafed red with wind and rain. The narrow chinstrap held the cap firmly on his head, the medallion between the peak and the crown with its S twined through the Celtic G shining more vividly tonight against the darkened cloth. He carried his carbide bicycle lamp in his hand, big and silver, its blue jet of gas still burning, he left it to Willie to quench, quickly discarding his cycling clothes. The rain had penetrated the cape and pull-ups. There were dark patches of wet on the trousers, and on the tunic with its array of silver buttons, the three stripes of his rank on the sleeve.

"Wet to the bloody skin," he complained. "A terrible night to have to cycle about like a fool."

The children were very still. He had an intense pity for

himself and would fly into a passion of reproaches if he got any provocation. They watched him take off his tunic and boots. His socks left wet prints on the cement when he stood up.

"All the clothes are aired," Elizabeth said as she gave them to him off the back of the chair. "You'd better change quick."

He changed in the dark hall that led down to the day-room door at the bottom of the stairs and was soon back at the fire in his dry shirt and trousers. He towelled his face, then the back of his neck, then his feet. He pulled on socks and a pair of boots he didn't bother to lace.

"A terrible night," he muttered at the fire. "Not fit for a dog to be out in."

"In what direction were you?" Elizabeth asked.

"Round be Derrada," he answered.

He disliked talking about his police work in the house. He only answered Elizabeth because he needed to talk.

"And you'd never guess who I met?" he went reluctantly on.

"Who?"

"The bastard Quirke."

"The Superintendent!" Her exclamation seemed a faint protest against the coarseness. "What had him out, do you think?"

"He was lukin' for a chance he didn't get, you can be sure!"

He began to recount the clash, speaking with a slow, gloating passion and constant mimicry.

"He stopped in front of me and pulled down the window and asked, 'Is that you, Reegan?'

" 'That's me, sir,' says I.

" 'And is there some trouble?'

" 'No, sir,' says I.

" 'And what has you out on a night like this?'

" 'I'm out on patrol, sir,' says I.

" 'But are you mad, Reegan? Are you stone mad? No man in his senses would be out cycling on a night like this

12

without grave reason. Good God, Reegan, don't you realize that all rules and regulations yield at a certain point to human discretion? Do you want to get your death, man, cycling about on a night like this?'

" 'Aye, aye, sir,' says I. 'But I'll not get the sack, sir.' "

No word was lost on the children who pretended to be busy with their exercises. It was an old feud between their father and Superintendent Quirke. They loved this savage mimicry and it frightened them. They heard him laugh fiendishly, "That shuk him! That's what tuk the wind outa his sails! That's what shut him up, believe me!"

Then he repeated Quirke in a high, squeaky voice, the accent so outrageously exaggerated that it no longer resembled anything human.

" 'Even regulations, Reegan, must yield at a certain point to human discretion—even the law!—even the law, Reegan! —must yield at a certain point to Human Discretion.' "

"But you're only causing annoyance and trouble for yourself," Elizabeth interrupted. "You'll be only bringing him the more down on you. For the sake of a few words couldn't you let it go with him? What does it all matter?"

"You mean it'll be all the same in the end?" he asked shrewdly. "We'll be all nice and quiet when we're dead and gone—and nothin'll matter then? Is that it?"

She did not answer. She felt she could care no longer. She knew he'd go his own way, he'd heed no one, opposition would make him only more determined.

"You never give a thought for anybody," spun angrily over in her mind but she did not speak it. She feared she still loved him, and he seemed to care hardly at all, as if he had married a housekeeper. She watched him pull the jumper she had knitted for him over his head and draw on his old tunic, leaving the collar unclasped at the throat, the silver buckle of the belt swinging loosely on its black catches. It was more than four years now since she'd first met him, when she was home on convalescence from the London Hospital, worn out after nursing through the Blitz. She had come to the barracks to get some of her papers put in order.

13

He happened to be on his own in the dayroom when she came. It was twelve, for the Angelus had rung as she left her bicycle against the barrack wall.

"It must have been a terror there in London durin' the bombin'?" he had asked, a conventional thing to ask any one who had been there at the time and she smiled back the equally conventional, "You get used to it after a time. You go on almost as if nothing was happening after the first few scares."

"It's like a fella hangin', I suppose," he laughed. "He hasn't much of a choice. But what amazes me, though, is that one of those rich Americans didn't run off with a girl like you on us."

She blushed hot at the flattery. He seemed so handsome to her in his blue uniform. He came to the door to see her out. She saw him watch from the barrack window as she cycled out the short avenue and turned left up the village.

The desire for such a day could drag one out of a sickness, it was so true to the middle of the summer. She felt so full of longing and happiness that she crossed from the shop to the chapel when she'd got the groceries for the house. The eternal medals and rosary beads were waiting on the spikes of the gate for whoever had lost them; the evergreens did not even sway in their sleep in the churchyard, where bees droned between the graves from dandelion to white clover; and the laurelled path between the brown flagstones looked so worn smooth that she felt she was walking on them again with her bare feet of school confession evenings through the summer holidays.

The midday glare was dimmed within, the church as cool as the stone touch of its holy water font, but she could get herself to say no formal prayer, all her habits and acceptances lost in an impassioned tumult of remembering.

A cart was rocking past on the road when she came out, its driver sunk deep in the hay on top of the load, a straw hat pulled down over his face. The way his body rolled to every rock and sway of the cart he could have been asleep in the sunshine. The reins hung slack. A cloud of flies swarmed about the mare's head and her black coat was stained with sweat all along the lines of the harness, but they rolled on as if they had eternity for their journey.

Whether he was ashamed or not to pass the shops so sleepily in the broad middle of the day, he started awake at the chapel gate and noticed Elizabeth.

"Powerful weather we're havin'," he shouted down, and it came to her as a prayer of praise, she never had such longing to live for ever.

She was helping her mother and brother on their small farm then, and they had opposed her marriage to Reegan from the beginning.

"There's three childer and his wife is barely cauld in the grave, remember. That's no aisy house to be walkin' into! An' what'll the neighbours say about it? Himself can be no angel neither, not if quarter of the accounts be true," her brother had said one autumn night in the kitchen while their mother stirred the coals on the hearth and supported him by her half-silence.

"Take heed to what he says! Marryin' isn't something, believe me, that can be jumped into today and outa tomorrow. It's wan bed you have to sleep on whether it's hard or soft, wance you make it. An' remember, as he tauld you, it's no aisy house to be walkin' into, but I'm sayin' nothin'. It's for your God above to direct you!"

Elizabeth knew it would suit them if she stayed, stayed to nurse her mother as she crippled, the mother who had seemed so old when she died three months ago that not even her children had wept at the funeral, she meant as little as a flower that has withered in a vase behind curtains through the winter when it's discovered and lifted out on a day in spring.

And it would have suited her brother who'd never marry if she had to stop and keep house for him, but she did not stop. She married Reegan. She was determined to grasp at a life of her own desiring, no longer content to drag through with her repetitive days, neither happy nor unhappy, merely passing them in the wearying spirit of service; and the more

15

the calls of duty tried to tie her down to this life the more intolerably burdensome it became.

She'd not stay on this small farm among the hills, shut away from living by its pigsties and byres and the rutted lane that twisted out to the road between stone walls. She would marry Reegan, or she'd go back to London if she could ever forget the evening she came away from the operating theatre with Sister Murphy.

"I lit three candles today in St. Anne's before the Blessed Virgin," the frail Sister had said.

"Are you praying for something special? Or is there something worrying you, Brigid?" Elizabeth asked out of politeness.

"If I tell you, you'll not mention it to anybody, will you?"

"No. Why should I want to? But, maybe then it might be better not to tell me at all. . . ."

"But you'll not mention it to anybody?"

"No! No!"

"I am praying to Her to send me a man—some nice, decent person."

Elizabeth stared at her in astonishment, but this frail woman of more than fifty had never been more serious in her life. She had blurted it out with such sudden, confiding joy. It seemed obscene for a minute; yet, when Elizabeth thought, the desire itself was not ludicrous, no more than a young girl's, but only the ferocious ruthlessness of life had made it in time seem so. Hardly fifteen years separated the two women. Elizabeth had blanched before this vision of herself growing old and blind with the pain of ludicrous longing. She had few hesitations about marrying and she believed she loved Reegan. The children weren't hostile, even if they'd remained somewhat reserved. And for a time she was happy, extremely happy at first.

When Reegan had his clothes changed he felt new and clean before the fire, drowsily tired after miles of pedalling through the rain. He was in high good humour as he pulled his chair up to his meal on the table, but he wasn't easy until he had asserted himself against Elizabeth's, "Couldn't you

16

let it go for once with the Superintendent? You'll be only bringing him down on top of you?"

"When we're dead it'll be all the same," he asserted. "But bejasus we're not altogether in that state yet! It's still God for us all and may the devil take the hindmost. Isn't that right, Willie?"

Elizabeth said nothing. She gathered up his wet clothes and put them to dry. She listened to him talk with the three children.

"What did ye learn at school today?"

They were puzzled, nothing new or individual coming to their minds out of the long, grey rigmarole that had been drummed all day in school, one dry fact the same as the next.

"English, Irish . . ." Willie began, hesitant.

"And sums," continued Reegan, laughing. "Shure that tells nothin'. Did ye learn anything new? Did ye learn anything that ye didn't know yesterday?"

He saw by the boy's embarrassment that he'd be able to tell him nothing, so he turned to the girls, almost clumsily kind, "Can the lassies tell me anything when this great fool of ours only goes to school to recreate himself?"

Neither could they think of anything. They had experienced nothing. All they'd heard was fact after fact. That nine nines were eighty-one. That the London they didn't know was built on the Thames they didn't know.

"Shure ye might as well be stoppin' at home and be givin' Elizabeth here a hand about the house," he teased, rather gently, a merriment in his blue eyes.

"Do ye know why ye go to school at all?"

"To learn," Willie ventured again, with renewed courage.

"To learn what?"

"Lessons."

Reegan laughed. He felt a great sense of his superiority, not so much over the children, he took that for granted, but over every one who had anything to do with them.

"You'll never get wit, Willie! Were you never tauld that you go to school to learn to think for yourself and not give two tuppenny curses for what anybody else is thinkin'?"

17

"And a lot of good that'd do them," Elizabeth put in dryly; it shook Reegan, then amused him.

"A lot of good it did for any of us," he laughed.

"We might as well have been learnin' our facts and figures and come out in every other way just as God sent us in—as long as we learned how to bow the knee and kiss the ring. If we had to learn how to do that we were right bejasus! And we'd have all got on like a house on fire! Isn't that right, Elizabeth?"

"That's perfectly right," she agreed, glad he was happy.

He made the sign of the cross as he finished his meal. He'd never known mental prayer, so his lips shaped the words of the Grace as he repeated them to himself. He sat facing the fire again, beginning to feel how intimate he'd been with them ever since he came into the house tonight, his mind still hot after the clash with Quirke, and he fiercely wanted to be separate and alone again. The pain and frustration that the shame of intimacy brings started to nag him to desperation. He didn't want to talk any more, nor even read the newspaper. He would have to go down to Casey in the dayroom before ten and fill his report into the Patrol Book, but that could wait its turn. All he wanted now was to lounge before the fire and lose himself in the fantastic flaming of the branches: how they spat or leaped or burst in a shower of sparks, changing from pale red to white to shifting copper, taking on shapes as strange as burning cities. The children's steel nibs scratched in the silence when Elizabeth wasn't moving. She knew the mood he was in and lingered over the little jobs tonight, stirring the porridge for the morning and watching the cake brown in the oven, putting off the time when she'd take her darning or library book and sit with him, when the drowsy boredom of the hours before bedtime would begin.

Down the hallway the dayroom door opened and Casey's iron-shod boots rang on the cement. They thought he might be rushing out again into the rain for a bucket of turf, but the even, ponderous steps all policemen acquire came towards them in the kitchen. He tapped on the door and

18

waited for the disturbed Reegan's, "Come in", before he entered. He was over six feet, as tall as Reegan, but bald, and his face had the waxen pallor of candles. The eyes alone were bright, though all surface, without any resting-place. He carried the heavy Patrol Book under his arm.

"God bless all here," he greeted.

"And you too, Ned," they returned.

Reegan was glad of the disturbance. Minutes ago he'd wanted nothing but to be left alone, but he was more than glad by this to be disturbed out of broodings that were becoming more lonely and desperate. He pulled his own chair to one side, eager to make room at the fire.

"Don't trouble to move yourself, Sergeant," Casey assured, "I'll work me way in all right, don't you worry. I just thought that if I carted you up the book it'd save you the trouble of comin' down."

"That's powerful," Reegan praised. "I'd be down long ago only I couldn't tear meself away from the fire here."

"And small blame to you! The devil himself wouldn't venture down to that joint on a night like this. I stuffed a few auld coats against the butt of the door but the draughts still go creepin' up the legs of yer britches like wet rats.

"God's truth," he continued, "I was gettin' the willies down there on me own: lukin' at the same bloody wonders all the evenin' in the fire and expectin' to be lifted outa me standin' at any minute be the phone!"

Then suddenly he felt he was complaining too much about himself and stopped and tried to turn the conversation with all the awkwardness of over-consciousness.

"And tell me, did you meet anything strange or startlin' on your travels, Sergeant?"

"Aye!" Reegan tried to joke. "I met something all right —whether you can call it strange or startlin' or not is another matter."

He was attempting a levity he didn't feel, it left greater feeling of anger and frustration behind it than violent speech.

"What did you meet with, Sergeant?"

"Did you ever hear of His Imperial Majesty, John James Quirke? Did you?"

"Jay," Casey exclaimed in real amazement. "You never met the Super, did you? What was takin' him out on an evenin' like this?"

Reegan began to recount the clash; and it had become more extravagant, more comic and vicious since the first telling. When he finished he shouted, "That shuk him, believe me! That's what tuk the wind outa his sails!" and as he shouted he tried to catch Casey's face unaware, trying to read into his mind.

"Bejay, Sergeant, but he'll have it in for us from this on. He'll do nothing but wait his chance. You can sit on that for certain comfort. As sure as there's a foot on a duck, Sergeant!"

"But what do I care? Why should I care about the bastard?" Reegan ground back.

Elizabeth drifted from between them. She gathered the sagging fire together and heaped on fresh wood. The blast of heat on her face made her sway with sleep. She felt how ill she was—and still Reegan's voice stabbed into the quiet of the big barrack kitchen, harsh with mockery and violence.

She lifted the kettle and filled it from the bucket of spring water on the scullery table, cold and damp there, the table littered with cabbage leaves and the peelings of turnips that she'd been too tired to tidy away; if anything, the rain drummed more heavily on the low roof—sometimes it seemed as if it might never cease, the way it beat down in these western nights. She replaced the old raincoat of the children's against the bottom of the door as she came in and lowered the kettle so that it hung full in the flames.

Soon it would start to murmur over the blazing fire, then break into a steady hum, as if into song. She saw the lamplight, so softly golden on the dark blinds that were drawn against the night. And she could have cried out at Reegan for some peace.

Were their days not sufficiently difficult to keep in order as they were without calling in disaster? Quirke had the heavy hand of authority behind him and Reegan could only ruin himself. And if he got the sack! What then? What then?

Her woman's days had no need of change. They were full and too busy, wanting nothing but to be loved. There was the shrill alarm clock at eight in the barracks morning and the raking of the ashes over the living coals close to midnight: between these two instants, as between tides, came the retreating nights of renewal and the chores of the days on which her strength was spent again, one always unfinished and two more eternally waiting, yet so colourless and small that only on a reel of film projected slowly could they be separated and named; and as no one noticed them they were never praised.

She cleared her throat as she stooped over the fire, reached for the hankie in the fold of her sleeve. It wasn't there. She spat softly, without thinking. The mucus hissed against the hot ashes. She shuddered as a tiny mushroom of the pale timber ash drifted up. How she'd always hated Reegan's spitting on the floor, then trying to rub it into the cement with a drag of his boot! Now she was no better! And to plague her, a vision of herself in London before the war flashed on her mind, a spring Sunday in London, when the light is grey and gentle as anything on earth. She had come out the great black hospital gates, a red tartan scarf thrown back on her shoulder; and turned right, up the marvellous width of Whitechapel Road, away from the crowds milling into the Lane, for it was the morning. Now she was spitting like any common slut in a barrack kitchen. It was with the abjection of a beaten animal that she lifted her knitting and sat down close to Casey and the three children, who had finished their exercises and come into the circle about the fire.

Reegan sat at the table, filling his report into the Patrol Book. They were silent as he wrote till Casey asked the children:

"Ye're finished the auld lessons?"

"All's finished," they told him quietly.

"And ye have them all off?"

21

"Aye."

"Well, that's the way to be. Be able to puzzle the school-master."

"I wouldn't be sure they're that well known," said Elizabeth.

"Well, you'll get nothin' without the learnin' these days. Pass the exams. That's what gets people on. That and swindlin'. I didn't do much of either meself. More's the pity. And signs are on it!"

They laughed at Casey's rueful grin. He brought a wonderful ease with him sometimes into the house, the black hands of the clock would take wings. They loved to sit with him at the fire, listening to the talk, feeling the marvellous minutes melt like sweetness in the mouth for ever.

Reegan wrote quickly at the table, to the well-practised formula, and only when he came to describe the weather had he to pause. He wasn't sure of the wind's direction. He remembered catching his breath at the way it clawed at his face and chest as he turned downhill from Ardcare; and then a mile farther on of the same straight road it came behind him, making the bicycle shift like a boat in full sail, its course warped in some way by the solid beech trees behind the demesne wall.

"What way is the wind blowin', Ned? Is it from the south-west?"

"About that," Casey pondered to answer. "It was comin' from Moran's Bay when I was out for the turf. It seems about the only direction it knows how to blow from," he added with a dry laugh.

Reegan was satisfied and turned back to finish his report but the wind's direction continued to amuse Casey.

"Where does the south-west wind come from, William Reegan?" he asked in the tones of a pompous schoolmaster.

"From the Atlantic Ocean," Willie entered into the game, all the children's faces, and even Elizabeth's bright at the clown's face Casey had on for the performance.

"Very good, young Reegan! And can you tell me now what it gathers on its long journey across the oceans?"

22

"It gathers moisture," Willie choked.

"Very right, my boy! I see you are one boy who comes to school to learn something other than villainy and rascality. And then as I have repeated day-in, day-out, while the hairs of me head turned grey, it strikes against the mountains, rises to a great height, and pisses down on the poor unfortunates who earn their daily bread by the sweat of their brows in this holy, catholic, and apostolic country of Ireland."

There was a stifled roar of laughter as Reegan wrote, frowning to keep his concentration.

"You're a terrible man, Ned," chaffed Elizabeth.

"But it's the God's truth!" he protested. "You know what Cromwell said: Get roasted alive in hell or drownded and perished in Connaught."

Naturally timid, the little comic success seemed to release him from the burden of himself. Everything was relaxed and easy as Reegan closed the Patrol Book and pulled his chair in among them, but even so Casey shirked asking for Una to spend the night with his wife, and he'd have to ask soon or it would be too late. Reegan could be moody and strange. At any time he might resent this constant call on Una. A refusal could shatter Casey's ease of mind for the whole night. His nervous fear came out in the painfully round-about, "The Missus was wonderin' if it'd be all right for Una to come up with me when I'm goin' up for the bit of supper, for to stop the night."

Tonight he had no cause for fear.

"Shure she can go. But that's the woman's territory. Whatever she says," deferred Reegan.

Elizabeth had no real say, though this social deference pleased her so, and she tried to catch Reegan's eyes with a smile of gratefulness as she assented, "She can, of course. Her nightdress is ready there in the press."

Una couldn't conceal her delight, though she tried. Nor could Sheila conceal her terror of the loneliness in the cold room. Both tried to suppress any expression of their feelings. They knew their places. They were simply pawns. And this

23

world of their father and Casey and Elizabeth was as unknowable to them as the intolerable world of God is to the grown, if they have not dulled their sense of the mystery of life with the business or distractions of the day and the hour. All the two black-haired girls could do was sit there and wait, coming and going as they were willed.

"I don't like troublin' you all the time like this," Casey shuffled.

Elizabeth stopped it. "Don't be talkin' foolish. Una thinks she can't get up half quick enough. Isn't that right, Una?"

The dark child smiled and blushed. No more.

"We don't know what we'd do only for Una. We'd be lost. That woman of mine would go off her head if she had to stop all night in that house on her own."

"And no one would blame her," Elizabeth managed to end.

Casey's embarrassment was over. He was as happy as he could be. He looked at the clock and it was already nine. He had nothing more to do before he slept, nothing but the repetitions that had become more than his nature. He'd bring Una with him when he went for his supper; kiss his wife at the door when he left again for the barracks a half-hour later: she'd stand with her hand on the edge of the door until she had heard the white gate that led on to the avenue clang behind him, it was her habit. Then the rest of the night was plain sailing: bring down the mattress and blankets from upstairs and make up his bed beneath the phone, lock the door, put the key on the sill, take out his beads to say a decade of the rosary with his few night prayers, set the alarm for the morning, rake the fire, turn down the oil lamp on the wall before he got into bed. He was at least master of these repetitions, they had no power to disturb him, he knew them in his blood; and they ran there like a drug.

"What about a game of cards? It's ages since we had a game," he said, now that he was no longer troubled. A pack of cards was found behind a statue of St Therese on the sideboard, the folding card-table fixed in the centre of the hearth. The cards were dealt and played. Elizabeth kept the scores on the inside of a torn Gold Flake packet. There was no tension in the play, no stakes, only the children excited as the night was cheated and hurried to its mid-hour.

From the outside the heavy porch door was shouldered open, small stones wedged beneath its bottom grinding on the concrete, the knocker clattering through the barracks. Steps lingered about the door of the dayroom before they came up the hall. They held their hands instinctively upright to listen.

"That's Jim's steps for sure," Casey said before Brennan knocked and entered.

He was small for a policeman, the bare five feet nine of the regulations, his face thin, and the bones standing out. He looked overcome in the heavy woollen greatcoat.

"A terrible night that's in it," he said.

"A terrible night."

The voices echoed him, more or less in unison, the hoarse chant of a prayer.

"I saw the light turned low in the dayroom. I was thinkin' ye'd all be here."

And he left his flashlamp down on the window-sill, his greatcoat and cap on the pedal sewing-machine just beneath. There was no further need of the cards. They were raked up and the green table lifted out.

"You let no grass grow under yer feet tonight, Jim?" he was asked, for it wasn't yet ten, and it was always later than ten when the policemen came to make their reports and sign themselves out for the night.

"I was makin' a bird cradle all the evenin' with the lads," he explained. "We just managed to make it a minute ago there. So I thought it might be as well to face out for here at wance and be finished with it for the night."

They could see him on his knees in the kitchen of their rooms across the river, most of his eight children gathered round, building the cradle out of sallies and the cement coloured rods of elder. When the snow came they'd set it on the street. And all through the hard weather they'd have cold thrushes and blackbirds.

"We got a great strong cradle med," he added. "None better in Ireland!"

The others smiled, Brennan's intense pride in everything that came into his possession was a barrack joke, it was artless as a child's.

"The best woman in Ireland to get a bargain," he'd say when his wife came from town on a shopping Saturday; and when he came home himself with the little yellowed bundle of Early York in spring, the plants still knotted in their ragged belt of straw, he had already, "A hundred of the best heads of cabbage in Ireland. Without question or doubt!"

"And how is Mrs Brennan's cold?" asked Elizabeth quietly.

"She's still coughin' away. A fierce rasp in her chest. But nothin'll get that woman of mine to stay up in bed," he complained proudly.

"She'd be wiser to stop. Is she takin' anything for it?"

"She rubs on a bit of Vick at night. That's all I ever see her do. She always says a cauld has to run its course."

"The bed's the only man," advised Casey. "It's the only place you can keep your temperature even. She needn't think that she can't be done without—the very best of us can be done without. So she's as well to take it aisy. Time and tide, they say, waits for no man, nor woman neither."

It was the end, this litany of truisms, draining away whatever little life the conversation ever had. In the way women are so quick to sense, Elizabeth knew it was the time to do things. She got cups and saucers from the dresser, bread from the white enamelled bread box, tea out of a paper bag on the mantelpiece. They took the cups in their hands at the fire, and a plate of buttered soda bread was passed about.

Mullins came as they were eating. He was no older than the others, but red and swollen, a raw smell of porter on his breath, though he appeared more depressed than tipsy.

"A wild night!" he said. "It seems I'm the last of the Mohicans."

"But the last shall be first, remember," Casey couldn't

resist quoting. With his weak laugh it came like a sneer of derision. Mullins stiffened at the door with resentment.

"Aye!" he answered inarticulately back. "And the first might be last."

"Don't be standin' there, John. There's a cup of tea just waiting for you," Elizabeth urged.

She pulled out a chair and Reegan, who had been taking less and less part in the conversation, just lying in a bored stupor in the chair, laughed, "It's not who's first or last counts in this house. It's to be in time for the tay. That's what counts. And you couldn't have timed it nicer, John!" as the ungainly old policeman sat down.

It took all the hatred that the gibe brought. Mullins laughed so tipsily that the cup rocked over and back on his saucer.

"Bejasus!" he swore. "It seems I med it on the eleventh hour, surely."

Reegan began to tell his clash with Quirke to Brennan and Mullins, Casey forced to listen again; and the tones of violence had now taken the resonance of a constant theme repeating itself through the evening.

They listened nervously to his frustration and spleen wear itself to the end of its telling. When he finished Mullins burst out in drunken passion that, "They can't ride rough-shod over us these days. Them days are gone. They can try it on. But that's all—bejasus!"

"You'd be surprised what they can do," Casey argued with unusual conviction. "Things don't change that quick. They might luk different, that's all. But if you *wance* cross them they'll get rid of you, no matter whether they can or they can't. They'll find ways and means, don't worry. Who do you think the Chief Super's goin' to stand up for? For John Mullins or Mr. Quirke? Power, let me tell you, always stands up for power."

"But what do I care? What the hell do I care?" Reegan shouted and it was another argument.

Examples began to be quoted, old case histories dragged up for it to end as it began—with nothing proven, no one's

27

convictions altered in any way, it becoming simply the brute clash of ego against ego, any care for tolerance or meaning or truth ground under their blind passion to dominate. And the one trophy they all had to carry away was a gnawing resentment of each other's lonely and passing world.

Even that resentment went quickly as a sudden liking can when Brennan steered the antagonism to a safe stop against the boy, "What does young Willie think of all this? Will he join the Force when he grows up?"

"Not if he has any sense in his skull," Reegan intervened. He spoke with the hotness of argument. The others were cooled and tired of it now.

"But do you think will he be the measurement?" Casey asked, preferring to ignore the challenge.

"We'll have to put a stone on his head, that's what we'll have to do soon with the way he's growin' up on us," Mullins said kindly and then he laughed. "But I'm afraid he'll never be *thick* enough."

"Thirty-six inches across the chest, Willie, and a yard thick with solid ignorance like the fella from Connemara; then five feet nine inches against the wall in your stockin' feet and you're right for the Force, Willie. All the requirements laid down by the regulations."

The pun was a favourite that never grew worn, always bringing back to them the six months they spent training in the Depot when they were nineteen or twenty, in the first days of the Irish Free State.

The British had withdrawn. The Capital was in a fever of excitement and change. New classes were forming, blacksmiths and clerks filling the highest offices in the turn of an hour. Some who had worried how their next loaf or day might come were attending ceremonial functions. There was a brand new tricolour to wave high; a language of their own to learn; new anthems of faith-and-fatherland to beat on the drum of the multitude; but most of all, unseen and savage behind these floral screens, was the struggle for the numbered seats of power.

These police recruits walking the Phoenix Park in the

evenings, or on the lighted trams that went down past Phibsboro' to the music halls, what were their dreams? They knew that lightning promotion could come to the favoured. They saw the young girls stand to watch them from the pavements as they marched to Mass on Sunday mornings.

Now they sat and remembered, thirty years later, waiting to go to their homes in the rain.

"Some of the auld drill sergeants were a terror," Casey comically mused as if he was enjoying bitterness itself. "Do ye remember By Garrup?"

"Ah, Jasus," Mullins swore. "As if any mortal could forget him. . . ."

" 'By Garrup, look at the creel of turf on Mullins's back,' he used roar, the auld bastard! 'You're not on the bog now, Mullins—By Garrup! Head to the front! Right wheel! Chests out! Ye're not carryin' yeer auld dyin' grandmothers up the stairs on yeer backs now, By Garrup! Mark time! Lift the knees!'

"Oh, the auld bastard," Mullins roared. They all joined him, loving few things better than these caricatures. The night that had hung about them like a responsibility seemed now too short, it was nearly wasted now and it seemed to be so quickly on the march.

"Do you mind Spats at the law classes," Casey continued. "The concate of the boyo!

"A legal masterpiece, gentlemen of the jury, is the proper distribution of the proper quantity of ink on the proper number of white pages. That, gentlemen, is simply, solely and singularly the constitution of any masterpiece."

"But wasn't he said to be wan of the cleverest men in Ireland?" Brennan interrupted suddenly. "Wasn't he a B.A. and a barrister?"

The interruption annoyed Casey intensely. He had been a conductor for a few months on the Dublin trams before joining the police.

"A barrister! What's a barrister? A chancer of the first water," he derided. "Hundreds of them are walkin' round

Dublin without a sole on their shoes. They'd hardly have even their tram fare!"

"But don't some of them make more than £5,000 a year?"

"Yes—some of them!—many are called, James, but few are chosen, as you and I should know at this stage of our existence," Casey quoted in such a funereal and sanctified tone that it left no doubt about what he thought of Brennan's offering.

Brennan had been silent till then. He was a poor mimic. Neither could he sing. He had often tried, patrolling the roads alone, but catching the flat tones of his own voice he'd grow embarrassed and silent again. He envied Casey and Mullins their flow of talk, their ability to shine in company, and he did not know that those content to listen are rarest of all. He felt bored to distraction at having to sit silent for so long. He was determined to get a foothold in the conversation.

"Isn't it strange," he said, "that with all the men that ever went into the Depot none of them were exactly six feet?"

"That's right," Mullins asserted. "No man ever born was exactly six feet. It's because Jesus Christ was exactly six feet and no man since could be the same height. That's why it's supposed to be!"

He had taken the words out of Brennan's mouth, who twisted on the chair with annoyance and frustration.

"I often heard that," Elizabeth joined, more to counteract Reegan's bored restlessness and silence than any wish of her own to speak.

"It's like the Blessed Virgin and Original Sin," Brennan rushed out again and went on to quote out of the Catechism. *"The Blessed Virgin Mary by a singular privilege of grace was preserved free from original sin and that privilege is called her Immaculate Conception."*

"Six feet is the ideal height for a man," Mullins asserted again. "Anything bigger is gettin' too big. While anything smaller is gettin' too small. It's the ideal height for a man."

"Kelly, the Boy from Killann," said Casey, "was seven feet with some inches to spare.

30

"Seven feet was his height with some inches to spare
And he looked like a king in command,"

he quoted out of the marching song.

There was immediate feeling of blasphemy. The song connected up with Jesus Christ, though Casey had meant no harm, he said it just because it happened into his head and he'd decided to say something. In the subsequent uneasiness the time was noticed. It was five to eleven.

"There'll be murder," Casey jumped. "That woman of mine'll be expectin' me for this past hour."

He put on his cap and coat in the dayroom. Elizabeth hurried Una so that she was waiting for him at the door. She wore wellingtons and had the parcel of her nightdress clasped inside her blue raincoat.

"It's time for any respectable man to be makin' home," either Brennan or Mullins said and they went down to sign the books and left almost on the others' heels.

Reegan rose from the fire and pulled back the circle of chairs. His hair was tousled from scratching it with sleep, the collar of the tunic still unclasped, his feet loose in the boots.

"It's a good cursed job that those don't decide to come up many nights," he complained.

His face was ugly with resentment.

"Oh, it wasn't so much harm, was it?" Elizabeth pleaded. "The nights are often long enough on us."

"But were you listenin' to that rubbish?—Jesus Christ and Kelly, the Boy from Killann. Sufferin' duck, but did you hear that rubbish?"

He was shouting. Elizabeth had to gather herself together before answering quietly, "It's only a saying that He was six feet tall. Does it matter very much? Did you never hear it?"

"Of course I heard it," he cried, beside himself. "I'm not deaf, unfortunately. If you listened long enough to everything said around here you'd soon hear the Devil himself talkin'."

Then he grew quieter and said without passion, as if

31

brooding, "Surely you're not gettin' like the rest of them, girl?"

She drew closer. She felt herself no longer a woman growing old. She wasn't conscious of herself any more, of whatever beauty had been left her any more than her infirmities, for she was needed.

"No, but does it matter what they say?" she said. "Hadn't the night to pass?"

The night had to pass, but not in that manner, was how he reacted. He turned towards the radio that stood on a small shelf of its own, some bills and letters scattered beside its wet battery, between the sideboard and curtained medicine press.

"Such rubbish to have to listen to," he muttered. "And in front of the childer. . . . And the same tunes night-in, night-out, the whole bloody year round."

He switched on the radio. The Sweepstake programme was ending. To soft music a honeyed voice was persuading, "It makes no difference where you are—You can wish upon a star."

It should all make you want to cry. You were lonely. The night was dark and deep. You must have some wish or longing. The life you lead, the nine to five at the office, the drudgery of a farm, the daily round, cannot be endured without hope.

"So now before you sleep make up your mind to buy a Sweepstake ticket and the first prize of £50,000 out of a total of £200,000 in prizes on this year's Grand National may be yours."

The music rose for the young night. It was Venice, the voice intoned. There was moonlight on the sleeping canals as the power of longing was given full sway. A boy and a girl drift in their boat. There is a rustle of silken music from the late-night taverns. They clasp each other's hands in the boat. The starlight is in her hair and his face is lifted to hers in the moonlight. He is singing softly and his voice drifts across the calm water. It is Venice and their night of love. . . .

In spite of themselves they felt half-engulfed by this in-

32

duced flood of sentimentality and sick despair. Reegan switched it off as the speaking voice faded for a baritone to ease the boy's song of love into the music. The house was dead still.

"The news is long over," he said. "Are ye all ready for the prayers? We should have them said ages ago."

He took a little cloth purse from his watch pocket and let the beads run into his palm. He put a newspaper down on the cement and knelt with his elbows on the table, facing his reflection in the sideboard mirror.

Elizabeth's and the children's beads were kept in an ornamental white vase on the dresser. Willie climbed on a chair to get them from the top shelf. Elizabeth's beads were a Franciscan brown, their own pale mother-of-pearl with silver crosses that they'd been given for their First Communion.

They blessed themselves together and he began:

"*Thou, O Lord, will open my lips*",

"*And my tongue shall announce Thy praise*," they responded.

They droned into the *Apostles' Creed*. Then *Our Fathers* and *Hail Marys* and *Glory be to the Fathers* were repeated over and over in their relentless monotony, without urge or passion, no call of love or answer, the voices simply murmuring away in a habit or death, their minds not on what they said, but blank or wandering or dreaming over their own lives.

Elizabeth's fingers slipped heedlessly along the brown beads. No one noticed that she'd said eleven Hail Marys in her decade. She had tried once or twice to shake herself to attention and had lapsed back again.

She felt tired and sick, her head thudding, and she put her hands to her breasts more than once in awareness of the cysts there. She knelt with her head low between her elbows in the chair, changing position for any distraction, the words she repeated as intrusive as dust in her mouth while the pain of weariness obtruded itself over everything that made up her consciousness.

She knew she must see a doctor, but she'd known that months before, and she had done nothing. She'd first discovered the cysts last August as she dried herself at Malone's Island, a bathing-place in the lake, not more than ten minutes through the meadows; and she remembered her fright and incomprehension when she touched the right breast again with the towel and how the noise of singing steel from the sawmill in the woods pierced every other sound in the evening.

What the doctor would do was simple. He'd send her for a biopsy. She might be told the truth or she might not when they got the result back, depending on them and on herself. If she had cancer she'd be sent for treatment. She had been a nurse. She had no illusions about what would happen.

She had been only away from the house once since she was married. She shuddered at how miserable she'd been those three days, the first blight on her happiness.

A cousin had invited her to her wedding in Dublin. She'd no desire to go, but that she had been remembered so surprised her with delight that she told them about the letter at the dinner hour.

"You might as well take the chance when you get it. It mightn't be offered again. It'd be a break for you. It'd take you out of yourself for a few days," she was pressed to go.

"But look at the cost! The train fare. The hotel. A wedding present for Nuala. And how on earth would I get past those shop windows full of things without spending every penny we have?" she laughed.

"Never you mind, girl. If the money's wanted it'll be always found," Reegan said.

"Why don't you go, Elizabeth, when you get the chance?" Willie asked wonderingly.

"Who'd look after the place while I was away, Willie?"

"That's a poor excuse," Reegan said. "There's no fear of the auld barracks takin' flight while you're away, though more's the pity!"

"And what if some one ran away with you when I was gone?" she asked flirtatiously.

"Not a fear, girl," he laughed. "Every dog for his day but you, you girl, it's your day."

She was flattered and satisfied. She would not go. Here they had need of her. What would she be at the wedding? A seat at the bottom of the breakfast-table, a relative who had married a widower in the country, a parable to those who had known her as a young girl.

"I think you should go, Elizabeth. I'd go if I was in your place, definitely," Willie persuaded with obstinate persistence.

"But who'd cook and wash and bake and sew, Willie?"

"We would, Elizabeth. We'd stop from school in turn. We could buy loaves. . . ."

"You only think you could, Willie," she tried to laugh it off nervously.

"We'd manage somehow," he enthused, heedless of his child's place in the house, he gestured excitedly with his hands and went on too quickly to be stopped.

"I think you'd be foolish to miss Dublin. Not many people ever get to Dublin. For the few days we'd be well able to manage. Shure, Elizabeth, didn't we manage for ages before you ever came?"

It fell as natural as a blessing, "Didn't we manage for ages before you ever came?" And they'd manage, too, if she was gone. She stood with the shock. She must have been holding something for she remembered not to let it fall. Then she broke down.

She thought she'd never be able to climb the stairs to her room, the things of the house gathering in against her; she thanked God that the dayroom door wasn't open on her way.

She heard Reegan shout in the kitchen.

"Now do you see what you have done? Now do you see what you have done? Jesus Christ, can you not keep your mouth shut for wan minute of the day?"

Then the boy's terrified protest, "I didn't mean anything! I didn't mean any harm, Daddy."

35

Reegan's shouts again, "Will you never understand? Will you never grow up? Will you never understand that women look on things different to men?"

She heard his feet follow her on the hollow stairs. She was sitting on the bed's edge when he came into the room. She could not lift her head. He'd look as unreal as all people pleading.

"The lad meant nothing. He was only thinkin' that we'd be able to give you a holiday at last. Shure you know yourself that we'd never be able to get on without you?"

He put his hands on her shoulders, she'd no wish to create a scene, she dried her face with her sleeve.

"I couldn't help it," she said, looking at him with a nervous smile. "But it doesn't matter. It was only that it came so sudden."

"Would you like to go to the wedding? The lad was only wantin' to please you. . . ."

"Maybe, I should go," she had tried to look bright. She had not wanted to go. It had been simply easier to go than to stay then.

She felt the pain at last was easing. The rosary was droning to its end in the kitchen. The decades were over. Reegan was sing-songing,

Mystical Rose
Tower of David
Tower of Ivory
House of Gold.

His face a mask without expression, staring as if tranced at its image in the big sideboard mirror, his fingers even now instinctively moving on the beads, the voice completely toneless that repeated Her praises, their continual "Pray for us", like punctuating murmurs of sleep.

"The Dedication of the Christian Family," began the last prayers, the trimmings.

Prayer for the Canonization of Blessed Oliver Plunkett—whose scorched head, they remembered reading on the leaflet, was on show in a church in Drogheda.

36

Prayers for all they were bound to pray for in duty, promise or charity.

Prayer for a happy death.

And the last prayer, the last terrible acknowledgement, the long iambic stresses relentlessly sledged:

O Jesus, I must die, I know not where nor when nor how, but if I die in mortal sin I go to hell for all eternity.

The newspapers were lifted, the beads and chairs returned to their places. They heard Casey come back from his supper. "Rush! Rush!" Reegan said to the boy and girl. "Off to bed! Ye'll be asleep all day in school tomorrow if you don't rush."

Some red bricks had been set to warm at the fire. Willie slipped them into a pair of heavy woollen socks with the tongs. He lit the candles in their tin holders and they were ready to be kissed good night.

Sheila ran to Elizabeth. Reegan was sitting in front of the fire and the boy went close up to him, between his open knees. Hands came on his shoulders.

"Good night, Willie. God guard you."

"Good night, Daddy."

He lifted the hot bricks and said at the door, "Good night, Elizabeth."

"Good night, Willie."

At last they were in the hall, their fluttering candles lighting up the darkness. Casey was coming down the stairs, a pile of the dark grey police blankets in his arms, the top and bottom edges braided with official green thread. He had to feel out his steps very carefully because of his load. They waited on him at the foot of the stairs with the candles.

"Ye're off to bed," he said. "Hot bricks and all to keep ye warm."

"Good night, Guard Casey," they answered simply.

He turned to them laughing, the whiteness of his bald head thrust over the pile of blankets into their candle-light.

> '*Good night,*
> *Sleep tight,*
> *And mind the fleas don't bite,*"

he recited.

They smiled with polite servility, but it was the end of the night, and his pleasantness went through them like a shiver of cold. They watched him cruelly as he shaped sideways to manœuvre his load of blankets through the dayroom door. They took his place on the stairs, the paint completely worn away in the centre of the steps, and even the wood shredding and a little hollowed by years of feet. They climbed without speaking a word. When they got near the top they could see their images with candles and bricks mounting into the night on the black shine of the window. It was directly at the head of the stairs, facing out on the huge sycamore between the house and the river. There was no sign of moon or star, only two children with candles reflected out of its black depth, raindrops slipping down the glass without, where the masses of wind struggled and reeled in the night.

Willie went with Sheila into her room. On nights like these they were never at ease with each other.

"Will you be afraid now, Sheila?" he asked.

"I'll leave the candle lit," she said.

"And do you want the door open?"

He knew by the way she said "Aye" that she was almost dumb with fear.

"Well, you want nothing else so?"

An importance had crept into his voice, the situation making him feel and act like a grown person.

"No," Sheila said. "Nothing."

"Well, good night so, Sheila."

"Good night, Willie."

Downstairs Elizabeth strained Reegan's barley water into a mug with a little blue circle above its handle. He drank it sitting before the dying fire, blowing at it sometimes, for it was hot. He loved drawing out these last minutes. The thought of Quirke didn't trouble him any more than the

38

thought of his own life and death. All things became remote and far away, speculations that might involve him one day, but they had no power over him now, and these minutes were his rest of peace.

"Is the cat out?" he asked.

"She didn't come in at all tonight," Elizabeth answered.

"Are the hens shut in?"

"They are."

"Do you want me to go out for anything?"

"No. There's nothing wanting."

He rose, put the mug down on the table, and went and bolted the scullery door. She was setting the table for the morning when he came in.

"Don't stay long now," he said on his way to bed, because she'd found it hard to sleep since she grew uneasy about her breasts, and often sat reading for hours in the stillness after he'd go, books Willie brought her from the lending library in the school, a few books she'd brought with her from London and kept always locked in her trunk upstairs, books that'd grown in her life as if they'd been grafted there, that she'd sometimes only to handle again to experience blindingly.

"No. I won't be a minute after you. When I rake the fire."

At the hall door he noticed the intense strained look on her face.

"You look tired out. You're killin' yourself workin' too hard."

And then he asked as if he had been given vision, "Are you sure you're feelin' well, girl?"

"Don't be foolish," she tried to laugh. "How could I work too hard with the few things that'd have to be done in this house! When I rake the fire I'll be in bed."

"Don't be long so, that readin' at night'd drive a person crackers," he said and left for his bed.

She put a few wet sods of turf on the fire, then covered it with ashes. She heard Casey noisily shifting his bed down in the dayroom, soon Reegan's boots clattered overhead on the ceiling and she blew out the lamp and followed him to their room.

39

2

The alarm woke her out of a state that wasn't deep enough to call it sleep. The night was still outside, and the room in total darkness with the blind of the one window down, the air raw with frost. The evenings of the wet February had gone; Lent was in, the days closing up an early Easter.

By sheer force of instinct and habit she reached across the shape of bedclothes that was Reegan and stopped the clock's dance on the table. Then she fell back, though she knew it could only make it harder than ever to rise in the end, as tired as if she'd never slept. Reegan hadn't woken; his elbow brushed her as he changed sides, the surface of his sleep no more than trembled by the alarm.

"If you go to bed tired and wake up tired," began to twitch like a nerve in her mind, and stayed there in its mystifying repetition till she fixed it among the ad. columns of many magazines and newspapers, "If you go to bed tired and wake up tired drink Bourna-Vita." She grimaced in recognition and settled herself deeper in the warmth. There had been another night of frost, she could tell by the air on her face. She didn't know how she'd managed to get up since the frosts came, but even before then it was becoming a more desperate struggle with every fresh morning.

A few more minutes, she told herself, she'd stay: Reegan hadn't woken: there was no noise of the children stirring in the next rooms; but, oh, the longer she enjoyed the stolen sweetness of these minutes the more it had to become a tearing of her flesh out of the bedclothes in the end. And she used to love rising into these March mornings, to let up the blinds gently in the silence and find the night not fully gone and the world white with frost. She'd unbolt the door to break the ice on the barrel with the edge of the basin and gasp with waking as her hands brought the frozen water to her face.

The mornings of these last weeks had been one long flinching from the cold and the day, what used to be the adventure once all changed to the drudgery she could barely get herself to face. She'd ask for nothing better than to lie on in bed and not to have to face anything, but these small reprieves she gave herself were always adding up till she rose in the last minute and the mornings were all a rush.

Suddenly she remembered: this was not any morning, it was the morning of the Circuit Court. She'd set the alarm for early, for twenty past seven. The room was still pitch dark, nothing was stirring.

How had she lain there for even these few minutes without it entering her mind? She had even checked his clothes the last thing in the kitchen the night before, and it had been on her mind between the fitful snatches of sleep she'd got during the night. Here she'd been playing a game of rising and it was a court day. Her dread of the cold and her weariness were gone in a flash: she was out of bed and dressed and moving through the dark to the door without being conscious that she'd managed to rise. She didn't let up the blind or shut the bedroom door fully so as not to make noise. She could hear Reegan's breathing as she left. She would not wake him until she was ready.

The house was quiet as death and dark as she came down, her slippers loud on the hollow stairs, her hand sliding down the wooden railing to guide her way; when it came against the large round knob at the bottom her foot searched out for the solid concrete. Here she could touch the dayroom door. She could hear nothing behind the shut door, but the smell of Mullins's smoked Woodbines came. She trailed her fingers along the wall as she came up the hallway to avoid knocking against the collapsible form that was laid against it. When she let up the blinds a little light came in. The bare whiteness of the field sloping down to the river and the hill

41

beyond shone against the dark. She lit the small glass oil lamp and turned to rake the coals out of the ashes.

She worked quickly and well and without thinking much. She didn't wash herself or brush her hair or go outside till she had to get water out of the barrel for Reegan's shaving. The cold made her wince as she broke the ice, and she saw their black cat dart in through the door she'd left open; she came in afraid to find her thieving, but she was only waiting to wrap her frozen fur about Elizabeth's legs and purred and cried loudly till she was given a saucer of milk in the scullery.

The children were rising, their feet were padding on the boards overhead. The kettle was boiling, the shaving water, the slices of bacon laid on the pan ready for frying, the table set. The morning's work was almost done; her sense of purpose, of things needing her to do them, failing fast. There wasn't enough in front of her now to keep her going headlong: she didn't want to wash or brush her hair and she could not bear the look of her face in the mirror; and when the children came with a rush of life into the kitchen it made her only more oppressively aware of her sickness. "There was frost, Elizabeth?" their cries came. "We'll be able to slide on Malone's pond if it keeps up."

She could only answer them with tired assent. There seemed no end to their excitement and curiosity. She wondered if they'd wake Reegan.

"Daddy's off to court today?"

"Yes."

"Is it time for him to get up, Elizabeth?"

"Can I go up to call him?"

"Me, Elizabeth, I'll go up!"

"Let Sheila go up so," she said to Una.

"Then I can quench the lamp, Elizabeth? It's no good any more, it's too bright."

"I'll shine his boots, Elizabeth."

Elizabeth, Elizabeth, Elizabeth, Elizabeth, it seemed without end. Sheila was racing up the stairs. The blinded darkness met her with a shock. She stood at the door and called,

"Daddy, it's time to get up," but she got no answer and she had to tiptoe to the window and let up the blind so that the light poured in.

"Daddy, it's time to get up," she timidly rocked his shoulder.

She had to rock harder and raise her voice.

"It's the day for the court, Daddy."

He grunted, and then suddenly opened his eyes. She felt the wild fright of his eyes opened on her and not recognizing her and then the slow remembering and the dawning there of the world he lived in. At last he knew who she was.

"It's time to get up, Daddy."

"It's you, Sheila," he rubbed the back of his hand across his eyes. "What day is today, Sheila?"

"Thursday, Daddy. It's the day of the court."

He took a moment to absorb what she said and then his eyes searched swiftly for the clock on the table: it was five past eight. "Christ, I forgot," he swore as he jumped out of bed. "Another blasted day in town."

He was downstairs almost with her in his collarless shirt and trousers and stockinged feet. He stopped to listen at the dayroom door: but there was no noise of Mullins moving.

"You must have been up early," he praised Elizabeth when he felt the kitchen warm with the blazing fire.

"I thought not to wake you," she replied.

"Is there water boiled?"

"It's ready—when you want it. . . ."

He took down the plain wooden box that held his shaving-kit from the top of the medicine press and opened it on the sewing-machine to get his cut-throat razor and he stroked it over and back on a strip of fine leather tacked to the side of the press. After he'd tested its sharpness he laid it carefully on a newspaper in the window and searched the box for the brush and stick of soap.

Elizabeth poured the hot water into the basin in the scullery, watched the steam rapidly rise up to cloud the mirror in the window, and took a clean towel from the clothes-horse to hand to one of the waiting girls.

"When he's finished," she said, for the ritual of these court mornings never varied.

The child waited till the scraping of the razor stopped and he was sousing himself with water. She was beside him when he turned, his eyes blind with soap, the large hands groping.

They were quiet in the kitchen as he sat to his breakfast, but the alarm had gone down in the dayroom. Mullins was up, pounding upstairs with mattress and load of bedclothes, dragging the iron bed in against the wall of the lock-up. His poker and tongs banged on the concrete as he set the fire going. They heard him unlock the outside door and the boots go on the frozen ground down to the ashpit at the bottom of the garden, with his bucket and piss-pot.

He came up to the kitchen in his greatcoat and cap a little later. His red face was burning blue, the pores plainly visible in the swollen flesh. He hadn't washed.

"That's a powerful smell, the fryin', Elizabeth, on a frosty morning. It has me driven wild already with the hunger. Freeze the arse of a brass monkey, this mornin' would. A holy terror to get out of bed," he spoke.

"That's six days of frost," she said, the social makeweight of these comings and goings was always left to Elizabeth.

"Six days surely, though anything's better than the wet. But wouldn't we be worse off if we had nothing at all to be complainin' about," he remarked and chuckled over his own wit at the door.

"That's true, I suppose," she smiled.

"We're all off today," he said. "Casey'll be holdin' the fort on his own."

He turned to Reegan and stated that he was going to get his breakfast and shine himself up for the court, he'd be back soon after nine to leave the books in order and go with them to the town.

"The door's left open, so you'll hear the phone if be·any miracle it rings. The day in town'll be a bit of a change," he said.

Reegan continued with his meal in silence after Mullins

went. Sometimes he watched out past the sycamore and netting-wire to the white field that went down to the river, the calm strip of black water moving through the whiteness, and the thorn hedge half-way up the white hill beyond. Sometimes he watched his own face eating in the sideboard mirror, completely silent. He disliked Elizabeth asking, "Are there many cases today?" "Not many," he said.

He'd give her no information. His mind had been a painless blank, watching his own face and the images of white field and river and white hill, and not relating them to anything and not thinking. Now she had forced her way into this total blankness and disturbed him with thought of her and the day.

"Not many," was meant to cut her out again but he could not.

"I only wanted to know whether you'd be home early for your dinner or not," he had to listen to her injured tones. He had to wake to some sense that she'd been hurt.

"Only one big case—last month's crash at the quarry," he imparted. "It'll depend on when it's called. We might be out in an hour and we might be there till night. If we're not home before two you'll know we'll be fairly late."

She nodded. There were tears in her eyes that she held back. She felt her strength draining and sat on the side of one of the wooden chairs, her arm on its back. It was early morning, excited with the preparations for the court, and she was as worn as if she'd been on her feet for days. She felt herself go weak. She had to grip the back of the chair fiercely, use all her determination not to go down. She could not let herself collapse. The fit passed; but she'd not be able to go on long like this, not more than days now; in the desperation she took her courage in both hands.

"Would you call at the doctor's and ask him what would be a good time to see him tomorrow?" she asked quietly. "I think I'd better go for a check-up."

The asking brought a dramatic silence that she shrank from, even the children turned quiet to fix her with their attention. She was drooped and deathly pale.

"You don't look well," he said with unthinking cruelty. "You've not been yourself since Christmas."

"I don't think it's anything," she protested. "It's only to make sure."

She was haggard.

"I'll tell him to come out," he said.

"No, no. It'd cost too much."

"Cost," he derided angrily. "We're not paupers."

"No. There'd be no sense in him coming. I'm well able to cycle. And I'd like the day in town."

She tried to brush it off as nothing. With all her will she rose from the chair. She lifted off the boiling kettle, put on a saucepan.

"It's nothing at all," she smiled casually with every muscle in her face. "It's only to be sure."

She stood still, making a pretence of tending the fire. She could hear her heart beating. She regretted having ever spoken.

She saw Reegan rise to change into his best boots, the ones Una had polished. He sheathed the razor and put his shaving things back in the box to take out the button brush and the brass stick and tin of Silvo. There began the scrupulous brushing of his tunic and greatcoat and cap, the buttons drawn together in a row on the brass stick and coated with Silvo, the letting it dry and then the shining, even the medallions on the collar and cap, the whistle chain that went across the tunic to the breast pocket, were polished till they shone like brightnesses. And last of all the black baton sheath was shone; the baton—a short vicious stick of polished hickory filled with lead, the grooved surface tapering to where a leather thong hung from the handle for securing it about the wrist in action—was placed in the sheath and hung from the belt of the tunic. He squared himself before the sideboard mirror, shaved and handsome, stuffing the fresh hankie she handed him up his sleeve.

He turned his back for their inspection. There wasn't a speck on the uniform.

"He'll not be able to find much fault today," he said.

No one could, he was shining.

"Will I leave your bike round at the dayroom door?" Willie wanted to know.

"Do, and see if the tyres are pumped," he was told.

Down in the dayroom the window was lifted up and the key taken from the sill, it was Brennan, for the next minute Casey appeared through the archway. The time was exactly nine. Reegan had to go down to them to sign and call the roll. He'd not return to the kitchen unless he'd forgotten something, but leave with the others from the dayroom.

"Are you sure you don't want the doctor out?" he asked Elizabeth as he kissed her good-bye.

"No. I'll go in tomorrow."

"Are you sure?" he repeated. He was worried. She hadn't been a day ill in bed since they were married. Her haggard appearance, her wanting to see the doctor, disturbed him with the memory of his first wife who had died in childbirth. Elizabeth could not die, he told himself; it was impossible that two could die; it would be ludicrous.

"Are you sure?" he pressed her.

"I am quite certain," she said.

He kissed her and went, she'd have to see the children ready for school, Casey and Brennan were waiting for him in the dayroom. He called the roll and marked Mullins present in his absence, who didn't come till twenty past, and when he'd done the signings connected with his completed b.o. duty they left. They wheeled their bicycles through the black gateway to the avenue and mounted there. Five bare sycamores lined the avenue from the gate to the road and at the last tree they turned right for the bridge and the town, Reegan and Mullins cycling together in front, Brennan behind because of the law prohibiting more than two to cycle abreast, Casey watching them cross the bridge from the window, a blue procession of three in the morning.

The village was waking. The green mail car came: then the newsboy from the Dublin train, the cylinders of paper piled high on his carrier bicycle. A tractor with ploughs on its trailer went past at speed, and some carts. There was

47

blasting in the council quarries: four muffled explosions sounded and the thud-thud of blown rocks falling. The screaming rise-and-fall of the saws came without ceasing from the woods across the lake. A riverboat went down towards the Shannon with the first load of the day.

Willie had to go to the dayroom to discover if Casey wanted any messages done before school, and he was sent for twenty Gold Flake and *The Express* and *Independent*.

Casey had a big fire down and the sunshine lit up the red and black inkstains between the ledgers on the table. The room was bare and clean, nothing but the table and yellow chairs, the stripped iron bed in against the wall of the lock-up, old records in filing clips on the walls, piles of ledgers on the green shelf up over the bed, the phone and rainfall chart on the wall close to the green mantelpiece. He kept the boy talking about football when he returned till Sheila came knocking that it was time for school. He then put on his greatcoat and went out to the rain-gauge in the garden to try to measure the few drops of moisture that had collected in the bottle since the morning before and entered his findings on the chart beside the phone immediately he got back. It was cold in spite of the sun and he shivered and rubbed his hands together when he'd hung the coat on the rack. He pulled one of the chairs up to the blazing fire, settled down the cushion that he always brought with him on these b.o. days, and sat into it with a sigh of comfort—to read the newspapers from cover to cover.

When the children had gone and she had washed and swept and dusted, Elizabeth sat with a book in the big arm-chair by the fire to grasp at an interval of pure rest. Such a quietness had come into the house that she felt she could touch it with her hands. There was no stir from the dayroom, where Casey was sunk in the newspapers; the noise of the occasional traffic on the roads, the constant sawing from the woods came and were lost in the quietness she felt about her. The whiteness was burning rapidly off the fields outside, brilliant and glittering on the short grass as it vanished; and the daffodils that yesterday she had arranged in the white vase on the sill were a wonder of yellowness in the sunshine, the heads massed together above the cold green stems disappearing into the mouth of the vase. In the silence the clock beside the statue of St Therese on the sideboard beat like a living thing. This'd be the only time of the day she might get some grip and vision on the desperate activity of her life. She was Elizabeth Reegan: a woman in her forties: sitting in a chair with a book from the council library in her hand that she hadn't opened: watching certain things like the sewing-machine and the vase of daffodils and a circle still white with frost under the shade of the sycamore tree between the house and the river: alive in this barrack kitchen, with Casey down in the dayroom: with a little time to herself before she'd have to get another meal ready: with a life on her hands that was losing the last vestiges of its purpose and meaning: with hard cysts within her breast she feared were cancer. . . . In spite of her effort to stay calm she rose in a panic. She looked at the mantelpiece and clothes-horse and sideboard and doors and windows. She was alone in this great barrack kitchen. She could scream and it'd only bring Casey hurrying up to see what had happened: and all she could tell him was that nothing had happened, nothing at all, she had only become frightened, frightened of nothing. Reegan was at court, the children were at school, she was in the kitchen, and did all these things mean anything?

She had believed she could live for days in happiness here in the small acts of love, she needing them, and they in need of her. She'd more than enough of London that time, no desire left for anything there, no place she wanted to go to after she'd finish in the theatre or wards, the people she wanted to talk to grown fewer and fewer, her work repetitive and menial and boring—and had she married Reegan because she had been simply sick of living at the time and forced to create some illusion of happiness about him so that she might be able to go on? She'd no child of her own now. She'd achieved no intimacy with Reegan. He was growing more and more restless. He, too, was sick, sick of authority and the police, sick of obeying orders, threatening

49

to break up this life of theirs in the barracks, but did it matter so much now? Did it matter where they went, whether one thing happened more than another? It seemed to matter less and less. An hour ago she'd been on the brink of collapse and if she finally collapsed did anything matter?

She should never have sat down, she told herself: she should have kept on her feet, working, her mind fixed on the small jobs she could master. A simple trap this half-hour of peace and quiet was, she'd have had more peace if she'd kept busy to the point of physical breaking-strain. She couldn't ever hope to get any ordered vision on her life. Things were changing, going out of her control, grinding remorselessly forward with every passing moment.

As she stood hopelessly there she saw Mrs Casey come through the old stone archway that was covered with ivy and cotoneaster, the incredibly shiny leaves still on the crawling branches, the last of the scarlet berries devoured in the December snows. The woman coming was in her late twenties, tall and pale, her flaxen hair drawn straight back in a bun, wearing spectacles with fine gold rims. She turned in towards the dayroom and Elizabeth heard the door open and shut and her voice in conversation with Casey's. She'd have her with her for most of the morning, she knew. She must surely be twenty years younger than Casey and it wasn't easy for her in this small village. Mullins's wife and Brennan's never lost a chance to make her feel her childlessness, parading their own large families before her like manifestoes. They never tried this with Elizabeth: she was too detached; her age and years in London gave her position in their eyes; and with Reegan's three children she hadn't the appearance of either the leisure or money that could rouse their envy.

The dayroom door opened and she came up the hallway as she always did—smoking.

"They're gone to court today, Elizabeth," she greeted.

"Ned is on his own today," Elizabeth answered in the same manner.

50

"Readin' the papers. He's talkin' about comin' up to you after the dinner to listen to some soccer match or other on the B.B.C."

She sat and threw the wasted cigarette into the fire, the cork tip stained with the crimson lipstick she wore. "Isn't it strange you don't smoke, Elizabeth? Nearly all doctors and nurses are heavy smokers," she said as she lit another.

"I used," Elizabeth smiled in memory. "But never much, it was easy for me to give them up."

"We smoke forty a day—between us. It's a constant expense, that's the worst. We tried to give them up once for Lent, but it only lasted three days! There was nearly murder done. . . . They say that doctors and nurses smoke so much because it's antiseptic or something. It keeps away germs," she ended the digression to return to her first theme as if it was obsessional.

"I don't know why, perhaps it does," Elizabeth said, she found herself already bored. This conversation echoed a thousand others. When she first married Reegan she'd found the small world absorbing and beautiful: but it was no longer so—her initiation was over, her passion had spent itself, this world on which she'd used every charm to get accepted in was falling in ashes into her hands. She was shackled, a thieving animal held at last in this one field. She'd escaped out of London, she'd not escape out of this, she'd have to stand her ground here at last. She could scream, the desperation she'd experienced on her own coming back on this conversation.

"Do you not feel well, Elizabeth?" the strained intensity of her features was noticed.

"No," she could have shouted but she drilled herself. "I've been feeling tired lately. I don't think it's much, probably just run down, but I'm going in to see the doctor tomorrow."

"It's always better to be certain, you can't afford to take chances nowadays," she echoed Casey and asked, "Which of the doctors are you going to?"

"Dr Ryan—just the police doctor."

51

"I always get Dr Malone, though Ned thinks there's no one in the world like Dr Ryan."

"It won't matter very much anyhow. It'll probably be just another iron tonic," Elizabeth tried to close the conversation.

"I'll say a prayer anyhow!"

"That's nice," she smiled in gratitude.

A wave of feeling, pity or compassion, crossed her for the other woman, but then she was looking upon her as an inferior. And what had she herself to feel superior about, she asked; were not both of them in the same squalid fix? And was somebody's unawareness of the horror about them a reason to seethe with pity for them? Were they not far and far better off? Now a hatred was mastering everything and when she was asked, "Were you at first Mass last Sunday?" she knew she couldn't stand much more.

She nodded. She was at first Mass every Sunday, there were meals to get ready when Second was on.

"Did you see the three Murphys at the rails?" she continued. "They must have got early holidays from the Civil Service. They were all very clever, weren't they! They passed the exams.

"I think Mary has failed. Irene is the prettiest now. She was dressed in all lavender, and it says in *Woman* that it's the latest fashion in Paris now."

Elizabeth hadn't noticed them particularly. She used to love watching the young girls home from the city parade to Communion, especially at Easter, when many came; it used excite her envy and curiosity, so much so that when she'd come from Mass she'd always want to talk about them to Reegan; it'd give her back the time when she too was one of them, but he'd never care to listen. Nothing, she knew, can exist in the social days of people without attention, her excitement would be gone before the breakfast was over.

How often was she aware of being present at Mass now! The murmuring of prayers, the rising and standing and kneeling and sitting down, the smells of incense and wet raincoats and candles burning would set a sleepy rhythm going through her blood and drift her into the sickly limbo of her own dreams.

"Do you think it's right that Irene's the prettiest now?" Mrs Casey was pressing.

Elizabeth agreed desperately and got up. She put on the kettle, taking automatic part in the conversation as she waited for it to boil. She made tea and put three cups and some bread on the table.

"We better call up Ned," she invited.

"So many will be too much trouble!"

"One more! What difference will it make? It'd better to have twenty if it'd save us the trouble of worrying about it."

Mrs Casey called from the door, and when he came out of the dayroom she said flirtatiously, "You're wanted up here."

"It seems I'm a wanted man so," he punned as he came. "It's as bad as being in *Fogra Tora*."

He saw three cups on the table, the plate of buttered bread.

"You're great, Elizabeth," he praised, "but you shouldn't have gone to that trouble."

"You're an important man today," she kept up the game, smiling at why on earth these elaborate acceptances had always to arise in Ireland; in the London she had known the offer would be simply accepted at once or refused.

"I'm the most important man in the house today, without question or doubt," he laboured on. "The sole guardian of the fortress! The phone never even rang, not to talk of anybody calling."

"It'd give you the willies," his wife shivered.

"Not enough money," he explained. "Not half the men in the woods are working. It's the same with the council quarries: the tarrin' of the roads is doin' away with the stones, and the bogs only last for the summer."

"What was it like in Skerries?" Elizabeth asked about his last station, where he'd met and married Teresa.

"The East Coast is good," he said. "There was great life there, near the city; the market gardening, places you

53

couldn't throw a stone without breaking glass; the fishing-boats, and the tourists in the summer. Too busy we were at times, but not so busy that I couldn't meet me Waterloo," he laughed towards his wife.

"It wasn't always that story," she flashed. "Do you remember the first night you left me home?"

He made a rueful face, that was all.

"We were dancing in the Pavilion," she continued spiritedly to Elizabeth. "Nothing would do him but to get me out of it before it was over.

" 'It's too hot in here. And you can't dance with the floor crowded, Teresa,' " she mimicked.

"So he brought me down by the harbour and put me up against Joe May's gable. You could still hear the music from the Pavilion and it was comin' across the water from Red Island too, Mick Delahunty playing there that night. There was a big moon over the masts of the fishin' fleet. I knew he was mad for a court."

Elizabeth laughed lowly. She looked at Casey's embarrassed face and bald head as pale and waxed as candles. She'd have given dearly to see him mad for a court.

"And just as he was kissin' me," she went excitedly on, caught up in the flow of her story, "I pulled back me head and I said: 'Do you see the moon, Ned?'

"You'd laugh till your dyin' day, Elizabeth, if you saw the cut of his face as he searched for the moon. And do you know what he said when he found it?" she rocked in a convulsive fit of laughing on the chair.

"What?" Elizabeth had to prompt.

"He said the moon was beautiful," she roared at last, holding her sides as the fit hurt.

"That's a nice story to tell on anybody, isn't it?" Casey appealed, he was ill at ease, and Elizabeth feared one of those embarrassed silences till his wife retorted, "I might never have married you only for that."

"You might never have been asked," he was able to return and then they laughed quietly together, easy again.

They talked another three or four minutes and then Casey

rose, "Elizabeth will want to get the children's lunch. We're only keeping her from her work."

"Can I help you to wash or anything, Elizabeth?" she offered.

Elizabeth refused. They left. The dayroom door shut. She heard them laugh together.

"He said the moon was beautiful," she pondered for a still moment, then quickly cast it out to get on with her work. She had less than an hour to prepare the children's lunch. They had but a half-hour from school and ten minutes of it went going and coming. Their meal would have to be on the table when they came to her, running.

She put down potatoes and hurried out to the garden for some curly cabbage, the plot just inside the gate at the lavatory, along the netting-wire. Away towards the road and avenue was a rectangle of blackcurrant bushes, the beaten black earth of last year's potato ridges about it, a strip of wild ground along the river from the ashpit to the bridge at the bottom, lined with tall ash trees and the spaces between them choked with briar and water sally. Across the avenue were the few shops of the village, hidden by sycamores: the church alone stood out visible, areas of stone and glass and slate showing between breaks in the old graveyard evergreens.

The woman who rang the Angelus came across the bridge on her bicycle. Elizabeth knew it was almost twelve, and she had enough leaves plucked. She waved to the passing woman but was not noticed. The sacristan's wife rode in the stiff poised way people ride who have learned it in their later age, with no ease of mastery, only a ferocious attention fixed on the bike and road, as if determination alone can achieve everything. Elizabeth smiled to herself. The spirit was willing and marvellous was surely the text of the small riding exhibition, she supposed; but the poor flesh had simply more than it could take.

Tomorrow she'd have to show her own flesh to the doctor! The detached smiling went. She couldn't bear to think about it, she'd have to show her own ageing flesh to the doctor, and it was no use trying to think anything, it was too painful, it all got on the same claustrophobic road back to yourself, it was the trick always played you in the end.

She shut the gate, hurried over the gravel to the house. The few hens she kept gathered about her legs when they saw her come with the basin. She hushed them away. The Angelus rang when she was inside. She did not stop her work to pray. She'd discovered when she stood still, when nothing immediate was there to force her on, anaemia and tiredness and despair swayed in her like sleep or death.

She kept on, she put the greens down with some slices of bacon, strained the boiled potatoes, laid the table; and when the three children came at twenty-five to one, warm and panting, pulling out their chairs to cry for food, they had not a moment to wait.

"How did things go today?" she asked as she always did while they were eating.

"I got a sweet and Willie got two slaps," Una cried.

"What did you get the slaps for, Willie?"

"For talking," Una answered.

"I didn't ask you," she saw the boy with his head low, on the point of tears.

"She missed her spellings but she got no slaps because she's the teacher's pet," he accused.

"I'm not!"

"You are!"

' It doesn't matter. These things happen," she quietened them more by her tone than words. She was on their side, that was all that mattered.

"And how is Sheila?" she didn't forget.

"Sheila is well. No slaps today," the small girl smiled, knowing in the child's way that she was the youngest and the favourite.

Elizabeth was silent now, filled with the rich feeling of care and love. They had need of her, and she would guard them. But they were devouring their meal. They were rushing to get back. With their mouths full of the last scraps

56

they were calling, "Good-bye, Elizabeth! Good-bye, Elizabeth!" their feet already running to grasp the minutes left of play before the bell rang, hardly aware of her existence.

She mashed their leftover potatoes with some meal for the hens and fed them in old rusty ovens down beside the netting-wire. She washed the dishes and then found she couldn't go on: she had bread to bake yet, some old clothes to mend, but she felt sick and sat without any will to do anything. She saw Mrs Casey come through the archway with Casey's lunch and she remembered the morning. She had not seen or heard her leave the dayroom to prepare the lunch. The world was going about its business no matter what she thought or felt. The day was already half-gone. She rose and took some food. Afterwards she was better able to face into the afternoon, but without any joy.

She got flour out of the bin, soda and salt and sour milk out of the press, and started to knead the dough in the tin basin. It was her will alone kept her working. She could see no purpose, no anything, and she could not go on blindly now and without needing answers and reasons as she could once. Her tiredness was growing into the fearful apprehension that she'd lost all power of feeling: she could no longer feel the sticky dampness of the stuff she was kneading with her hands or taste it if she touched it with her tongue or see it other than through a clear covering of glass—it felt as if the surfaces of her body had turned dead. She was existing far within the recesses of the dead walls and gaping out in mute horror. She tried again to bring herself to the surface: to break out of the grip of tiredness and despairing reflection: to live only in the chores and repetitions she knew; and in this plodding way she kept on till the children came from school.

Their coming gave her a new lease of energy. She buttered and put jam on their slices of bread, to talk with them and smile. They had come hungry and shouting into the kitchen, she'd forgotten about herself, becoming the living miracle of the cripple who walks, having lost thought of his infirmity in one moment of passion.

57

"If we tidy the scullery table will you let us go to play with the Mullinses on the quay?"

She'd to smile at how it began with the effort of bribery, their father would not let them go if he was here, she was an easier mark.

"Will you promise to be back in an hour?"

She knew they'd promise anything They spent a bare minute over the scullery table, then were gone. She didn't hear them answer her warning, "Don't play on the edge of the quay," as they went. It had been a landing-stage for the provision boats of the nineteenth century, coming up the Shannon with cargoes of salt and flour and tea and tobacco and barrels of beer; covered now with grass and weeds, only used by the farmers as a dipping-place for sheep and the houseboats that called in summer, the granite wall and four metal bollards the last traces of its history.

The river was twenty feet deep there, no protection on the wall, and the granite slimy and sheer. She began to grow uneasy. If any of them fell in with Reegan away at court, it was she who had given them permission. She thought of going to the bridge to call them home, but what was the use? She couldn't now. They were gone. It was unlikely that anything would happen.

Casey came to listen to the soccer match, leaving a chair against the dayroom door so that he'd hear the phone if it rang or anyone came. He took the sport pages from the newspapers he brought and offered the rest to Elizabeth with the apology, "What I've here would be of no interest to you!"

"Was there anything strange today?" she asked as she took the pages.

"No—nothing strange. The same old stuff but you read them all the same, don't you?"

"And had you callers?" she changed.

"Peter Mulligan," he named a farmer. "He wanted a licence to cut trees."

"Is it difficult to get a licence now?" the conversation

58

continued while he waited for the football to begin. The radio had been turned on, it was playing a sleepy waltz.

"What are licences for only for gettin'?" he laughed cynically. "Unless I wanted to stop him, that's all! And why would I stop anybody from gettin' anything, Elizabeth?"

"There'll be no trees soon," she more mused to herself than answered.

"There'll be no country soon, never mind trees, if you ask me, Elizabeth! But I suppose there'll be always some eejit left to sound *The Last Post*. That's how it's always supposed to be, isn't it?"

The waltz ended. The commentary was announced. Casey had no further interest in the conversation. He pulled up a chair to the radio and with twenty Gold Flake, a box of matches and the sport pages settled himself in anticipation of existing pleasurably for the next hour on the voice coming over the air.

Elizabeth looked through the newspapers. The radio was low above the sawing in the distance. Surely the evening was coming, the light turning, blue with the cigarette-smoke, the aroma an evocation of a thousand evenings where her life had happened while cigarettes were smoked. The starkness of individual minutes passing among accidental doors and windows and chairs and flowers and trees, cigarette-smoke or the light growing brilliant and fading losing their pain, gathered into oneness in the vision of her whole life passing in its total mystery. A girl child growing up on a small farm, the blood of puberty, the shock of the first sexual act, the long years in London, her marriage back into this enclosed place happening as would her death in moments where cigarettes were smoked. No one, not even herself, could measure it by slide or rule. No one could place a finger on it in judgement and say this or that without all they said being just easy trash. Her life was either under the unimaginable God or the equally unimaginable nothing; but in that reality it was under no lesser thing; and the reality continued, careless of whether the human accident was a child waking up in terror or two people bored together,

59

whether it was the rejoicing of a marriage or a man listening to the radio and smoking and a woman turning the pages of a newspaper.

She rose to pile wood on the fire in a deep joy, to sprinkle and sweep the floor. Casey started up and tried to shrink in against the wall when he saw her with the brush. She'd to assure him several times that he wasn't in the way before he'd sit again and he'd put himself to so much inconvenience for her that she felt she owed it to him to ask, "Is the match good?"

He described it as if accuracy was a matter of life and death: its importance in the League Table, if Wolves lost the teams it'd bring back into the running; the stars, the transfers, the internationals, the three Irishmen playing. . . .

It seemed he could go on for ever but frenzied noises from the commentator and background cheering glued him again to the set.

"It's a goal," he shouted. "One all. Now we're in for the fireworks!"

He lit another cigarette, and marked the time and score and the scorer down on the page of newspaper, sitting erect with excited attention, his ear close to the set so as not to lose a word.

Fragments drifted to Elizabeth as she idled over the sweeping.

"Throw in to Wolves. Smith takes it. Long pass out to Atkinson. The game opening out more now. Atkinson beats Morgan on the turn. Coming into the edge of the penalty area. Shoots——"

She saw Casey go tense and rise in the chair and then relax as the tones turned to an anticlimax of disappointment. "Oh, straight at O'Neill. O'Neill safely gathers, hops the ball, comes out to the edge of the penalty area. Long throw out to Henshaw. . . ."

It seemed that nothing could ever change. The sunshine, the curtains, the daffodils in the white vase on the sill, the voice rising and falling. She heard the chug-chug-chug of a riverboat coming downstream, hugging the black navigation sign at the mouth of the lake, the timber rising out of the hold, only the man at the tiller on deck, in greasy overalls and sailor cap. She read The Old Oak as it passed the house. The screen of vegetation between the boles of the ash trees shut it out of sight as its trail of foam swayed in the centre of the river and the water began to ramp against the banks.

Neither phone nor caller disturbed Casey as he listened, completely absorbed, searching the pages now and then for information. When it was over he announced the result to Elizabeth with the comment, "Not one of the forecasts were right!"

"The season will soon be over?" she entered into a conversation.

"In four weeks, with the Cup Final," he said, "and then it'll be the cricket and our own stalwarts of the G.A.A. on Sundays with Michael O'Hehir. "Bail o Dhia oraibh go leir a chairde Gael o Phairc an Chrocaigh. Hello everyone from Croke Park and this is Michael O'Hehir," he mimicked and they both laughed together, the performance marvellously ridiculous and accurate.

"Shure there'd have to be something," he said as he left, "or we'd all go off our rockers. All work and no play makes Jack a dull boy."

He was gone as the children came exultant and rosy-cheeked from playing on the quay, willing to do anything rather than submit to the discipline of their homework. She loathed this badgering and coaxing she had to do.

"We haven't much this evening—we'll have plenty of time after tea," they protested.

"But if you do them now you'll be finished and done with them for the whole evening," she reasoned.

"We'll have plenty of time after tea," the same old excuse came back and then the sulky cry from Willie, "Why do we have to do all these lessons anyhow?"

He'd need to write and read and add to live in modern society; to penpush his way to sixty-five in some city office; discipline his formless will and not to be for ever the child of his own longing, and there were other reasons, she knew.

61

And if they were let follow their own longings now they'd accuse back: "You never gave me a chance, Elizabeth! I didn't know what was right and you didn't care enough to show me," and they had the right, she supposed, to grow to knowledge of everything and perhaps the desperate satisfaction of knowing for certain that there is nothing that can be really known here and now.

But did these children want to get their way? Did they not in their hearts want her to enforce the rules of their lives so that they could assert themselves against them without real danger, they wanted to shake their fists at the skies but not for the skies to crash about their heads? They too had need of their laws and gods, they wanted to feel secure. It was all difficult and complicated, it might be this and it might be that, nothing real about the lives of people could ever be known, but she'd enough of thinking and reasoning and arguing for one evening.

"You must do your lessons now," she commanded firmly and they obeyed. She saw them unbuckle the blue cloth schoolbags she'd made them out of an old tunic of Reegan's, get the bottle of ink from the sideboard and bend over their blue-lined copies, and she felt as defeated as they did.

"I'll help you in anything you want," she tried to atone for the severity, and listened to their nibs scrape in the silence with anxiety. She was afraid her firmness would harden them against her till Sheila raised great dark eyes and asked her how to do a problem that she began to read out of the Arithmetic. She stooped over her to help. The small child soon understood. She was able to continue on her own. Then Una asked something else out of jealousy; and later, Willie, "Is b-e-a-u-t-i-f-u-l the way to spell beautiful, Elizabeth?"

She told him it was and asked how he wanted to use it. She felt she was part of their whole lives as they worked. She watched them for a few minutes in a perfect wonder of peace. Then she went to the window to touch the heads of the daffodils with her fingers. The sun had gone down close to the fir-tops across the lake. The level glare stained a red roadway on the water to the navigation signs and the grass of the river meadows was a low tangle of green and white light. It came so violently to the window that she'd soon to turn away, spelling the word Willie had asked her in inarticulate wonder. They were pestering her with questions. She forgot the cysts in her breasts, the cancer, the doctor, the changing moods that swept her day.

She laid the table for Reegan and hoped they wouldn't stay late drinking. Reegan seldom did: it gave him no release, only made him more silent and dissatisfied as he listened. It was worse if he talked, for he'd dominate, and was not wanted then. He would not stay but it was so easy to get caught in a drinking bout after the courts: he couldn't very well come home without Mullins and Brennan, because of the nuisance their wives would make.

The banging of the outside door and excited talk down in the dayroom eventually told her they were home. She hadn't long to listen for Reegan's feet in the hallway: she saw the children stiffen, they could tell by his step how the day had gone. She saw them turn to gaze at her with meaning quiet —as she had partly sensed herself, it hadn't gone well.

He said nothing when he came and they knew him too well to speak. He took gloves out of his greatcoat pocket with the quarter of Silver Mints he always brought and left them on the sewing-machine and hung his coat on the back of the door.

"There's some sweets there for you," he told them distantly; if he was in high humour he'd shout and ask them what they'd learned in school and throw sweets in the air to watch them scramble. Now he sat at the table and waited for his meal. The three children went without noise or rush to the sewing-machine and Willie divided them, two by two by two, into three little heaps, and they brought their share cupped in their hands to Elizabeth. She took a sweet from each and they went to their father, it was a kind of ceremony. He tried to be pleasant as he accepted their offering, and left the three sweets he took beside his arm at the tablecloth.

63

None of the others had yet gone home. Their excited voices came from the dayroom, discussing the day with Casey: who won and who lost, Judge O'Donovan's witticisms, the blunders, the personal animosities of the lawyers; sometimes going for the law books on the shelf to argue the decisions.

Elizabeth put a boiled egg before Reegan and poured out tea. He said, "Thanks," quietly and drew it to himself. "You had a long day," she said.

"The big case didn't come up till three. Hangin' around all day with our two hands as long as each other."

"Where did you get your lunch?"

"In the Bridge Café."

It was by the river, with a green front, and served substantial meals cheaply.

"How did the case go?" she was uneasy asking. He was in bad form, she could tell; he might resent her asking as petty curiosity; but surely he hadn't forgotten to call at the doctor's! He'd said nothing yet.

"A fine and a suspended sentence for dangerous driving. The drunken driving charge was squashed. He had a good solicitor, a good background, a good position, a university education. . . . What more could you ask?" he smiled with sardonic humour.

She saw the old sense of failure and frustration eating but she'd come to fear it hardly at all, or care. Her own life had grown as desperate.

"It's the way of the world," she said.

"It's the way surely," he laughed harshly, though coming out more, not trying to hold it all back within himself.

She watched him with tenderness. He was a strange person, she knew hardly anything about him, beyond the mere physical acts of intimacy. There had never been any real understanding between them: but was there ever such between people? He'd have none of the big questions: What do you think of life or the relationships between people or any of the other things that have no real answers? He trusted all that to the priests as he trusted a sick body to the doctors

64

and kept whatever observances were laid down as long as they didn't clash with his own passions.

Yet, it had survived far better than the deepest relationship of her adult life, though she had still Michael Halliday's letters locked in the wooden trunk in their bedroom and some of the books he'd given her. He'd been a doctor with her in the London Hospital and he changed her whole life. She'd listened to him for so many hours in the long London evenings that were lovely now in the memory; read the books he gave her; went with him to films and plays and concerts; and most of all he made her suffer, he put her through the frightful mill of love.

She saw the streaks of grey in Reegan's still blond hair, the images of grey and gold bringing the memory of a party, the twenty-first birthday party of a nurse from the hospital. She'd been invited by the girl and had brought Halliday. Though she hadn't known then the relationship was already well on its way to failure.

The girl's father, a clerk all his life in some tea company in Aldgate, rose late in the night to sing drunkenly to his wife:

> *Darling, I am growing old.*
> *Silver threads among the gold*
> *Shine upon thy brow today,*
> *Life is fading fast away,*
> *Yet my darling you will be*
> *Always young and fair to me. . . .*

The night was almost over. The chorus was taken up, tears smiling in many eyes, and it was then Halliday tried to shout in some drunken obscenity. Everybody there was drunk or tipsy; it didn't attract much attention, and she'd managed to stop him and get him home.

The next evening he apologized to her in a way.

"I'm sorry, dear Elizabeth," he said, "but if I was sufficiently drunk again and you not there I'd do it again."

"Why?" she asked. "What harm was it? Wasn't it a human thing enough to want to do?"

"You mean it's a universal emotion, as the professors put it, is that it, Elizabeth?" he asked maliciously.

She had not known then. She'd been confronted for the first time with a strange language and its mockery and she could only smile and wait.

"Everybody's full of that kind of thing," he said bitterly, "but it's not the truth. It rots your guts that way. You need real style to get away with something like that. And that old bastard after having bored and distracted that unfortunate woman for thirty years to get up as drunk as bejesus on his hind legs isn't my idea of style. It's an invitation to sink with him into his own swamp of a life. That's the kind of thing that kicks in your face on Friday and leads the choir at your funeral service Saturday morning."

She'd said nothing. There was nothing she could say. Mostly she was dominated by Halliday and content to listen.

She little thought then that she'd be as she was now: married in a barrack kitchen, watching the grey in another man's hair. It all came round if you could manage to survive long enough. Reegan was growing old, and so was she. There was nothing said or given or fulfilled in her life. He was eating his meal, unaware of her; he hadn't bothered or remembered about the doctor; he'd brought her nothing home, not even something as unimaginative and cheap as the bag of sweets he brought the children.

"Did you see the Superintendent?" she asked to avoid thinking her way into another depression.

"Aye," he admitted.

"Did things go any way well?"

"Nothing happened."

"Very little at all happened so," she yielded with such tired frustration that he looked. Her head was lowered over a shirt of Willie's. The needle shone as it was driven in and out of the cream stuff with mechanical precision.

He'd always felt her hostile to his private feud with Quirke, not that she ever reproached him openly, but he'd glimpsed it in stray words and silences. Once he had spoken about applying for a transfer and she had argued against it for the children's sake, "Whatever life they've built up here for themselves will be broken down if we move. There'll be new teachers, new friends. . . ."

He had just nodded and gone away and said nothing. So for the children's sake he was supposed to make a monkey out of his own life, he thought. No man had more than one life, the children would have to take their chance as he had to take his, he wasn't going to give it up for anybody's or anything's sake; but he'd decided that he didn't want a transfer then—it would be little better than changing one hairshirt for another. In plain clothes he'd leave when he left, it would be in nobody's uniform, and at his own choosing. He'd go about it in his own way, without reference to anybody. So he kept his mouth shut about his feelings and plans and frustrations, only confiding when the pressures became too great inside and another human being seemed possessed of more understanding than a bedroom wall.

Tonight he sensed that she had somehow changed: she'd oppose nothing and he wondered if it was possible that she might really want him to speak out. He saw her sewing away, and he laughed, a dry breaking laugh—she'd have her way.

"No. Nothing happened," he said. "Except what happened the last time and the time before and the time before that again.

" 'My Lord, it was a thoughtless act of the moment that this young man will suffer in his conscience for the remainder of his life,' " he began to parody but grew too bored or angry to continue.

"Such bullshit—and it never stops! It has no end. You should have heard O'Donovan's wisecracks today. He surpassed himself. He didn't miss one chance."

O'Donovan was the judge, waspish and one side of his face disfigured with a livid birthmark, never comfortable except in the display of his own wit, a composition of stabbing little references and allegories delivered with pompous sarcasm that played on small disadvantages; a kind of beating down that was surely meant to compensate for some private failure. Reegan had tasted the sting himself more than once.

"Two labourers home from England were up for drunken brawling and he said"—here Reegan began to mimic the cocksure tones of O'Donovan—"Labourers home from England who behave between jobs like film stars between pictures can't expect to get the same kind of admiring treatment.'

"Apparently some of the Hollywood stars were up for brawling in Los Angeles last week: which was supposed to give the whole point to the joke," Reegan explained. "And you should have heard them laughin' and the sound of it. Such a performance all day! If someone let off an honest shout of laughin' at any time you'd be able to hear a pin drop in that court. He'd never be forgiven! It reminded me at every turn of the school we went to and old Jockser Keenan—he fancied himself as an entertainer and we used to have to laugh for our lives all day."

"They're only men and not perfect," Elizabeth pleaded out of mere curiosity and not to seem too silent. Her voice carried no conviction. It sounded the platitude it was and no one could take it as opposition.

"That's right," he shouted. "You'd have some search for a saint in that crew, there's no mistake! But when I'm expected to dance to the tune, that's the trouble! What the hell do I get out of dancin' up?

"Nothing would do Quirke only come and talk to me. I got an hour of enforcin' the law, and rules and regulations and Acts of Parliament. He asked me did I read the article in this month's *Review* on The Road Traffic Act. What in-the-name-of-Jesus interest have I in The Road Traffic Act as me pay comes? And I'm sure I was supposed to play the game and say: 'I looked quickly through it, sir, when it came but I must have missed the article somehow. I'd have read anything as interestin' as that. I must look for it the very minute I go home. I'm terrible grateful to you for remindin' me about it, sir.' Jesus, it's so ridiculous," he swore.

"Then he asked me didn't I think O'Donovan had a great sense of humour. You should have seen him watch me face to try to see what I meant when I said, 'Yes, sir. He has a very fine sense of humour. He'd be able to make his livin' in a circus, sir!' ' Yes, Reegan. A circus! ' he said and you should have heard his accent. 'Yes, Reegan, a circus!' He was afraid somebody had seen through him, but he'll get on, make no mistake! He led the laughin' every time O'Donovan cracked out. It's the system of arselickin': whoever's on the bottom rung of the ladder must lick the arse above him till the last arse at the top is safely licked; they lick the arse above them and to keep their minds easy the buggers below must keep on lickin' theirs. The poor bastard at the bottom has always the worst end of the stick! It's in the natural order of things then, as Quirke would put it."

He spoke with vicious reasonableness but he could not keep it up. It bit too near the bone.

"I'm sick of it," he burst out. "Sick of saying:

'Yes, sir!

'No, sir!

'It looks so, sir.

'What do you think, sir?

'I think it might be the best way to do that, sir.' As I grow older I get sicker and sicker," he said with heat and pain. "I can't take much more of it, that's certain! I don't want to come just because some one else wants me, and have to go away when he doesn't; I want to come when I want to myself and go away for the same reason. Why should another bastard shove me about? I don't want to push anybody. But I'll not be pushed much longer and Jesus, I'm tellin' you that!"

Elizabeth was silent. She suspected that he'd be soon ashamed of having spoken at all, that was always the way with him, and she'd never heard him say so much before or so openly. Life for her these days happened much the same everywhere, she'd not enough illusions left, it had to be endured like a plague or transformed by acceptance but she said nothing. She went on sewing.

He sat silent at the table, his hands moving about his forehead and jaws with nervous excitement, until she asked cleverly, "Did Mullins come?"

"You can hear him down below," he said, glad of the escape route. "We had just the round, three drinks, and he came away with us. It's too near the first of the month for a spree."

He laughed. He was easier.

The talk of town and court, their father echoing the world that they would one day climb to out of the servitude of their childhood captured the three children; but eventually the anger and frustration became too wearing. They went to steal outside in this first lull. It was the last hour of daylight.

"Just to put water on the slide," they explained, when they were noticed going. "It's going to freeze heavy tonight."

"Mind you don't put it where someone will fall."

"It's on the river path. Nobody'll be walkin' there till the summer."

"Put coats on yourselves," Reegan at last took it into his head to play the part of father, "and no splashin' about of water. It's no time of the year yet for a wettin'."

A lovely blue dusk was on the water, a vapour of moon that'd climb to yellow light as the night came was already high. The sun had gone down to the rim of the hills they could not see beyond the woods, the spaces between the treetops burning with red light.

The sawmill came to a stop, then the stonecrusher in the quarries. Men called to each other and their voices came with haunting clarity across the frozen countryside. A bucket rattled where a woman was feeding calves in some yard. Groups of men from the quarries crossed the bridge on bicycles, their faces pale with the powdered limestone, the army haversacks that carried their sandwiches and bottles of tea wrapped in woollen socks slung from their shoulders. Tractors were ploughing in the distance, using their headlamps now; and the carts came crunching home

70

on the road, the men's faces white with dust, talking to their horses.

The children slid till they were warm and when they tired scattered buckets of water on the path and smoothed out bumps with an old shovel.

Elizabeth and Reegan were silent together within. She put aside the sewing as the light went. Then when she thought it was all too terrible and hopeless, that he'd gone to brood again over the court day, he asked with tenderness, "Are you feelin' anything better this evenin', my girl?"

He turned her face gently with his hands till their eyes met.

"Are you feelin' tired?" he asked.

She felt she could have no other wish but to fall into his arms and give way to starved emotions. And, still, she could not do that, it would be in no ways fair, neither to him nor to herself. Even if there was no such thing as control or private order, it was better to try to have a semblance, so that they might stay in some measure free, and not be all gathered into a total nothingness. She couldn't let herself fall into his arms, it'd obscure everything, it would be as if nothing had ever begun or happened.

"I feel full of pity for myself," she smiled. "I feel as tired as if the whole weight of the world was on my shoulders."

Once she'd admitted and mocked it the need to weep was gone, as if she'd mastered it by managing to stand upright in the admittance; but a part of her felt utterly cheated as they both smiled together.

"That's always the way when you're in the dumps," he said. "But there'll be no loss, you'll be all right."

"You saw the doctor?" she asked.

"Yes. I didn't want to tell you with the children there."

"What time did he say?"

"Ten to twelve are his surgery hours. They would be almost certain. But would it not be better to get him out? It's a long auld cycle. And I've only to go down to the phone to get him out."

"No—I'll go in the morning."

71

"If you're sure you want to," he conceded. "Will one of the girls stop from school?"

"No. Teresa Casey will be down later and I'll ask her to stop. She hasn't much to do and she feels she has to pay us back for Una going up nights. She has no way but those foolish presents. She'll be delighted and Ned can take his meals here till I come."

He disliked having such intimacy with anybody, but he agreed, he didn't really care enough not to let her have her way.

"We better call the children and have the rosary over early for once. It gets harder to kneel down the later it gets. It was a long day," he said quietly.

He went and she heard him call on the street, "The rosary! The rosary! The rosary!" and their shouts from the river path, "Coming, Daddy! Right! Coming, Daddy!"

The night was with them at last, the flames of the fire glittered on glass and delf, the crib on the mantelpiece bathed in the ghastly blood-red of the Sacred Heart lamp. She should take and light the lamp but their faces would fall if it was lit when they came. She'd leave it till the rosary was over. She'd have less scrutiny to fear in the uncertain firelight as she prayed. She took down the white vase that kept their beads as their feet came.

Tomorrow she'd see the doctor and she was frightened in spite of the tiredness and hopelessness. Everything might be already outside her control, nothing she could do would make the slightest difference. She could only wait there for it to happen, that was all. Whether she had cancer or not wasn't her whole life a waiting, the end would arrive sooner or later, twenty extra years meant nothing to the dead, but no, no, no. She couldn't face it. Time was only for the living. She wanted time, as much time as she could get, nothing was resolved yet or understood or put in order. She'd need years to gather the strewn bits of her life into the one Elizabeth. She did not know what way to turn, nothing seemed to depend on herself any more. She thought blindly since she could turn no way, the teeth of terror at her heart,

72

"I will pray. I will pray that things will be well. I will pray that things will be well."

They were with her in the kitchen now. She handed the children the pale mother-of-pearl with silver crosses and took out her own brown beads of wood.

Reegan got his beads from the little cloth purse he always carried in his watch pocket. He put a newspaper down on the cement and knelt with his elbows on the table, facing the dark mirror.

They blessed themselves together and he began:

"*Thou, O Lord, will open my lips*",

"*And my tongue shall announce Thy praise,*" they responded.

The even, religious tones continued in their unvarying monotony. *O Jesus, I must die! I know not where nor how. My happiness is as passing as my evenings and nights and days. I must travel the road of penance and prayer towards my Resurrection in Jesus Christ. It is my one joy and sweetness and hope, and if I will not believe in this Eternal Resurrection I must necessarily live within the gates of my own hell for ever.*

Reegan sang out the prayers as he sang them every evening of their lives and they were answered in chorus back, murmurs and patterns and repetitions that had never assumed light of meaning, as dark as the earth they walked, as habitual as their days.

"We offer the holy rosary of this night for a special intention," he dedicated before the Mysteries.

He didn't even pause, uttering the prayer in the same monotone as the prayers before and after, but it woke Elizabeth to immediate attention. Could it be possible that he was praying for her?

She felt delusion of happiness run with such sweetness in her for a moment that she felt blessed; but then was it for her he was praying? She couldn't know. She had no means of knowing. He wouldn't tell and she could never ask.

She felt the warm wood of the beads in her fingers. They were old and rather rare, she knew, and there was a relic of

73

St Teresa of Avila enclosed in the carved crucifix. She'd been given them by a priest she had nursed in London. Someone had brought them from Spain and they were more than a hundred years old, she remembered he had told her once.

3

They rose into another white morning, cold as the other days of frost, all of them helping her much, knowing she had to go to the doctor. She had slept little through the night and now she worked in a flame of nervous energy that she'd have to pay for yet. The morning went in a flash: the children gone to school, the roll call over in the dayroom, Reegan gone out on patrol. She never felt it go, she couldn't believe how it went so fast. She was dressed and Mrs Casey was smoothing down the back of her navy costume.

"You look wonderful today," she said, and it wasn't all flattery, the colour high in the usually pale cheeks, the vein in the side of her temple swollen and the eyes bright with fever. She'd know in the next few hours what she had avoided for months: she'd be alive and facing into the summer she loved without mortal anxiety, or she'd have cancer. She put on her dark overcoat and gloves and as she was ready for leaving Mrs Brennan came, a determined little woman with wiry black hair and sharp features that must have been pretty in a cold way once, but whatever luxury of flesh had bloomed there was worn down to skin and hard bone by this. She had heard Elizabeth was going to town and wanted a bottle from the chemist's for her youngest child. "Would you ever get it in Timlin's?" she asked and handed over the prescription rolled about a hard pile of silver. Her bright blue eyes lusted with curiosity as she offered conventional hopes about the visit to the doctor, but she was told nothing, and then the talk swung with deadly fixity to doctors and diseases and women's and children's ailments till Elizabeth couldn't escape quickly enough. She'd such a horror of the domestic talk of women

75

that she felt she must be lacking somehow, she got frightened sometimes, it could make her feel shut in a world of mere functional bodies, and she broke away with ill-concealed haste to be gone. It was such relief to feel the frost on her face and see the wide skies. They came with her to the door and went inside as she cycled round the barracks. Mullins heard her tyres come on the gravel and was at the window as she passed.

"Good luck, Elizabeth," he waved, the chest bursting out of the blue tunic, and she waved back.

"Old drunkard!" she smiled and was happy. She saw him close his fist and stiffen the arm as he waved for the last time: to have courage, and calling on God to stand up for all sorts of bastards. He'd have come into the kitchen to wish her luck if the women hadn't been there.

She could never see him without remembering how he had staggered in, one evening she was alone in the kitchen soon after being married. He had slumped down in the chair to wag a drunken finger and say, "Elizabeth, I can call you Elizabeth, can't I? Can you answer me this, 'lizabeth? *Who are they to say that we shall have no more cakes and ale?* That's what you might call a question, Elizabeth! A professor told me that, one Saturday night before an All Ireland Final, in Mooney's of Abbey Street, and he was drunk as I was! He was a powerful talker, could discourse on any subject under the sun! Did you ever see Mooney's of Abbey Street, it's a great place for meetin' people, and it's just opposite Wynn's Hotel where all the priests up from the country stop. There's nothin' in the world I like better, Elizabeth, than a good conversation over a pint."

She'd given him a meal, she remembered. No one could refuse him who had any heart. Not even if he had abused a hundred responsibilities. He'd shaken with laughing as he ate and said over and over, "*Who are they to say that we shall have no more cakes and ale?* That's what you might call a question, isn't it, Elizabeth? *Who are they to say that we shall have no more cakes and ale?* It gives a man heart to hear something the like of that even once in his life!"

76

She saw him at the window and waving and she over-flowed with gratitude as she bumped out the rutted avenue with the line of sycamores inside the garden wall and turned across the bridge for the town.

She had two miles of beaten dirt and stones, scattered by the traffic out of the potholes the council were always filling, till she reached the Dublin Road. Here the traffic began to pass and come against her incessantly. She hadn't to go far till she found she'd set her strength at least its equal. Even as far back as Christmas she had found it tough going, the day she went with Reegan for the children's Santa Claus and the fruit and spices and whiskey and things that would create their festival with the candles in all the windows of the houses Christmas Eve and the walk at night to the church ablaze with lights for midnight Mass.

Her clothes grew clammy with sweat as she cycled, and she felt the journey come down on her more like a weight. There were great beech trees between ash and oak and chestnut along the road and she started to count, numbering when the smooth white flesh showed out of the darker trunks in the distance, cycling past, her eyes already search-ing ahead for the next. There were five hills to go that she'd have to dismount under and walk. She turned and pushed and turned the pedals till they dwindled to four and three and two, with so many hills behind, till she was across the last; holding the handlebars as she free-wheeled down into the town, the solid block of the mountains beyond dominat-ing the slate roofs and the treetops.

It was twenty past eleven on the post office clock in Carrick Street and she left her bike against the wall there to walk to the doctor's house at the other end of the town.

She read on the brass plate: DR. J. RYAN, M.B., N.U.I. and climbed the steps between black railings to press the doorbell and was let in by a very made-up girl in her early twenties.

"Mrs Reegan," Elizabeth said.

"Was the doctor expecting you?"

"Yes."

77

"Would you come this way, please? He's rather busy this morning but I do not think you'll have long to wait. I shall tell him that you've come," with the practised smile and bow and opening of the door.

There were five women in the room, a youth, two children —all sitting round the big elliptical table with its vase of daffodils and quota of magazines.

They watched her find the most deserted corner of the table like a half-dazed animal and she was in no condition to observe them read her belly for pregnancy, her face and greying hair for age, the cost of the dark coat and the bag she carried, the third finger of her left hand when she took off her gloves.

Their curiosity soon exhausted itself. They did not know her. They were women from the poorer class of this ex-garrison town. The companies had gone, the windows smashed in the great stone barracks, but somehow their class remained—Browns and Gatebys and Rushfords and Boots and Woods—hanging idle about the streets; or temporary postmen or lorry helpers or hawkers of fish and newspapers—now that it was Britain's peace-time! But they had been Monty's Rats and in Normandy as their fathers had been at Mons and the Dardanelles. Already Friday Gateby's account of Dunkirk had become the local classic of the whole war. "It was a very dangerous place," he agreed, home for a few weeks' leave after the collapse. "A very dangerous place surely!"

With holy-water bottle and stole and speeches to the tune of *Soldiers of Old Ireland are We*, Wellington Parade became St Brigid's Terrace in white paint on a green plaque, but they went on breeding more than their fair share of illegitimates and going and coming from the Ulster Rifles and Inniskilling Fusiliers as if nothing had ever happened.

They continued with the conversation Elizabeth had interrupted. She listened quietly there, turning the pages of *The Word* that happened to lie at her hand till she was calm. When she raised her eyes she saw nothing on the faces that she hadn't seen in Whitechapel and the evenings in her own

78

barracks when the policemen gathered: the frightening impatience of the listening, holding back the dogs of their egos till they could unleash them to the sweet indulgence of their own unique complaint and wonder; the one or two who dominated and the ridden faces of the many who had learned to wait in the hope of getting a word of their own world in edgeways.

The two children played across the back of a chair, admonished every now and then by their mother. Only the youth seemed apart, biting at his finger-nails, and turning the pages and pages in front of him without reading.

She put some cooling scent on her hands and throat. She wasn't thinking of anything and she began to look more carefully through the magazines. The receptionist called another name: a woman rose and left. An old man, who looked like an army pensioner, was admitted. Another woman was called. They had started to go quickly and it was coming close to her own turn.

She might have been kneeling in the queue in front of the confessional and her turn to enter into the darkness behind the purple curtain coming closer and closer. You were sure you were ready and prepared and then you weren't any more when you got close, less and less sure the closer you got. Doubts came, the hunger for more time, the fear of anything final—you could never bring all your sins into one moment of confession and pardon, you had lost them, they had escaped, they were being replaced by the new. The nerves began to gnaw at the stomach, whispering that you were inadequate, simply always inadequate. The penny candles guttered in the spikes of their shrine; the silver sanctuary lamp cast down its light of blood, great arum lilies glowed in the white evocation of death on the altar; reverential feet on the flagstones tolled through the coughing and the stillness.

The wooden slide rattled shut across one grille, rattled open on the other. A woman's voice, "Bless me father, for I have sinned," and a tired priest's, "Continue, my child. . . . Is there anything else troubling you now, my child?"

The shutter shivered against the wall of the confession

box, there was no one now between you and the heavy curtain, your hand groped to pull it aside. It drew you to its darkness like the attraction of death but you wanted to start preparing for it all over again, quite safe at the other end of the queue, going through the five little formulas you knew so well; or you wanted to rush outside and vomit or something between the evergreens and tombstones.

She felt the strain of waiting the same as she moved closer to the moment when the receptionist would call her name. The images echoed no afterworld, there were no vistas of hell and heaven; but the mind and the heart and the stomach reacted as if they were all the one.

Her whole being was on the door when it opened, the pretty made-up face of the receptionist, the calling, "Mrs Reegan now!"

She moved to the door but had to retrace her steps in a fit of embarrassment for her handbag. At last she was standing on the black and white squares of the hall. The surgery door was open. Her name was quietly announced. The doctor rose from his desk to offer her his hand and a small modern armchair.

She did everything ingratiatingly, her eyes full of fear. She watched him walk across the grey carpet to the windows.

"Your husband was in yesterday," he chatted, "and he thought he might persuade you to call me out, but you preferred the outing, I see! It takes you out of the house, doesn't it, and it was a lovely morning for exercise. I don't take half enough exercise myself these days. A car spoils one, you can't post a letter without it in the finish, it gets such a grip on you. I see the other day where Eisenhower has taken to his bike: it's probably some publicity stunt to get the Yanks out of their automobiles. They say they're worried to death about the lack of exercise there. They're afraid they'll become a decadent race in the next generation, if they don't learn to take more exercise."

He adjusted the pale venetian blinds and returned to his chair at the desk. Then she recognized it all. He had noticed her fear when she came. He was putting her at her ease.

"You didn't mind the waiting?" he smiled as he sat down, pulling the chair sideways so as not to have to face her across the desk with inhibiting formality.

"No. Not at all," she answered.

"You must have patience so. I simply loathe waiting m if."

"Does there be so much every morning?" she kept up.

"Yes. Sometimes much more," he smiled with pride and she smiled and nodded too. He took up a biro to amuse his hands. There was a world of professional kindness and availability in his voice as he asked, "Well, can I help you?"

The priest would say, "Now tell me your sins, my child," but this room was full of light and not the dark enclosure of the box. She was sitting in a modern armchair and not kneeling on bare boards. There was a walnut clock on the mantelpiece with the inscription, *To Dr. and Mrs. James Ryan on their wedding from their friends at Mullingar G.C.* and not the white Christ on a crucifix above the grille. It was her body's sickness and not her soul's she was confessing now but as always there was the irrational fear and shame. She could not know where to begin. She was tired and anaemic. There were secret cysts in her breast.

"I've been feeling tired and run down," she said. She paused. He smiled her on.

"I thought it better to see you."

He nodded approval.

"Do you think might there be any cause? Is there anything you suspect? No?"

"There are some growing cysts in my right breast," she said and it surprised her that it came out in mere words.

She held his face in a scrutiny so passionate that it'd sift flickers into meanings. Nothing stirred there, neither eyes nor mouth, the hands played on with the biro. She saw seriousness, listening, readiness, understanding; but neither surprise nor alarm.

"Have you been aware of them for long?" he asked.

He did not even ask to see them yet. She pretended to count back.

"Last November," she diminished. "I felt as well as usual. Christmas was coming. There seemed so many things I had to do. It went on the long finger and slipped from day to day."

"Do not worry," he said. "We all put things on the long finger, foolish as it may be! Is there any pain?"

"No. Sometimes an awareness of something there, a discomfort, but not a pain."

"Can I see?" he asked at last.

She unbuttoned the blue coat of the costume and then the lace blouse that rose squarely to the throat in the V of the coat, unhooked her brassière. She let him guide her to the couch against the wall and lay down there.

There was the usual probing and asking of questions, "Here? There? Yes? Does it hurt?"

The breasts that her own hands had touched, the breasts that men had desired to touch by instinct and to seek their own sensual dreams of her there, now these professional hands sought their objective knowledge of her for a living. She dressed. They sat again. It was his responsibility to speak or stay silent.

"I don't think you have a thing to worry about but," and she knew the words that were coming, "from my examination I think it'd be better to send you for a hospital investigation, just to make certain."

"To hospital," she murmured in dejected acceptance.

"Were you ever there before?"

"Yes," she smiled. "For twenty years."

"You were a nurse before you married?" he started. "It was careless. I should have known. You should have told me."

The professional manner cracked a little, he had blundered, "Where?"

"In London mostly."

"Why, that's where I practised first. What part?"

It was a common pattern: a few years abroad to gather enough money to start his own practice at home. He had disliked it: it was no place to bring up children, you never

82

belonged, you were always Irish. "With the National Health a doctor's no more than a glorified clerk there and not half as well paid," he complained.

This slight accident of identification brought them closer but other patients were waiting.

"Is there any place you'd like to go?"

"No. Wherever you recommend."

"The County Hospital. Surgeon O'Hara there is quite good. If there's anything serious, which I'm almost certain there won't be, you'll be sent to Dublin. So you've nothing at all to worry about for the present. I'll ring Surgeon O'Hara immediately I see the last of the patients. It's better always not to waste any time. And I'll ring you at the barracks. I expect they'll find you a bed almost immediately."

She knew by his hand on her arm that the examination was over, that it was time for her to rise and go.

"How are you getting home?" he asked at the surgery door.

"A bicycle," she said. She felt a patient now, no longer free, having to live to instructions.

"If you'd wait I could leave you out on my way to the dispensary. I'd have contacted Surgeon O'Hara before then too."

"I'd rather shop and cycle," she said.

"You're running a temperature, you know. And then," he pondered and said: "I suppose it'll be all right," like a schoolmaster granting a concession.

"And the fee," she said.

"No. There's no hurry. We'll see about it later. It's all right."

"You'll not ring before I get home?" she asked.

"No. When I get back from the dispensary. . . . Would seven suit? My wife will ring the information if I have to be out."

"That would be lovely," she said. She had all that length of private time.

"They say we make poor patients. That we know too much and let our imaginations run riot," he flattered with

83

unconscious snobbery. "But I say that knowledge helps you to face up to the situation. It stands to reason that it must."

She smiled and nodded flattering approval. She had seen doctors and nurses ill and getting well again and dying as she had seen people from every other way of making a living getting well and dying too; and it made small difference. No one was very privileged in that position. Money and a blind faith in God were the most use but there came a point when pain obliterated the comfort of private rooms and special care as it did faith and hope. The young and old, the ugly and the beautiful, the failures and the successes took on such a resemblance to each other in physical suffering that it seemed to light a kind of truth. If anything made a difference it was the individual man and woman and that not very much. No one was good company sick. No one died well or got better well, they did it day by desperate day, and none of them wanted to do it alone, and it was no more strange than the fact that none of them had wanted to live alone. Doctors and nurses found they'd learned very little about suffering from the practice of their profession when it came to their own turn and she knew that neither she nor he were likely to be exceptions.

"At seven so," she heard him say.

"At seven," she nodded.

She was on the steps in the March sunlight, between the black railings, wondering if she still had her handbag, the door with the brass plate closing behind her. Not until seven would he ring. She had that much time. She came down the stone steps to the footpath, stood a moment at the corner of the railings and then she found herself walking desperate down Main Street. In flashes her mind brought her to stops. Where did Main Street lead to but to Bridge Street and Bridge Street led to St Patrick's Terrace or the Dublin Road and where in the name of Jesus did they lead but to other streets and roads and towns and countries? What could she do? Where could she go? She wanted to cry out in the street. She could face nothing.

And then her feet took over, carrying her forward, jostling

her against the shoppers; the mindless ease and constancy of their rhythm seeping into her blood with its illusion of habitual order, wore down her strength till it reduced her to a longing for a chair, and she went into a café at the Bridge and ordered coffee and cakes.

There was no use in worrying, she tried to tell herself as she sipped the wonderfully scalding coffee, there might be nothing the matter yet, the doctor had said that nothing'd be known till after the hospital examination. It had been inevitable that she'd have to go away to hospital from the beginning, that was why she'd put it off so long, but she could not reason. It involved her life in its death and the wave of terror came again.

What was her life? Was she ready to cry halt and leave? Had it achieved anything or been given any meaning? She was no more ready to die now than she had been twenty years ago. There was the after-life, hell and heaven and purgatory between, Jesus Christ on the right hand of God, but her childhood and adolescence over they had never lived as flesh in her mind, except when she dreamed. She had naïvely trusted that she'd be given some sign or confirmation before the end, or that she'd discover something, something she knew not what, some miracle of revelation perhaps, but she had been given nothing and had discovered nothing. She was as blind as she had ever been. She hadn't even started to be ready and she felt she had to try and grip the table or something, for it was absolutely inconceivable that she could die. What was it all about? Where was she going? What was she doing? What was it all about?

And then a single voice of memory broke across her agitation and she grew calm to listen. "What the hell is all this living and dying about anyway, Elizabeth? That's what I'd like to be told," Michael Halliday would beat out at a certain stage of drunkenness, especially in the months before the car crash on the Leytonstone Road that ended his life, when the affair between them had already failed. She had loved him. She had hung upon his words but they had

85

different meaning then, she had seen them as the end of love, she was seeing them now with her own life.

Names came. The London Hospital Tavern, The Star and Garter, The Blind Beggar in Whitechapel Road; the prettier pubs of the city with always the vases of red and yellow on the counter, their names like The Load of Hay enough to remember.

Halliday had fine black hair that took a sheen when brushed, brown eyes, and thick dark brows, hands that had never to toughen themselves to toil; the grain of his throat was coarse and with his pale skin she liked him best in blue.

In this café by the river images crowded every other source of life out of her mind. Her senses were shut. Her awareness of the café, the river coming white and broken between dark rocks in the arches beyond the side-windows, the shopping street shifting backwards and forwards outside the glass door were greyed away. She was in London, with Halliday, the enriched and indestructible days about her, "What the hell is all this living and dying about anyway, Elizabeth? That's what I'd like to know," removed to the fixity of death and memory and coming now like a quality of laughter.

She'd known him for months on the wards and in the theatre before he had asked her out. It wasn't easy for her to accept, though she had always liked him. He was a doctor, would probably be yet a surgeon: she was an Irish nurse, trained because it had seemed better than barmaid or skivvy, suffering every week, "So you're Irish, are you!" in the tone that it's a miracle you seem civilized. Going out with Halliday would cause the other nurses to hate her: she'd be grasping above her station; and he was an odd bird in the hospital, a bit mysterious and apart, belonging to no set, but known as a drinker, not much liked, the herd instinct immediately smelling an outsider, and he was to blame himself, for he went to no trouble to pay it the lip service with which it is often satisfied. But Elizabeth went out with him. She didn't care what they said or thought, she'd been already coming into herself. She was less and less awed by

86

the conversations and people and things that had dominated her earlier life. She was already reading, getting books out of the little public library beside Aldgate East Station, beginning to see her life in its passage, it'd end and never repeat itself, and she felt it unique and all the days precious. If she lived the life other people lived, looked on it the way they looked, she'd have no life of her own. She did not want an ensured imitation of other people's lives any more, she wanted her own, and with the wild greed of youth. Safe examples that had gone before were no use—her mother and father and the nurses about her—she could break her way out of the whole set-up. The impossible became turned by fierce desire into the possible, the whole world beginning again as it always has to do when a single human being discovers his or her uniqueness, everything becoming strange and vital and wondrous in this the only moment of real innocence, when after having slept for ever in the habits of other lives, suddenly, one morning, the first morning of the world, she had woken up to herself.

She had loved Halliday and had counted no cost. She could feel again her excitement bringing him back the first real books she'd been ever given and crying, "But they're real! They're not stories even. They're about my life."

"No, dear Elizabeth. Not exactly," he laughed, but sharing her wild delight. "You feel and see them with your own life, so much that it becomes real as your own, but it's not yours. It's somebody else's, Elizabeth. All real lives are profoundly different and profoundly the same. Sweet Jesus, Elizabeth, *profoundly* is an awful balls of a word, isn't it? But there's very few either real books or people. They're few and far between," he ended savagely.

"They're the same and different?" she asked.

He laughed and began to explain. They'd talk and argue the long evening. He had changed her whole life, it was as if he'd put windows there, so that she could see out on her own world.

The richness and happiness of that summer and early autumn! People woke and laughed when she came about, sensing the life and rejoicing within her. When she was leg-weary in the sweating wards she had only to say, "Isn't it marvellous that I'll be meeting Michael at seven and all this will be as far away as Asia?" to be renewed.

The excitement of seeing him waiting in the distance, reading an evening newspaper, or if she had arrived the first the throbbing of her heart when only a few minutes passed. The concerts, the theatres, the first restaurants she had ever been in with wine and waiters and the menus in the French she did not know, where eating became a marvellous ceremony, and how Halliday would laugh when he saw her pretending to read the card and saying, "I'll have whatever you're having, Michael," and blushing as she put it down. The walks in the evenings in the great parks that London has, the greensward lovely between the huge plane trees, moving with crowds; and talking together or staying silent over their glasses in pubs with doors open so that the cool of the late summer evening came in.

Three week-ends they spent. . . . But was there use, remembering can go on for ever. It changed, it came to nothing. Halliday changed, as quietly as a blue sky can turn to cloud. She suffered the agonies of fear and hope and suspicion and hurt vanity, becoming wildly jealous. She had thought there must be some other woman.

"No, no, there's nobody," he protested.

"But you've changed towards me?"

"No. I love you, dearest Elizabeth. How could anything have changed?"

It fell with such sweetness on her ears that she wanted to be blind and believe, but she knew in her heart he had changed. She couldn't be content, though she wanted nothing else but this blind happiness.

"No. That is not the truth. There must be someone else. I know it. Why do you want to fool me?"

He looked at her. He wondered how much she suspected and knew.

"No. No woman will believe that there's not another woman, but there's not! I tell you there isn't, Elizabeth!"

88

"There must be something. I know there must be something. You do not love me any more?" she pleaded, her lips shaking.

He looked at her. He suffered whether to tell her or not. She was young and the most beautiful person he had ever met but he didn't love her any more, and he wondered if he ever had.

"You couldn't understand. It'd be no use," he blundered stupidly.

"Do you think I'm too stupid?" she cried, her eyes brimming.

"No, no, no!" He was distressed and harried. "I don't think you'd believe it! You're too beautiful."

"That you do not love me?"

"That there's nothing, simply nothing!"

"How nothing? Why can't you speak straight? Why must you always talk in riddles?"

"That there's nothing," he almost shouted, goaded into passion. "That there is nothing and nobody in my stupid life. Nothing at all, absolutely nothing. Women have to believe in life, but some men are different."

Tears slipped down her cheeks. She couldn't understand, it had no meaning. How could something stay alive on nothing? He was telling her that he loved her no more, that was all she understood. And she winced years later in the café in this small town at the memory of the flood of pain and desperation and total defeat that had come down about her. They had gone out for the evening, to a little Kensington bar, it had red carpets, blue plates and copper or brass goblets hung around the walls. They were sitting in wooden alcoves out from the farthest wall, their glasses on the bench between them. It could return with such shocking vividness.

She had wanted to run away and couldn't and only the public place kept her from breaking into a complete mess. She had asked hopelessly again, "You do not love me?" and his voice was definite, "No, no. I'm sorry, Elizabeth. It wouldn't be fair to you, it'd only make it far worse in the end and to do this is harder for me than to go on."

She had nearly pleaded: to let it go on, to let it persist under any kind of illusion, anything that'd lighten this terrible nightmare. She tried to hold herself calm. She had wanted to shout or scream. She had turned the glass about and about on the bench.

"You told me that you loved me," she became calm enough to accuse though it seemed more part of insane musing than any accusation. "You told me that you loved me!"

"I loved you. I could not have lived without you. In the weeks before I met you the thought of calling it all a cursed day followed me about like my own shadow. You're the most beautiful person I ever got to know. You brought a kind of laughing into my life, I can't even attempt to understand. I began to believe in everything again. I used to think about you all day and then it went and I started to sink back into my own shit again. I could do or feel nothing. Not even you had any meaning. I thought you might never notice it."

"And it is still the same?"

"Yes."

He saw she was shocked and broken but the threads had become too involved with his own life and he couldn't stop.

"These last weeks have been nothing but torture—that I'd come to the end of my own tether and used you to get a short breather. That I used you so as not to have to face my own mess. That I seduced you because I was seduced myself by my own fucking lust."

Then he woke fully to its effect on her and he tried to jerk her back.

"O, but you are beautiful, Elizabeth. None of this is your fault. . . ."

Why couldn't he have let her go on in her illusions? Everything was stripped down to the bone now and there was the pure nothingness that he'd spoken about. Nothing could ever stay alive, nothing could go on living.

He was dragging her to attention by pulling at her wrist. "Do you understand now that there's no other woman?"

She nodded. She was trying to get some grip on herself. She hadn't given it all up as lost yet. She'd fight him.

"There's the books and music," she ventured quietly, her voice betraying nothing of the hope she trusted to it, of the balance of fear and hope that tore her heart.

"No, no, no," he denied. "You woke that and it died too. I discovered what I was at twenty in your enthusiasm. When there's no curiosity any more, when you're seeing the world through other people's eyes, deaf and dumb and blind yourself, no two worlds the least alike, what are books and music then? Nothing, nothing at all, an extension of the fraud, that's all!"

She was silent. Her heart sank in the acceptance of death. She started when she heard him ask, "Will you marry me, Elizabeth? Will you marry me now, Elizabeth?"

"Are you trying to make a fool of me?" her vanity had been hurt to quick life.

"No! How can you say that, Elizabeth? I mean will you marry me after what I told you? Will you, Elizabeth?"

He was serious then; but how could she marry him? He had forced her to see further than marrying for a house and position and children. She had seen the happy solution of her whole world in love and mutual sympathy. She could give her share, but he couldn't or wouldn't, and it was quite as useless as if there was nothing on either side. He had destroyed her happiness. She'd never be able to believe even in a dream of happiness again.

"No," she shook her head. "It'd be impossible now."

"Is there no hope, no hope at all?"

She shook her head, her eyes blind with tears.

"Would you have married me if I hadn't told you?" he was driven by egotistical curiosity to see what other road his life might have taken.

"I do not know," she refused.

"Only a fool tells everything," he complained bitterly, beginning to be dogged by longing for what he had destroyed. "You can tell nothing. It takes a moron to believe he'll ever find someone who'll understand."

She couldn't recall much of the next few weeks. They became swallowed up in a merciful and protective fog. She saw Halliday almost every evening. She didn't know what'd become of her if she couldn't see him. This terrifying need to see him took possession of her, she had to know that he was always available. She was helpless. She would be devoured by the need till she'd be able to find her own feet.

Then she reacted to the lash of hurt vanity, and to recover herself out of the bondage of love. She was still in subjection to him, but she'd recover. She'd smash that subjection, she'd hate him, he was the cause of all her suffering; when she got completely free of him she'd never see him again. She'd be mistress then. And she steeled herself to do without him, destroying the need within herself with the poison of hate and resentment, but in the meantime she saw him constantly, his complete despair coming out in those evenings. He'd go to plays and concerts no more. The only place he could feel free was in pubs, and he was drinking heavily.

"I came from what's called a medical family," he derided one evening. "So when my turn came I walked the long grey line too, 'privileged to peer down microscopes for a number of years at all the bacteria in the human corpus,' as a certain ass expressed it. I'd enough illusions myself then to sink a battleship, for never did such a wide-eyed ass arrive at any university! Alleviation of suffering, scientific advancement and all that kind of lark! The prize of the collection was to get a bedside seat at *The Human Drama of Suffering*, to live and work close to the brass tacks of life. You see I was a pessimistic bastard even then, a volume of Housman in my hip pocket! Soldier-to-the-war-returning and all that slush! Byjesus, I was never set for such a shocker, the whole drama is in your own fucking suffering, the other poor chaps are egomaniacs all! No desire to give you the inside story there, byjesus! Only bribe and blackmail you into taking their carcass as solemnly as they take it themselves! Sweet Jesus, Elizabeth, it's too uproarious! Wouldn't an M.Sf. be the degree of degrees, Elizabeth—Master of Suffering! Wouldn't it go beautiful with a cap and gown? And, byjesus, what a record number of candidates you'd have the day the arch-angel G jollies all the old centuries up with that bugle of his," he roared, his hands at his sides because they hurt.

He didn't care whether he shocked her or not. He had given up all hope of his life ever getting strength and purpose through her. No, no, no, he argued with himself; she'd not be always there in the evenings when he'd come home tired. She'd not be there to excite him with her dressing-up to go out to the parks and restaurants and theatres and shops and pubs. She'd not be there when a mad fit of sexual desire came, to blind it in the darkness of her womb before it grew to desperate sight enough to see his life moving in a hell of loneliness between a dark birth and as dark a death. Nor would he have her woman's breathing by his side when he woke at night or have her to talk to when he needed someone; or be able to walk with her through the morning market, sharing the buying of eggs and bread and butter.

He had dreamed of bringing her to the South he'd fallen in love with in the long holidays from the universities: Chalon on the way down, Lyons, Valence, Avignon, Nîmes, Montpellier, Sete across the marshlands high above the Mediterranean; poplars and the road glowing white between the open vineyards, the cicadas beating and the earth and sky throbbing together in the noonday as you went on to Carcassonne to sit with a glass of wine in the evening at a sidewalk table and wonder how long more you could make your money last out. Even the naming of the towns brought fierce longing and he had dreamed then of bringing back a girl like Elizabeth with him to show her it all. And he hated this dream of happiness as only something can be hated that's so deep within a person that it's painful not to want.

"Sweet Jesus, Halliday, it's too much," he would swear silently. "You want to bring a girl back with you to watch over your dead youth, no less, and all that kind of shit! To have her breathing by your side when you wake up in the nights! Jesus, Halliday, it'd do for a literary fucking medical man, praising the job for the experience it gave him of life.

93

Sweet Jesus, Halliday, buck yourself up! You can't go down into that fucking swamp!"

So he set his face steadily on his real road, away from Elizabeth, and he would be tempted by dream of neither normality nor goodness nor any other social thing. He often wanted to hurt her now, but she was growing free. His drinking worsened into a steady gloom, he was seldom able to stand up by pub close; and, "What the hell is all this living and dying about anyway?" would come as a scream of frustration and hate at some time or other of those grisly evenings. Then came the car crash on the Leytonstone Road to solve nothing and everything: the inquest; his people's invitation to Elizabeth to go to visit them, which she never accepted; and his burial in her own mind till the day she'd die.

"What is all this living and dying about anyway?" came almost as flesh of her own thought at last in this small-town café, but it had been Halliday's question in the beginning, it had never been hers alone. Even if she hadn't cancer she was still growing old and it was more than time to face up to the last problems; but weren't they so inevitable and obvious that they were better ignored? Were the real problems faced and solved or declared insoluble or were they not simply lived in the changes of her life? She could live her life through in its mystery, without any purpose, except to watch and bear witness. She did not care. She was alive and being was her ridiculous glory as well as her pain.

The waitress came and took the cup and plate away and she knew it was time for her to pay and go. She had to leave Mrs Brennan's prescription with the chemist and do her shopping. She was told the prescription would be made up in a half-hour and so as not to mix the little pile of cash that she unrolled out of the paper with her own money she asked if she could pay then. She had to smile as she handed it over—for it was exactly right.

It did not take her long to do the shopping and she got no pleasure from wandering on her own between the windows. The tiredness was returning, people with whom she knew she could have no conversation were stopping her to talk, draining away the little life she had left for her own things. The only real conversations, anyhow, she ever had were with the people she had loved, and if she had God's energy she could possibly love everybody, but she had even less and less of her human share. She had to keep it for her own things or she'd be nothing. She had been lavish once, looking round for things to give herself to, and she did not regret any of the giving but she couldn't do it any more. She had to be what she would have despised once—careful! She had nothing against these social pleasantries of weather and births and marriages and success and failure, the falls of the humble dices of life, but she didn't care enough. They were not exciting any more. She couldn't care for everything. Her love had contracted to just a few things. It might be squalid and true but hadn't the love the same quality of herself as it had in the beginning? What more did it matter? What did it matter if these social exchanges had reduced themselves to the nightmarish vision of the idiotic and barely comprehensible gestures and grimaces of face and head and hand people make when they try to communicate through a closed window. *They* did not exist any more, but *she* did.

She got away as quickly as possible each time. She had her shopping done. She came back to Timlin's for Mrs Brennan's prescription and had to wait a while, sitting on the chair between the weighing-machine and the Kodak girl, quiet and very clean there with the rubber advertising mats down, and not many came. She put the bottle she had already paid for in her bag when it was ready and left. At the bottom of Main Street she met the woman who kept the sweet shop beside the chapel in the village, the fourth person this day she had to stand to speak to.

"We had a good day for coming to town," it went. "How did you get in? How'll you get home? Will it be long till you're going?"

She was going now. She was in a hurry. She was delighted to have met the other woman, they must have a long talk some time, but not just now, she simply had to rush. She had been in town all morning. She should have been gone an hour ago.

And she was free, crossing the bridge with her shopping-bag, and her bicycle was where she'd left it, at the post office. A slight wind had risen that blew with her. She climbed uphill out of the town and mounted the bike above it, her push-push-push on the pedals lulling her into the temporary effort and peace of its rhythm. Even when she had to walk the hills the conversations that began within her kept far from the cysts in her breasts, light and musing and futile.

"Why are you pushing this bike, Elizabeth?"

"To go home, of course!"

"But why do you want to get home?"

"Because I want to get home!"

"But why?"

"That's the why!"

"That's a stupid child's answer!"

She went along the demesne wall Reegan had patrolled on that wet night in February, swollen green with ivy, the great beech trees stirring behind. Cars met and passed her, bicycles, a tractor, a coal lorry from the pits, three timber lorries. The rooks were mating in the bare sycamores about the Protestant Church and cawing and flapping clumsily about overhead.

"All answers are stupid and questions too," the game continued in her head. "I am pushing the bike because I am pushing because I am pushing. I am going home because I am going home because I am going home."

"But you must have some reason!"

"I want to go home."

"But why?"

"But why?"

"But why ask? That's it: why ask? I'm going home. I'm alive. That's obvious, isn't it?"

Men were gathered about tractors and a solitary horse at the forge beside the crossroads where she turned down the dirt track to the village. A cylinder of Calor gas was out on the street, the blacksmith or more mechanic now since he'd come home from Birmingham goggled as he stooped over a broken plough, the explosion of blue and white light shocking her passing eyes as the acetylene in his hand made contact with the steel.

She could see the village as she came downhill, the light staring her in the face, the woods across the lake, the mountains beyond with the sheds and gashes of the coal pits on the slopes, the river flowing through into the Shannon lowlands. The long pastures with black cattle and sheep, stone walls and thorn bushes came to meet her; and in a tillage field a tractor was ploughing monotonously backwards and forwards with its shadow.

"I am coming home and I am alive," it at last decided and started to go over and over in her mind till it tired away.

Mullins was asleep by the fire and was not woken by her tyres passing the dayroom window on the gravel, but the two dark-haired girls came chasing, "We were watching the window for you, Elizabeth. We thought you must have got a puncture, Elizabeth," and to carry the shopping-bag proudly in. Mrs Casey was there with a cigarette and smiling.

She gave them the sweets she brought and they cried out with excitement as the ceremony of dividing them began and the offering of their portions to Mrs Casey and then Elizabeth.

There was no use sidetracking the young woman's curiosity. She told her that she was going into hospital for examination. She didn't give any intimate information. Nothing would be known until she went into hospital, she said. She came with the other woman to the door after they had made cups of tea and thanked her there. She watched her go and she didn't turn left through the archway but crossed the bridge towards the great stone house where the Brennans had rooms. The wind, Elizabeth thought, had risen: the days of frost were about to turn to spring rain.

Inside she heaped wood and turf on the fire, filled the kettle, hung it to boil, put some slices of bacon that were

97

too salty in a bowl of warm water, all the time waiting for Reegan to come home. The hands of the clock were crawling up to five. At seven the doctor would ring. Surely Reegan would be home before then, surely she would not have to take the call on her own.

The children went out to play on the avenue. She heard their shouts about the archway. The minutes beat by in the stillness, the slow minutes waiting for him to come home; more than sixty minutes, for his blue uniformed bulk did not pass through the window light till it was almost six. The whole day had gone in waiting for this or that: it had torn her nerves, and all boiled into sudden hatred of Reegan. "Didn't he know that she had been to the doctor? Couldn't he make it his business to wait home for her? The patrols were not that necessary? What right had he to keep her suffering like this?" had gnawed all reason and vision away by the time he came.

His feet sounded on the cement of the street where the barrels stood under the eavespipes. He lifted off his cap and put it carelessly down on the sideboard, unbuttoning his greatcoat.

"You got back all right, Elizabeth," he greeted smiling, and then he saw her waiting for him, her face tensed, the hour spent resenting his delay making it the image of the reproach she had not yet uttered.

"I was waiting here this past hour," she cried with the maniacal temper of a child.

It was the last thing he had expected. He'd seen small flashes of resentment, and these but seldom, but never such an explosion. In his blind way he felt something terrible must have happened.

When she heard her own frustrated voice and saw him stand so shocked and frozen her feeling burst in tears. He came towards her and he was awkward. She felt ashamed. She'd betrayed herself. She'd let the stupid passion of resentment rise up through the frustration and strain of her life in this day and she had given full vent to it on Reegan for keeping her waiting. What right had she to expect Reegan to wait at home for her? She'd no right to expect anything. She hadn't even the right to live.

Reegan didn't know what to do but he did the right thing by instinct: he came to her. His first wife that he'd taken from the Show Dance in Sligo had often been like this, he'd have to pet and pleasure her or else affirm his male strength, and everything would come out all right in the embracing or sexual intercourse that always followed as naturally as sun after a shower. Elizabeth was different. He had never got close enough to be able to predict her but he was attentive and careful now and it was right.

"I didn't think," he said. "I never thought of this," and then with stultifying awkwardness, "I love you, Elizabeth. It doesn't make any difference, this! You know I love you, Elizabeth."

She sobbed. Then he kissed her. She kissed him back. Tears blinded her eyes. She could not see, and now she was drowning in this emotional swoon. She must grip herself. She must, somehow, try to stand upright.

"What did the doctor say?" his common sense came with the pure relief of the first daylight.

"He said that I'll have to go into hospital for examination. He's afraid I may have cancer. He's phoning at seven, he's arranged about a bed in the County Hospital."

She had said everything in her reaction from the breakdown. She wouldn't have to use the sign language of concealment and fear any more, it was a miracle how she'd managed to tell everything. Reegan was shaken now.

"He said you may have cancer?" he repeated, not able to believe. He'd seen his first wife in the morgue and had experienced little except a desire never to see a dead face again. She was gone, he was frightened, his whole life would be upside down.

How could two wives die on the same man? It was incredible.

"He said you *may* have cancer," he repeated, flinching at the clear viciousness of the word, "but he doesn't know."

"He doesn't know," she started with painful hope.

99

"Where, does he think?"

"In the breast. There are cysts there. They may be malignant. . . ."

"When did you notice them?"

"A few weeks ago," she lied.

"You never told?" he reproached.

"I thought that they were nothing," she tried to excuse. "I didn't want to cause you more trouble. I was feeling tired and didn't know till he said. . . ."

She was near breaking again. She saw his eyes on her breasts in morbid fascination. No, he couldn't want to see them now, she cried within herself: the church in which they had married had proclaimed them one flesh, but no, no, no. . . . People rotted apart. With fierce relief she heard the children come. It was half six. She'd been alone with Reegan all that length of time and it seemed gathered into the intensity of a single moment. At seven the doctor would ring and she had many things to do before then. She put the steeped slices of bacon on the pan. Rain spat at her when she went out to the barrels for water. That was why the children must have come in, she thought. She heard the unearthly cry of the foxes in their season from the brushwoods along the river. It always filled her with terror, this raw cry of animal heat. She smelled the bacon frying as pure sweetness when she closed the door. There was a white cloth on the table, cups, sugar, bread, butter. The kettle was singing on the fire. They had even chairs to sit in. Soon the children would light the lamp with her, draw the blinds against that night. Mullins was coming up the hallway.

"That frying has me driven mad, Elizabeth. I can't stand it any longer. I'm off for the auld tea. So I'll leave the door open and you'll be able to hear the phone or anyone knocking," he said as if he had never known himself to say it before.

"Brennan didn't come?" Reegan asked.

"He must have got held up!"

"You should have gone before," Reegan said. "You should have gone at six. I'd have told you to go only I thought Brennan had relieved you."

"Don't worry, Sergeant. The auld appetite is the better for it. Hunger is good sauce," he laughed. "And these things'll all right themselves in a hundred years, isn't that it?"

"Leave the key on the sill," Reegan called, "in case Brennan comes."

"He's not likely to come now but I'll leave it there. Well, I'm off at last in God's truth," he laughed, did a kind of dance shuffle with his feet, swept off his cap in mock flourish, and was gone whistling down the hallway.

"It's better they're makin' them these days," Reegan smiled dryly and they were at ease again.

They took their evening meal. Elizabeth couldn't take her eyes off Reegan. What was he thinking? His face was a mask. Was he fed up with her? Was he thinking of the hospital bills? Was he thinking that this was another shackle to hold him longer in the police? Was he regretting ever marrying her?

"It'll be a devil to get to sleep for the next weeks with that cryin'," was all he remarked as the mating call of the foxes came loud and fierce from the brushwoods.

At exactly seven the phone rang and he asked: "Will you go down, Elizabeth?"

"No. You go down," she said.

The ringing came above his boots on the cement as he went, above his boots on the boards of the dayroom. He did not shut the door. They heard his, "Hello", as the ringing stopped.

"Is there something wrong, Elizabeth?" Willie asked, sensing the tenseness.

"Why?" she responded neurotically.

"No why, Elizabeth. I just thought with the phone and that," he bent his head, rebuffed.

Her whole attention was on the conversation between Reegan and the doctor. The barracks was dead still, but she could hear nothing, the doctor obviously doing most of the talking, the little Reegan said muffled by the receiver.

Then it was over. The receiver clicked as it was laid back in its cradle.

There was that terrible moment of searching blank features for information when he came, information that was given seconds later, "He got a bed for tomorrow. The ambulance will be here at four," he said.

"The ambulance," she repeated, with visions of the cream van with the red cross coming in the avenue.

"The whole village will know," she said.

He came close to her. Then he saw the three children gazing with open curiosity. He stopped to shout, "Have you no lessons to do tonight? Have you nothing to do but stand there?" and he watched them pretend to go to their school-bags.

"It doesn't matter, everybody gets the ambulance, it's there for us as well as the next," he said. "I can't go to-morrow and it'll be better and quicker that way. He says you may be only a few days there. What does it matter about them knowin'? They'll know anyhow, nothing can be kept secret in a place as small as this."

He wouldn't ask Quirke for a free day, it would seem like asking a favour, she suspected; but there was no charity in that thinking. The children were staring again in open curiosity.

"It doesn't really matter," she said. "You're quite right. And, it'd be better to tell the children now."

"I am going away to hospital tomorrow," she confided. "Not for long. Only for a few days."

Tears came in their eyes. Their own mother had gone to hospital years ago and never came back. She had gone to heaven.

They hadn't seen coffin or hearse or anything. She'd been taken from the hospital to the church in the evening and buried the next afternoon. The slow funeral bell had tolled both times, they'd heard noise of heavy traffic, the blinds of the house were down in the broad daylight, but they'd seen nothing. Afterwards, they were allowed out to play on the avenue.

Two men they knew who often brought them down the river meadows came in the avenue with fishing-rods. They rushed to meet them, "Will you bring us down the meadow today?"

The pair of men were put ill at ease. They searched each other's face.

"Not today. Some other day."

"Please, please, please . . . You brought us before?"

"Did you not hear about your mother?"

"They told us. She is being buried now, but they said we could play. Please, can we go?"

"Not today," they refused. "Some other day. And we'll catch a big pike," and they watched them go with longing, the flowers shining out of the thick greenness of the meadows, white stones on the shore of the river, the cattle standing with the water to their bellies in the heat and the fish rising.

The people came from the funeral and they had asked, "When is Mammy coming back from heaven?"

"When God tells her. Very soon, if you pray to God."

They'd got tired asking and getting the same answer. Elizabeth had come and they'd almost forgotten. Now it was Elizabeth who was going to hospital.

"I'll be only a few days there," she persuaded. "You must finish your exercises for school tomorrow. If you don't do them now, how can I expect you to do them when I'm away?"

They brushed their tears and settled themselves to their work.

"That's the way," she encouraged. "You were making a big thing out of nothing."

Reegan had moved to the window, made to feel out of place by the delicacy of the scene between the woman and children.

"It's all right about the ambulance," he said.

"It's all right," she answered.

The blinds were down, the lamp lit, the children at their exercises, and the night repeating itself in the same order of so many nights. Once she had wanted to protect this calm flow of life against Reegan, she'd succeeded, and what did it matter? Did it make any real difference? Tomorrow night she'd be in a hospital bed and this'd continue or break up without her.

She started to lay out the things she'd need there and she then went to their bedroom. It was lonely and intensely quiet in the room, with the flame of the small glass oil-lamp blowing in the draughts.

She unlocked the wooden trunk she'd brought about with her all her life. It held bundles of letters and photos and certificates and testimonials, a medal she had won in her final examination, some books, a withered plane leaf, a copybook of lecture notes, and other things that'd be junk to everybody else—except what her hands sought, a roll of money.

So she hadn't trusted much, she'd been afraid. Was this why it had failed? she pondered. With this money she could always be in London in the morning. She had not given herself fully, she had always been essentially free.

"You can only give one thing really to anybody—that's money. Love and sympathy and all that kind of stuff is just moonshine and ballsology. Give a person money and tell them to take a tour for themselves. Tell them to go and look about themselves. That's all you can do, if you feel yourself moved," she had heard Halliday say bitterly once. Many of the letters in the trunk were his, all the books. She did not know. She might never get back to this house. Maybe, she should destroy these things now, she'd hate anybody else reading through them, but then what did the dead care? She locked the trunk, leaving everything undisturbed, except the money she took. She'd take it to the hospital. But when she saw Reegan and the children in the bare kitchen she began to be tortured with what was still too present to be called remorse, she should tell them, they were all together, it was their money as much as hers; but she could not, she wished she had long ago, it'd be too complicated and dreadful now to tell. And if it all came out when she was dead, how could she be hurt then? She would not even think. "No, no, no, no," came on her breath, the echo of the mind's refusal to endure more torture.

Mullins came. "I got back at last," he stated.

"No one came since," Reegan informed him.

"You could sit down there for a year and nothing'd happen and then the once you'd take a chance you'd be caught out," Mullins said and stood awkwardly there till he managed to say, "I hope you don't think that I'm too full of curiosity, but is it right that you're goin' to the hospital, Elizabeth?"

She met Reegan's eyes: he had said that nothing could be kept secret in a place as small as this.

"I have to go tomorrow," she said.

"I'm very sorry to hear that but I hope it'll be all right."

"It's only for a check-up."

"With the help of God it'll be nothing and if there's anything I can do . . ." he offered.

"No, no. Thank you, John. It'll be only for a few days."

"I'm glad to hear it's not serious," and he had nothing more to say and still no excuse to go with ease. He stood there waiting for something to release him. The children watched. It was Reegan who finally relieved the awkwardness.

"Will you put me out on patrol? It'll save me going down to the books."

"Where?" Mullins beamed to life.

"Some of the bog roads. Some place where not even Quirke's huarin' car can get."

"So it's a patrol of the imagination so," Mullins laughed the barrack joke.

"A patrol of the imagination!" Reegan laughed agreement.

"As sound as a bell so! It'll be done while Johnny Atchinson is thrashin' ashes in Johnny Atchinson's ash hole! I bet you not even Willie'd say that quick without talkin' about arse holes. . . ."

He was his old self. He laughed as he pounded down the hallway and the house shivered with the way he let the dayroom door slam.

"Some people should ride round this house on bulldozers," Reegan said as he put down a newspaper on the cement and let the beads run into his palm. "We better get the prayers over because, unless I'm mistaken, this house'll be full of women soon."

They came before Elizabeth had her packing finished, all the policemen's wives, Mrs Casey and Mrs Brennan and Mrs Mullins. They were excited, the intolerable vacuum of their own lives filled with speculation about the drama they already saw circling about this new wound.

"It's only for a few days. It's only for an examination," Elizabeth tried to keep it from taking wild flight, but they were impatient of any curb. They went over the list of things she'd need. They offered the loan of some things of their own. They talked about their experiences in hospitals and doctors and nurses and diseases. They gave pieces of advice. Tea was made. The children were sent to bed.

Reegan had no part in the conversation. He moved restlessly about the house, not wanting to leave Elizabeth on her own.

Ten came and there was no sign of them going. He turned on the radio full blast to listen to the news and let it blare away up to eleven through the Sweepstake programme.

Eventually he found a pair of shoes to mend and it became a real battle. The ludicrously loud belting of the nails above the radio music and the deliberate scraping of the last on the cement made it painful to try to talk but they stayed militantly on till he gave up.

Elizabeth felt herself near madness by the time it was over. She didn't wait to listen to his curses when they'd gone. She let him do all the small jobs she'd always done herself before sleep, and struggled to their room without caring what kind of unconsciousness overcame her there as long as it came quickly.

4

The ambulance took her away at four the next day and spring came about the barracks that week as it always did, in a single Saturday: bundles of Early York, hundredweights of seed potatoes and the colourful packets of flower and vegetable seed the children collected coming from the Saturday market. Spades and forks and shovels, cobwebs on the handles, were brought out into the daylight; the ball of fishing-line that kept the ridges straight was found after a long search, beneath the stairs. In the night Reegan sat with a bag of the seed potatoes by his side, turning each potato slowly in the lamplight so as to see the eyes with the white sprouts coming, and there was the sound of the knife slicing and the plopping of the splits into the bucket between his legs.

Mullins and Brennan were splitting the seed in their kitchens exactly as he was there, and Monday they'd be planting in the conacre they rented each year from the farmers about the village. Reegan alone had the use of the barrack garden, but he'd not be able to spend as much time there as they would in the fields—it was open to the village road and anybody passing. The other two would do nothing but plant in the next weeks, all their patrols would be *patrols of the imagination* as they joked, carried out on these plots of ground. They knew Reegan didn't care and always a child was posted on the bridge to warn them if Quirke or the Chief Super appeared. They couldn't afford to buy vegetables and potatoes for their large families: their existence was so bare as it was that Mullins was never more than a few days on the spree when they were getting credit in the shops or borrowing or going hungry.

Casey hated manual work. It was as much as his wife could do to get him to mow the lawn and keep the weeds out of the gravel and dig the beds for the roses she put down so as not to be shamed by the school-teacher who had the next rooms. Not having children to feed he wasn't forced to take part in this burst of spring industry; he still brought his cushion down with him on b.o. days, kept his gloves on when he wheeled or rode the bicycle, read newspapers and listened to the end of the season's soccer and the boxing matches and *Sports Stadium* on Friday nights; and he fenced, "It's a bloomin' bad country that can't afford one gentleman!" when Mullins or more seldom Brennan chaffed.

This was the time when poor Brennan's *best-in-Ireland* act started up for the year in real earnest and it went on obliviously till the crops were lifted in October. "Ten ridges, twenty-nine yards long, meself and the lads put down yesterday. Not a better day's work was done in Ireland," he'd boast at roll-call, while the others winked and smiled.

Reegan was happy too in this spring, the frustrations and poisons of his life flowing into the clay he worked.

It was good to be ravenously hungry in these late March and April evenings with the smell of frying coming from the kitchen! Would it be the usual eggs and bacon, or might they have thought of getting the luxury of fresh liver or herrings, if the vans brought some to the shops? It was such satisfaction to drag his feet through the gate and look back as he shut it at an amount of black clay stirred, so many ridges shaped and planted; his body was tired and suffused with warmth, the hot blood running against the frost, and there was no one to tell him the work wasn't done fully right, they were his own ridges, he had made them for himself. And these evenings could be so peaceful when the sawing and stone-crushing stopped and the bikes and the carts and the tractors had gone home. The last of the sun was in the fir tops, the lake a still mirror of light, so close to nightfall that the birds had taken their positions in the branches, only an angry squawking now and again announcing that the unsatisfied ones were trying to move.

He'd wash the dried sweat away inside in front of the scullery mirror and change into fresh clothes before he sat to eat in the lamplight, he'd laugh and make fun with the children and feel the rich communion of being at peace with everything in the world. Never did he get this satisfaction out of pushing a pen through reports or patrolling roads or giving evidence on a court day.

All his people had farmed small holdings or gone to America and if he had followed in their feet he'd have spent his life with spade and shovel on the farm he had grown up on or he'd have left it to his brother and gone out to an uncle in Boston. But he'd been born into a generation wild with ideals: they'd free Ireland, they'd be a nation once again: he was fighting with a flying column in the hills when he was little more than a boy, he donned the uniform of the Garda Siochana and swore to preserve the peace of The Irish Free State when it was declared in 1920, getting petty promotion immediately because he'd won officer's rank in the fighting, but there he stayed—to watch the Civil War and the years that followed in silent disgust, remaining on because he saw nothing else worth doing. Marriage and children had tethered him in this village, and the children remembered the bitterness of his laugh the day he threw them his medal with the coloured ribbon for their play. He was obeying officers younger than himself, he who had been in charge of ambushes before he was twenty.

That movement in his youth had changed his life. He didn't know where he might be now or how he might be making a living but for those years, but he felt he could not have fared much worse, no matter what other way it had turned out. But he'd change it yet, he thought passionately. All he wanted was money. If he had enough money he could kick the job into their teeth and go. He'd almost enough scraped together for that as it was but now Elizabeth was ill. He should have gone while he was still single; but he'd not give up—he'd clear out to blazes yet, every year he had made money out of turf and this year he rented more turf banks than ever, starting to strip them the day after he had the potatoes and early cabbage planted. He'd go free yet out into some life of his own: or he'd learn why. He was growing old and he had never been his own boss.

That week-end he brought Elizabeth home. They had taken the biopsy of the breast and sent it to Dublin for analysis. The final diagnoses had come back: she had cancer.

As the next-of-kin Reegan saw the surgeon the Saturday he took her home. He was told she'd have to go to Dublin to have the operation: she'd be let home for only a few days, until such time as a bed was ready, the only reason she was being allowed out at all was that she had pleaded to be let spend the spare days she had between the hospitals in her home.

He wouldn't say what her chances were—she had definitely a slight chance. If the operation proved successful she might live for ten or even more years. If it wasn't—a year, two years, he didn't care to say, he had only taken the biopsy, he was forwarding all his particulars to the Dublin surgeon. He could assure Reegan that she would be in the best hands in the country.

The formality of it was terrifying, the man's hand-tailored grey suit and greying hair, the formal kindness of his voice. A thousand times easier to lie in a ditch with a rifle and watch down the road at the lorries coming: you had the heat of some purpose, a job to do, and to some extent your life was in your own hands: but this, this. . . . It was too horrifying, a man or woman no more than a caged rat being given over to scientific experiment. He thought the interview would never be over. He wanted to forget, forget, forget. This wasn't life or it was all a hell of a flop. It was no use doing anything: it'd be better to take a gun and blow your brains out there and then, but at least Elizabeth was waiting smiling for him, and he couldn't get her quickly enough away and home.

The five days she was there proved too many. She had to follow instructions, take medicines, stay in bed late, do none of the tasks that had become her life in the house. She was living and sitting there and it was going on without her. The policemen's wives were constantly in. She had no life whatever then, just chit and chat, skidding along this social surface. She knew she must have cancer. Moments, when she'd suddenly grow conscious that she must be only sitting here and waiting, she'd be seized with terror that it would all end like this, a mere interruption of these banalities and nothing more.

The nights were worse, when she was awake with Reegan and could discuss nothing. Oh, if she could only discuss the operation she was about to face and discover what they both felt! And if they got that far together they might be able to go back to the beginning and unravel something out. There never had been even any real discussion, not to speak of understanding, and while each of them alone was nothing there might be no knowing what both of them might find together. No, she could not even begin when they were awake, silence lay between them like a knife; and he was slaving at the turf-banks these days as well as doing his police work, and was mostly asleep, no sound but some aboriginal muttering rising now and then to his lips, the same that would rise to hers out of the black mysteries of her own sleep.

So it continued till she went, they did not even make simple sexual contact because his hands would come against the bandages. Few were waiting at the town station that morning she went. A cold wind blew down the tracks but the little red-brick building, old and rather pretty, had last year's holiday posters and narcissi and daffodils tossing between the bare rods of the fuchsias in the beds.

"It's cold for April," she shivered, her eyes resting on the features they knew too well to experience any more.

"It's better to have it now than a bad summer," clicked as automatically out as if she had put a coin in a slot.

"But if we could have it both ways!" the words forced other words.

"That'd be perfect," it continued, "but with the weather this country has we're lucky to get it any way at all."

111

"There's not many travelling," she looked about her after a silence.

"No. Never in the morning. We're lucky not to be on the three twenty-five. It's like a cattle train these days and them all for the night-boat," he said.

"There'll be soon nobody left in the country," she murmured what was being said everywhere.

A signalman crossed the tracks with a white hoop, and Reegan took his watch out of the little pocket that kept his beads.

"Another few minutes," he said. "It's due in four minutes."

"Is it going well, the watch?" she asked very quietly.

"It hasn't broken for four years."

"And it's very old, isn't it?"

"More than twice my age. There are no parts for it any more. It costs a fortune if it breaks. It was bought in New York. My father gave it to me when I joined the police. *Elgin*," he read off the white face with its numerals and hands of blue steel. She had these details before and she asked as she asked more than once before, "Will you keep it?"

"For my time," he laughed as he always did. "Willie can do what he likes with it when it comes to his turn."

The diesel in the distance turned to a powerful roar as it came closer, the signalman exchanged the white hoop for what seemed an identical hoop with the driver, it must be some safety device. Reegan put her cases on the rack and they sat facing each other at one of the windows of an almost empty carriage.

The train pulled out of the station. Trees, fields, houses, telegraph-poles jerking on wires, thorn hedges, cattle, sheep, men, women, horses and sows with their litters started to move across the calm glass; a piece of platform was held still for three minutes at every wayside station and for ten at Mullingar.

She had cancer, she was going for a serious operation, and it was so frighteningly ordinary. The best years of her life were spent and all she'd managed to do was reach this moment in this train. "Trees, fields, houses, telegraph-poles, Elizabeth Reegan, cattle, horses, sheep," throbbed in her head to the train's rhythm as they flashed past. They seemed so unimportant, she and Reegan and people; after a struggle of a lifetime they managed to get in a train or some place, "Trees, fields, houses, Elizabeth Reegan", beating like madness in their heads as the train beat on to its terminus.

She was going weak, and it was the stuffy heat of the carriage, she told herself. She must try and talk. She must try and ask Reegan something. She must break this even drumming of, "Trees, fields, houses, Elizabeth Reegan", to the beat of the train. She'd collapse or go crazy if she couldn't stop it soon, she'd have to try and start a conversation, she'd ask, "Have we many more miles to go?" and it would be a beginning. "Have we many more miles to go?" she asked and he answered. From Westland Row they got a taxi to the hospital. She knew every inch of this squalid station and the street outside: the Cumberland and Grosvenor hotels, the dingy bed-and-breakfasts, the metal bridge, and the notice above the entrance at the traffic lights.

How the lights of this city used to glow in the night when the little boat train taking her back to London after Christmas came in and out of the countryside and winter dark. The putting-on of overcoats and the taking of cases off the racks and the scramble across the platform to get on the train that went the last eight miles out to the boat. Always girls weeping, as she had wept the first time too, hard to know you cannot hide for ever in the womb and the home, you have to get out to face the world.

Often she had wanted to lie down at dawn and die on this platform after the night-ride across England and Wales, the crossing from Holyhead, the fight off the boat through the Customs at Dun Laoghaire, the fight for the seats on the train for here, carriaged home those 23rd of December nights like cattle.

Suddenly, she'd remember she was going home. She could lie in bed late in the mornings, she hadn't to tramp

113

from bed to bed on the wards for three whole weeks more. The ones she loved and hadn't seen for a year would be waiting with a hired car and shy, lighted faces outside the red-brick station, coloured bulbs in the Christmas tree and whiskey on the porter's breath, and they'd lift her off the train and take her home.

They'd be shy at first, thinking she must grow grand and away from them in a great city like London, and she making things more awkward still by telling them what they could not believe—that she was growing more and more the simple human being that had been forced to leave them the first day.

The sheer ecstasy of laying out the presents on the deal table in the lamplight. She'd have spent every penny of money and imagination and now was the hour of indulgence, the blessed ecstasy of giving and being accepted in love, tears lighting her eyes as she watched their faces while they stripped away the festival paper, patterned with red berries and the green, spiked leaves of the holly. Every gift was wrapped in yards of paper so that their imaginations would have chance to make a glory out of the poor thing she had brought, she had gone without things for herself to bring these presents, gone without for weeks before Christmas. And she would do it again. She would do it again and again and again.

Soon they'd force her to sit to her meal and they'd even remembered the dishes she used like best as a child. Now was their turn. They had her present. She gave sharp cries as she tore away the twine and paper, "What is it? What can it be?" and it was there and she was breathing, "Oh, it is too much and so lovely", as she lifted the shining bracelet and they gathered about to gloat over her happiness.

They were a big family and she was young then, and full of life, which is the only youth, and far rarer than beauty. They'd sit together about the blazing pile of ash on the hearth and she'd make them go over every scrap of local news. She'd tell them about London. They'd laugh much. The whiskey and sherry bottles that were kept for Occasions would be brought out of hiding and someone would sing: because Elizabeth was home.

What did it matter that it had all slowly broken up and separation had come before even the first death? It didn't matter, she must affirm that—it made no difference! Only her happiness mattered. She'd been given all that much happiness and she wanted to praise and give thanks.

She was not really going in a common taxi to a common death. She had a rich life, and she could remember. She'd suffer a thousand anythings for one such Christmas again.

She reached over and took Reegan's hand, her face alive with joy, and he held it uneasily. He couldn't understand. She was at the gates of the hospital and the defeated woman that had faced him in the train was gone. He was uneasy and couldn't understand.

The hospital was in its own grounds, trees partly shutting it away from the city; a new state hospital, modern and American, several rectangles of flat roofs in geometric design, the walls more glass than concrete.

They didn't notice much as they paid the taxi and asked the way with their cases to the reception desk. Elizabeth's name was checked on the list of admittances for the day and they were sent to wait in a kind of hall or corridor facing four official doors. A few little groups already waited there about their own patient, all lonely-looking and humble and watching. The doors opened and people in white coats came out to call their names off a file in their turn.

Elizabeth was strained and tense by the time the formalities were finished. The last she had to do was check in her things at the desk and get a receipt. A porter was waiting to take her to her ward. She had to say good-bye to Reegan.

"Is there anything else, Elizabeth?" he asked. She watched his face and coat and hands with the swollen veins. She was quiet with fear. She might never see his greying hair again, the two deep lines over the forehead, the steel blue eyes, the scar on the upper lip, the short throat, the gaberdine coat he wore, the veins swollen on the back of his hands. She might never even see this corridor where they were standing. She

115

might never get out alive. When she took leave of his lips she might be moving into death.

"I'll tell the children," he said when she didn't speak.

"Buy them something. Say I sent it back," she managed.

"That's all right. There's nothing else, is there?"

"No. Not that I can think. There's nothing else."

"Don't worry, Elizabeth. All you have to do is get well soon. Some Thursday we'll come up on the excursion ticket, the four of us. We'll all write before then. We'll ring the day of the operation. . . ."

He saw her wince. He was conscious of the porter waiting. "There's nothing more so?" he puzzled for the last time. "Good-bye, Elizabeth, everything will be all right," and they kissed in the stiff public way of hospital farewells, as bad actors would.

She could say nothing. He came with her to the lift, let go her hand at the entrance, the porter pressing one of the lighted buttons for the door to slide between them.

When the door had shut and the lift rose he lingered, pervaded by that sense of vague melancholy that can be as powerfully evoked by the singing of *Good-bye to the White Horse Inn* as by a real departure. Their lives were flowing apart and she was alone and he was alone and it was somehow sad and weepycreepy.

Through one of the glass doors he saw a pair of patients in dressing-gowns and slippers talking at a radiator. One was drawing for the other on his bandaged throat what must have been the incisions the surgeon had made. Then the other started to trace another pattern across his stomach, making great slashes with his fingers. One had cancer of the throat, the other stomach cancer, Reegan deduced. He watched the white bandages on the throat in morbid fascination: that man would choke to death one of these days! And the really lunatic part of this dumb show was that they were both as excited as blazes, working hand and lip as if they were trying to make up for ages of silence. It was quite enough to shake him out of his mood of melancholy and send him on his way.

He walked quick as he could, down the tree-bordered avenue, past the little lodge at the gates with the two round lamps on the piers that came on at night, and got on the first bus to the Pillar.

He had something to eat in O'Connell Street, bought three fountain pencils with the inscription *Present from Dublin* as he had promised Elizabeth, and then loitered about the streets with the fascination of country people for faces, the thousands of faces that poured past, not one that he knew; strange to understand that they were all subdued and absorbed in their own lives, that such constant friction of bodies didn't cause them to strangle each other or copulate in mass.

He got tired tramping and standing about, his feet not used to the asphalt, but he had hours to kill before his train went. In this city he'd been trained, in the Depot in the Phoenix Park, and he inquired the numbers of the buses for there and got on one.

Findlater's Church, Dorset Street, Phibsboro, St Peter's Church, the Cattle Market; and as the bus went, the rows of plane trees seemed to run the length of the Circular Road to the Wellington rising out of the Park and join branches about its base there.

The Depot was behind its railing. A group of recruits were drilling under the clock on the square and it hadn't even changed its black hands. Two policemen stood with their thumbs hooked in their tunic pockets outside the guard-house, coming lazily to attention to salute the cars that went in and out. Reegan watched and listened greedily, the bellowed commands, the even stamping of the boots, the buttons flashing when they wheeled, his life at twenty echoed there.

"The poor humpers!" he muttered and it didn't take it long to turn to the frustration of his own situation. Ever since he'd come up against the fact that life just doesn't hand you out things because you happen to want them, he'd carried a grudge. He'd never understand that it's an extremely limited bastard as far as satisfaction goes: and he

117

saw the fault in the strip of green and gold with the white between flying over the Depot, symbolizing the institution of Eire now as it had done as good for his dream once, and this drilling square turning out men to keep its peace in the blue uniform that he'd have to wear when the train took him out of the city and home.

The tests found Elizabeth worn and anaemic, her heart had weakened, she had to be given blood transfusions and let rest. The day before the operation the anaesthetist introduced himself to make his examination, and late in the evening the chaplain came to hear her confession.

She confessed to a usual rigmarole of sins already confessed and forgiven in her past life. She didn't love or hate enough, she thought, to commit them any more; she hadn't envy as she hadn't desire enough left; and who was she to curse! She only got more and more frightened as the days went. She had failed and despaired and given up so many times in the last months, and good God, how little she trusted! She had neither words nor formulas to parrot out the catalogue of this state, and how could something so much the living state of herself be state of sin? She seemed to have grown into it rather than fallen from anything away, she could not be sorry. She met the priest's gaze with a gaze as steady as his own: he was a man too, he knew nothing more than she knew, and if she couldn't find words for herself in her loneliness how could they be got out of a double confusion; and words, she knew, didn't profoundly matter anyhow; nor did human understanding, because it understood nothing.

She met him face to face and assured him that she had nothing on her mind, she was grateful for his solicitude, but she had absolutely no worries. He seemed to dislike her gaze as steady and sure as his own. He told her peevishly that she had no need to be grateful for what was his duty. She bent her eyes. He may not have had an easy day, she thought: she heard the words of absolution, and he was gone to another bed.

118

He was gone. The aluminium of a trolley shone under the blaze of the electric lights beside the sterilizing room. She heard a low moan, a rattle of a newspaper, what sounded like a buckle rang against one of the beds, the rubber foot-soles of a nurse padded down the ward, some one laughed. The walls were the green of a rock sweet she'd been crazy about as a child: from the heart of the city the traffic roared, a great sea of noise. She muffled a sob. Tomorrow morning the anaesthetist would put her into a sleep she might never come out of. Oh, if she could clutch and suck every physical thing around her into her being, so that they'd never be parted; she couldn't let go of these things, it was inconceivable that she could die!

A nurse came to her bed, a black-haired country girl, who said, "We're giving you something that'll let you have a good night's rest, Mrs Reegan. We must have you in good shape for tomorrow," and she was at last able to smile and wonder whether the tablets were blessed seconal or sonerzol as she fell asleep.

She was screened off the next morning and a nurse, gowned and masked and with a sterile trolley by, began to prepare her skin for the operation. Both armpits were shaved; the area of both breasts, the arms to the wrists and belly to below the navel were washed, painted with iodine, and covered with a sterile towel. She stiffened with fear as the screens were pulled about the bed and then fear itself was displaced by the loathsome shame of having to expose her body to be handled and shaved and washed.

This nurse at her bedside felt no disgust or shame, she tried to tell herself; she had long become practised and in-different, it was just another job in her day she could do well, as it had been the same once for Elizabeth in her days on the wards in London.

So why should she be shamed because it was her own body this time—was she shamed when this same body was excreted by her mother or when it had strutted in the rouge of its youth? No, if she wasn't shamed then, neither could she be now, she had to accept all or nothing, she couldn't go away with the pretty bits and turn up her nose at the rest, and why should any one be shamed by anything if they weren't shamed by everything! They helped her into an open-back gown. She put on white theatre socks and cap and was covered with a theatre pack, dressed as if for some old rite, horribly unreal, and then she was given atropine. The drug went quickly to her head: she began to laugh and talk; everything was bathed in a light of loveliness and wonder as the porter, with the nurse at her side, wheeled her out of the ward and down the corridors towards the theatre.

Hours later a nurse was urging her back to consciousness.

"Wake up! You must wake up. It's time you were awake! Wake up, Mrs Reegan! Wake up!"

She moaned, some unconscious protest stuttered on her lips, she tried to sink back.

The nurse increased her exertions, "Wake up! You must wake up out of that, Mrs Reegan! Wake up out of that," and slapping at her face.

She had to wake. Pain tore away the drugs and sleep. She moaned and cried as it engulfed her whole consciousness.

They had laid her on her side, her arm was in a sling and rested on a pillow, the bandages about her were saturated with blood.

"I can't stand it. Something . . . Give me something," she tried to moan.

The nurses left to bring back the ward sister. Together they examined the bandages and the tube that had been inserted at the completion of the operation.

"No. I don't think there's need to report," she heard the sister say and passed into a delirious state of semi-consciousness as they repacked the saturated dressing and replaced the breast bandage firmly again. They propped her up and put a pillow at the bottom of the bed so that she could push against it with her feet. She moaned for relief and was given morphia but it didn't make much difference for long. She moaned and cried. How on earth was she to stand this mangled body. The idea of pain had always terrified her, and now she felt nothing else.

She must escape. If she could get an overdose of drugs that'd sink her into a night of unfeeling, she didn't fear or care about death. "Oh, please God, send something," she prayed. "Send anything, anything that'll change this. Get me out of this hell."

Or if some one would only blow her brains out, she thought violently; or that the pain would get bad enough to break her.

Nobody would do anything. She could be sure of that. Another four hours would have to go by before they'd even give her more morphia. She'd just have to lie and suffer and wait.

But, Jesus Christ, she couldn't just lie there suffering and doing nothing, she'd have to try and do something, this wouldn't go on for ever, she knew from her nursing days that'd be a lot less in twenty-four hours, and in forty-eight it'd be almost gone, twenty-four hours wasn't long, it was only a day, and a day was very little in a lifetime.

The main thing was to try and distract or occupy her mind with something, if she could only do that she'd hardly feel much at all. She'd read or heard somewhere that to try and say thirteen times tables was a good trick to take your mind off your pain. They'd taught you far as twelve at school, these'd come easy, but you have to concentrate like hell to make up thirteen times, and it'd take your mind off whatever was happening to you. She ground her teeth. She could feel her heart beating against the bandages. Slow, slow, slow; each pulse rising to explode behind her forehead; going on till it would stop. She'd have to try and say thirteen times tables. Her body was on fire. She couldn't stand this as she was. She'd have to try and pass the time somehow.

"Thirteen ones are thirteen," she could have screamed as she counted out in her mind, and it was no use, she'd be better to fall back and just suffer; but that's only the first time, she persuaded herself; go on, you must go on. What are thirteen twos? Double the three and the one—go on: it's twenty-six, isn't it?

"Thirteen ones are thirteen.

121

"Thirteen twos are twenty-six.

"Thirteen threes are. . . ."

Go on, what are thirteen threes? I was never much good at figures, she tried to say; but still the voice urged, go on: because you're no good at figures is all the more reason for you to go on with them, you're unlikely to ever get to the end of the table, in fact they'll occupy you for the rest of your life if you want, and isn't that the most anyone could possibly hope for, it'd be awful to come to a successful end of something and be still suffering. So go on, Elizabeth; go on! Thirteen threes are what?

No, I'll not go on, I can't, she faltered. She was reduced to a few stone of agonized flesh and she'd be better just to lie there and be that and be no more. These tables were all a game and they hadn't managed to pass very much unfelt time for her. How much time had gone? Nine or was it seven or was it ten, it was definitely no more than ten heart-beats? A heart-beat was a second. Ten seconds had gone, six times that in a minute, 360 in an hour and an awful lot more in a day and still an awful lot more in a lifetime. She ground her teeth again and wept. She couldn't stand it, they must have mangled her whole body. She'd have to play some sort of games or pray or something, her state was too terrible to be just it. Oh, but if she could just get her hands now on an overdose of drugs or a loaded gun it'd solve everything, it'd solve everything as far as she was concerned, but she'd get her hands on neither weapon nor drug tonight.

"O God, if you relieve me of this pain I'll serve you with the rest of my life," she turned desperately to the last of all resorts.

She had never served God much, she had served herself all her life, but weren't the people who were serving God serving their lives too, there was a notion that nobody went to heaven or hell except they wanted to, she'd read it in a newspaper. Did it matter much? Did anything matter much? The one thing that mattered was for her to get shut of this body of hers by any way at all.

She'd been brought up in the fear of God but what remained most powerful in the memory was the church services, always beautiful, especially in Holy Week; witnessed so often in the same unchanging pattern that they didn't come in broken recollections but flowed before the mind with the calm and grace and reassurance of all ritual, a nameless priest in black and white moving between the Stations of the Cross with a breviary, the altar boys in scarlet and white and the lights of the candles they carried glowing on the young faces, a small crowd beneath the gallery in one of those eternal March twilights. That was her religion. Certain phrases: *thirty pieces of silver, the lakeshore of Galilee* evoked events in the life of Christ. The soul went before the Judgement Seat as dramatically after death as it did in the awful scarlet and gold and black of the pictures on the walls in every house, as concretely as the remains went across the bridge to the graveyard in a motor hearse. Though it had never much to do with their lives, except the observances they had to keep: if they kept these their afterlife was as surely provided for as toil and marriage and care and a little luck would provide for the one here on earth. Everything was laid out and certain, no one needed to ask questions, and there was nothing to offer to anyone who stumbled outside its magic circle.

It was little use to Elizabeth as she lay racked with pain. She couldn't pray. *I believe, O God. Help my unbelief,* rose to her lips and sounded as dishonest as something intended to be overheard, she'd never made it part of her life, it was not in her own voice she spoke. The childhood terror of hell came back and she was afraid but she could not adapt herself to living now in its presence. She'd have to try to go on as she had come to live, without fear or hope or despair, there was a passing moment in life.

"O Jesus Christ, get me out of this fix. I can't stand it. God blast it! Blast it! Blast it," broke from her lips but it was nothing but wretched cries against her suffering.

She put her free hand to the railing of the bed, it was iron and cold as ice in her hand. If she could knock herself out

123

against that iron railing, if she could manage to do that it would all be marvellously over.

She had been through as much pain as this before. She had tried to knock herself unconscious against bed and wall before, and those nights had passed, they seemed nothing now. What she was suffering now would soon seem nothing too, she thought; though it did her no good, it was only this intolerable present that mattered. A nurse heard her cry and came to the bed.

"How do you feel, Mrs Reegan?"

"I can't stand it much more," she breathed. "Can you not give me something?"

"Try and bear it a little while more. It'll be better that way and when I give you something it may put you to sleep. You'll try another while, won't you?"

The voice was kind and Elizabeth tried to smile her old smile. She'd try to stick it out: and she had to smile again with bitter self-knowledge when the nurse had gone: she'd been seduced far more often throughout her life by goodness than by any evil, and now it was no different. She should have made such a nuisance of herself that they'd have to give her something—to get some relief was the one thing she craved.

Soon, soon it'd be over, it couldn't go on like this, and the next time she called they did give her morphia. It dulled the pain a little. Her night'd crawl towards morning by these four-hour stages, from dose of morphia to dose of morphia. The visitors arrived and left, the trolleys came with supper, the night staff relieved the day, the lights went out and the roar of traffic from the city never ceased, eased perhaps for a while in the small hours, and resumed with more fever than ever before the morning.

The hours went, without complications. The tube in the breast was rotated and eased somewhat in the afternoon of this next day. Her suffering grew much less. The tube was removed altogether the day afterwards, the real pain was all over. The breast was dressed each day, the tube opening touched with antiseptic till it began to heal, the alternate

124

sutures removed on the tenth day, and the remainder two days later. She had to be helped with her food and washing and clothes and hair these first days and she had to do arm exercises. Whenever she thought she was getting more than her share of the lash she had only to think back on the pit of suffering out of which she had just come for everything to be treasured and alive again. By the tenth day she could touch the back of her head with her hand and she had hours of happiness such as she never remembered.

The white sprouts of the potato seed forced their way through the earth about the barracks, grew leaves and green as they got the light, and the slender cabbage plants held their heads in the air. Most of the turf was cut and not firm enough to be handled. There was no rush. When the turf firmed their days would be a constant rush. Now they could sow beans and lettuce and parsley in little raked squares, and talk. A young pig that Mullins had been given as a bribe to keep his eyes shut to some stealing of timber he had noticed from the woods was much in those conversations.

He kept him in a shed that used hold old rubbish and his bicycle. He'd got a cartload of green rushes for bedding and levied buckets of skim milk each day from the creamery carts passing through the village; later in the year he'd get windfall apples to sweeten the bacon, he said; and he'd kill him in November.

Sometimes they talked about cancer and Elizabeth, they knew she had come through the operation, they expected a letter, and she'd be home. As always, the children sprinkled rushes and wild flowers on the doorstep for Our Lady's Eve and kicked away their boots to go barefoot, it was May.

The turf dried. Mullins and Brennan switched their *patrols of the imagination* to the bog, where Reegan already slaved. He had hired several banks and day labourers to do the cutting but he'd have to save the turf himself if he was to make much profit. He'd sell it in the town and if it went lucky it'd more than pay for Elizabeth and he'd be able to leave the police. He didn't want to have to go to the city

125

to open and shut swing doors in some ice-cream parlour to supplement what pension he'd get. He'd buy a small farm and work how he liked for himself. With what he had saved and the gratuity he was owed he should be able to do this if the turf paid for Elizabeth: he wasn't staying in the police till he was blind and weak at sixty, no matter what came or went, was the one thing he was certain of.

At daybreak he was out of bed to cycle the two miles to the bog, he'd work in a kind of frenzy there till eight, and rush back to shave and change into his uniform, gulp the breakfast the children would have prepared, to be in the dayroom to call the roll at nine.

Mrs Casey cooked their dinner all these days. Casey had his meal with them in the kitchen and was much loved by the children. He never forgot to pay them some attention, he was light and gay, and didn't oppress them with the sense that he was being slowly crucified by time and care, as many did.

They had to go to the bog every evening after school. The work was monotonous and tiresome, continual stooping to lift the sods off the ground into windrows and clamps, but not heavy, a child could do as much as a man. It was a novelty first, Reegan incited them with sweets and odd bottles of lemonade or an orange, but it was soon too much. They'd hear shouts of other children playing as they lifted dreary sod after sod. The mud matted in the hair of their legs and it was painful to rub it clean with hard sedge, standing to their knees in water to let it soften. Sometimes one of the little girls'd scream when the yellow of a frog's belly flashed before their eyes, leaping from under a sod they had moved; with terror they saw the black leeches crawl on the mud; they sucked blood, the old people said. They were left with no energy to face into their lessons and got into trouble in school the next day. Their faces began to shut, a mask on the weariness and bitterness, they laughed little, and started to grow twisted as the roots of a tree between rocks.

Reegan saw nothing. All he saw was turf saved and the money that'd give him the freedom he craved. He drove

126

them with the same passion that drove himself, without thinking that it might not be to them the road to the vision of sky and sun that he saw. Their faces shut. When they laughed it was with the bright metal of observant people, not with their hearts, and mostly they watched, nothing but watch.

Reegan drove himself mercilessly, working every chance he got during the day, and grew more greedy and careless, taking risks every new week that he would not have taken the week before, even though he knew Quirke was prowling.

Late one night he wrote to Elizabeth, his greatcoat was over the back of the chair, his peaked cap on the table where he wrote. He had worked all day at the turf and he had just finished a patrol to see that the pubs were closed. The children, and Brennan in the dayroom, were asleep. He paused several times as he wrote: to put his hand to his forehead and to gaze wearily at his face in the sideboard mirror. He had nothing to say to Elizabeth. He hoped she'd be home soon and then he had the pages to fill with gossip. He felt no connection with what he wrote, it was his duty— with the turf and potatoes and the money that'd get him out of the police he was connected, and they could bring him to violent life and excitement, but this letter didn't rouse anything, except his dislike of intimacy, and when it was finished the quiet conscience of having done his duty.

A letter arrived a week later from Elizabeth. She told him not to come to see her, she was happy and recovered, she'd be home by the end of June. It'd be silly to make the long journey to Dublin when she'd be so soon home, she said.

He took her at her word, and wrote two more laborious letters, nights he was barely able to keep his head from sliding down to the notepaper on the table. The strain of the work had him physically jaded and no end was in sight. When the clamps dried he'd have to cart them out to the road with borrowed donkeys. The lorries would take them from there to the town. He forced himself on and on, he could always find energy, so fierce this passion to get money and his freedom that it drove him like a whiplash. Only in the drawn sag of his face when he relaxed over his supper at the end of the rosary did the strain show, and in the increasing risks he took. He spent little time at his police work. He had gone lucky so far but it was unlikely to continue so for ever.

The potato stalks were a green sway of leaves in the garden, flecked with their tiny blossoms, blue of Kerr's Pinks, white of Arran Banners, red of Champions. June was nearly ended, in a week Elizabeth would be home, the children have holidays from school. Thunder showers and evenings when the midges swarmed out of the sycamores and the edges of a few potato leaves burned black with blight warned them it was time to spray.

On a Saturday Reegan told the children to put the spraying barrel out in the garden, fill it with water from the river, steep the bluestone he had left ready, and he'd spray when he got back off patrol.

They had to roll the wooden barrel, stand it on its end to work it through the gate at the lavatory. Half-way across they placed it at the foot of the ridges, where the wild part of the garden ran down to the ash trees and the river. They tramped a pass through the wild meadow and the nettles and briars between the trees to get with their buckets to the water. Through meal bags thrown across the mouth of the barrel and secured with twine they strained the water to catch grass-seed and leaves and dirt that could clog the machine. Then they tied the bag of bluestone to a pole and set it to steep and put down a pot of water to boil so that Reegan could melt the washing soda when he came home.

He was late, and changed out of his uniform as soon as he'd eaten, melted the soda, and hurried out to the waiting barrel without making his report or signing the books.

The bluestone had melted, the solution blue-green of the sea on a cloudy day, and as he spilled the washing soda in it changed to a miracle of rich turquoise, white foam boiling to the top and clinging to the pole with which he whirled the mixture round the sides of the barrel. Then he rested the knapsack sprayer on the edge of the barrel, took a small

128

delf jug to fill the can, and strapped it on his shoulders to spray, its copper covered under the blue coats of its years.

Brennan came out from b.o. duty in the dayroom and leaned over the netting-wire.

"That's what'll keep the blight away," he called.

"It's more than time too," Reegan shouted. "Some of the leaves are burned."

Brennan came into the garden to examine the blight on the leaves.

"It's time I sprayed my own so," he said. "I suppose I can bring the can with me tonight. Mullins'll be wantin' to spray too if he hears about the blight."

"Bring it tonight, surely," Reegan laughed.

He felt the pressure on the pump as he drove it down to his hip. He turned on the tap. The two jets hissed out on the leaves. The strong, matted stalks broke apart as he backed up the furrow, the leaves showing a dull silver where they were upturned. Pools of blue gathered in the hollows of the leaves, they glistened green with wet, and then started to drip heavily in the silence, the way trees drip after rain. He had sown these potatoes, covered them with mould again when the first leaves ventured into the spring frosts, kept the weeds from choking them till they grew tall and blossomed, now he was spraying them against the blight this calm evening and he was happy.

"What kind of a crop have you, Jim?" he asked out of mischief.

"The best crop you'd see on a day's walk," Brennan boasted. "They're as high as your hips and all blossom. That's why I'm so anxious about the sprayin'."

"O God!" Reegan laughed inwardly; though it wasn't fair, he thought—poor Brennan was far too gullible.

The spray rocked in the can on his back as it emptied and then started to suck and the jets to weaken. He went with it to the barrel. Brennan had gone inside: he had thought to tell Reegan about the report he didn't make and the books, but he was weak and afraid and Reegan could be too unpredictable.

The screaming of the saws rose and fell across the lake. The stalks were dripping. A few people rode by on bicycles. One of them said, "God bless the work," and Reegan answered, "And yours too, when you're at it," and then Quirke's Ford came across the bridge as carefully as any vehicle could come and turned in the avenue to stop at the barrack gate.

Reegan was rooted there with the spraying-can. He couldn't move. Then he panicked to escape, lie down in the furrows or race for the shelter of the ash trees? No, he couldn't do any of these, he might have been already seen, it'd be better to stand his ground and face it. What could Quirke do anyhow?

He wasn't able to continue spraying as if he hadn't seen the car. He had to stand still, listen to the door slam and feet on the gravel, wait for, "Good day, Sergeant."

"Good day, sir," he answered.

"I see you're doing some spraying," Quirke leaned his arms on the top of the netting-wire, gloves in his hand.

"That's right, sir. It's the weather for blight."

"You've good ones there too."

"They're not bad," Reegan managed a ghost of a smile.

"I'm just passing. I suppose I better go and sign these books."

"Right, sir," Reegan nodded and watched him go inside to Brennan and turned to spray in a fit of chagrin and desperation.

Everything in the day had gone dead, actual spray fell from the nozzles on actual leaves, and he tried to vent his frustration by pumping madly and damaging the locked stalks as he backed savagely up the furrows.

The pump sucked dry, he had to fill the can again, spilling the stuff in his need for violence. A heavy can burdened his back when he rose from the barrel and he couldn't keep his mind off Quirke going through the books in the dayroom and the dayroom door opened and shut and Quirke was at the netting-wire. Reegan had to turn off the pump and stand to talk or listen, as Quirke willed.

"I noticed, Sergeant, that you're still supposed to be out on patrol?" he demanded.

"It was three before I got back and I was in a rush to get this barrel out, it slipped my mind in the rush," he explained, fit to take Quirke by the throat as he listened to himself in the servile giving of explanation.

"It's all right this time, but don't let it happen again. In your position it gives bad example. If you and I don't do our work properly, how can we look to them to do theirs?"

"That's right, I suppose," Reegan agreed and a slow, cynical smile woke on his face. Quirke had expected a clash, it wouldn't have been the first, and what seemed this sudden agreeableness satisfied and flattered him, he looked on himself as a patient and reasonable man. Perhaps, at last, Reegan was taming down, he was getting some glimmer of sense.

"And what cases have you for next Thursday?" he changed affably, he wanted to show Reegan that they weren't enemies but in a team together, with a common cause and interest; and when Reegan outlined the few cases for him he began to discuss and explain Act this and Code that with a passion oblivious to everything but its petty object, while Reegan stood between the drills, the can on his back, the leakage seeping into his clothes. The listening smile faded to show frightening hatred as he listened, but he contrived to convert it into sufficient malicious cunning for Quirke not to notice.

"We have a fine reputation to uphold," Quirke was lecturing, "and if we don't uphold that reputation for ourselves nobody else will do it for us. In the years ahead we'll be seeking professional status and if we look upon ourselves as a depressed section of the community how will others look upon us? We must have pride in ourselves and in our work. And it's up to people like you and me, Sergeant, in posts of responsibility, to set the tone.

"At an inspection the other day I asked a certain member of the Force what he knew of The Dangerous Drugs Act.

"He looked at me in such a way as to suggest I had asked him the way to the moon. Then I inquired did he know any dangerous drugs, could he name me one? And you wouldn't credit the answer I got, Sergeant!"

"No," Reegan had to prompt.

"*Mrs Cullen's Powders*. He said *Mrs Cullen's Powders* was a dangerous drug. Can you credit that, Sergeant! What kind of respect can a man like that have for himself or his work? And that man would be the first to have his hand out for an increase of salary! And, I say, unless we raise the efficiency and morale of the Force, how can we expect to raise its status?"

Reegan listened to the moral righteousness without feeling anything but his hatred. This bastard has associated himself with the Police Force, he thought shrewdly; his notion of himself is inseparable from it. Why should he go against him when the wind wasn't blowing his way, he'd wait his chance, and then let him watch out; but why should he do the strongman when the wind wasn't blowing right, now he'd throw the bait of flattery, and watch the egotism swallow and grow hungry for more.

"There's not many men in the country realize that as you do, sir. They're not modern enough in their approach," he cast and watched Quirke blossom as he swallowed.

"I've seen saying it for years. We must raise our status first ourselves before we can hope to get anywhere, but none of them seem to realize it, Sergeant."

"That's right, sir," Reegan agreed; the slow, hard smile deep in the eyes.

"By the way, I heard your wife is in hospital. How is she?" Quirke grew to feel that he had indulged himself, and tried to switch the centre of interest to the other person, far too consciously and quickly.

"She's coming home next week, sir," Reegan's face was as inscrutable as a mask.

"I'm glad to hear that. I suppose it's time I was on my way. You'll want to finish your spraying. And don't forget to put those books right."

"No, sir," Reegan said.

"Good-bye so, Sergeant."

"Good-bye, sir," Reegan answered.

He waited till the car went. The straps were hurting his shoulders, his whole body was sore from having stood stiff for so long, the leakage had seeped through his clothes. Brennan came out of the dayroom as soon as the noise of the car had died. Reegan cursed as he eased the can from his shoulders and stretched his body.

"He stayed a long time talkin'," Brennan opened carefully.

"Aye. And me with the can on me back like any eejit."

Then Reegan laughed, it was mocking and very harsh.

"Do you know, Brennan, that you're my subordinate? Do you know that I have to give good example to you fellas?"

The small, thin policeman shifted on his feet, he went to say something but it was so confused that it didn't even reach his lips; he was upset and didn't know what to say, he looked terribly overcome beside the wire. He couldn't decide whether Reegan was serious or not. He was relieved when Reegan asked, "Did he tell you that the sergeant hadn't made his report in the book?"

"No. I saw him examine it but he said nothing."

"That's the stuff," Reegan jeered savagely. "That's the proper way to behave! Never undermine an officer's position before his men, isn't that it?"

"That's it," the puzzled and upset Brennan agreed as Reegan hooted, "We in authority must give the good example. We in posts of responsibility must set the tone. Ah, Jasus, it's a gas world, Brennan! There can be no mistake!"

"It's a gas world surely," Brennan agreed.

The lights were on in the church and women going by on the road to the Sodality Confessions when Reegan had the barrel of spray out and the can and barrel and jug washed clean of the poisonous stuff. He was tired and frustrated when he came into the meal the children had prepared, not able to bear to think how he had behaved with Quirke that day.

"Only a fool acts when he's caught out on the wrong foot," he reasoned. "Play them at their own game, that's the way! Wait easy for your chance. And, Jesus, when I get the chance that bastard'd want to watch out for himself. There's goin' to be more than the one day on this job."

He ate with the children hovering about in attendance, chewing slowly and not speaking; when he finished he went down to fill the books in the dayroom, bringing the knapsack sprayer to leave for Brennan to take home.

Elizabeth had recovered, the course of exercises were completed, she had the use of her arms again, these days beginning to be full of rich happiness, the wonder of herself and the things about her astonishing her at each turn. The marvel of the row of poplar trees outside the windows, their leaves quivering in their silver and green light; these women in the beds fighting to live in spite of their cancer; marvel of the shining trolleys and instruments and the young nurse telling about the dance she'd been at the night before. It frightened her to think that her life and herself were such rich and shocking gifts and almost all of the time she wasn't able to notice.

She had terror of change. Sometimes in the evenings cousins would come to visit her and she used dread the first sight of them in the corridor—they would come and destroy everything! And they wouldn't be five minutes at the bedside when the time was flying; the little charms and ruses she'd then have to use to try to prolong the visit to the last, her panic when the bell went and she was taking their hands— soon they'd be gone and her happiness could not be the same again.

She had such ease and peace and sense of everything being cared for: no fears, no worries, no hours of indecision; the same things were done at the same times every day; her meals came without her lifting a hand; nurses changed the tired sheets and they felt light and cool as air. She was plagued by no gnawing to see some guiding purpose in her days, she had to suffer no remorse for these hours spent in total idleness and comfort; for had she not given up her body to be healed and with it responsibility, so that this blessed ease was both her duty and her enjoyment.

Much of her time was spent idly dreaming. Reegan and the children and the policemen and the river flowing past the barracks and the ash trees. London, and she was one of a covey of girls crossing Whitechapel Road to get a train to take them to a dance in Cricklewood. The long, happy evenings when she used first go out with Halliday. Those nights on the wards during the war, the air-raid sirens worse than the bombs, and walking past the smoking craters in the mornings. Farther away mornings when she was a country child and rising with the larks to go down to the sheep paddocks with a sweet can for mushrooms, the grilling of them on a red coal, and Jesus just to taste them once more with salt and butter. Faces, faces from all the places and all the years, faces passed without a glance in the street one day and at the living centre of her life the next, and later to be no more than another displaced memory, made to flare in the mind again by some stray word or sight. Strange, it was all strange, she pondered to herself for hours; it was all so mysterious and strange and unknowable; and it did not burden her, she confronting it as dispassionately as it confronted her.

Then the nights came and the hours of dusk she loved, lamps of the cars would shoot up, a pair of glowing yellow eyes on a stretch of road on the Dublin mountains she could see through the poplars, and race down to the city. To what restaurant or theatre or marvellous place were they going? She could be in one of those cars, delicate perfume mingling with the cigarette-smoke and the warm leather, in love with a happy dream of someone, and going out to a lovely evening.

She'd have to smile: it was too ridiculous. An ignorant wife of a police sergeant lying with cancer in a hospital, watching cars on a mountain road to pass the time, and having such dreams, it was such a fantastic comedy, and when she'd grow tired of her own she could turn and watch the others play.

The visitors were coming, conscious of eyes watching them from all the beds, and making their entrance as stiltedly as if someone had thrust the flowers or chocolates or fruit into their arms and pushed them out beyond the footlights to play, *Keep your heart up, I'm comin' to visit you.*

Nearly twenty must have come and the fantastic thing was that no two had come the same; and what difference did it make that they had no spectators except in their own heated imaginations, for no one in the beds really cared how they made their little entrances or departures; and the people most concerned, the people they had come to visit, were too busy trying to make a good show of the receiving to notice anything else. Though how on earth could that be known, they were all involved in their life in the visit, and there was nothing besides?

What kind of entrance and departure would she herself make, Elizabeth thought and knew she'd escape none of the lunacy of living because she could sometimes see, she'd be as blind with life, as ridiculously human as any other when it came to her turn. She and they were involved together: they jigacted with millions of others across a screen's moment, passionately involved in their little selves and actions, each of them in their own mind the whole world and everything; all of them tragic figures in their death, there was no joke there byjesus, the whole world falling when they fell. It was so fantastic, and so miraculous that it could go in spite of having no known purpose, blind passion carrying it forward in spite of everything. She was able to smile with some of the purity of music. She was still and calm and surely this way she saw was a kind of human triumph, even though this mood, as all her moods, was soon to change.

A fortnight before she was due to go home she was given a course of radiotherapy and the after-effects of it in the evenings were to make her ill and miserable.

She knew that the carcinoma must be pretty far advanced

136

if they were giving her this, it destroyed the cells, they wouldn't be able to operate again. The chances must be all against her, she'd think; she'd go home out of this and be able to walk and work about for a little while and then one day the pains would get too much and she'd have to go to bed to wait to die. That was the way, that was mostly the way, most of them went that way, and she'd have to lie down that way too. She was no different, that was the terrible thing, she was no more than a fragment of the same squalid generality. She'd have to go home and walk about and lie down and wait the same as the rest. She shuddered, she felt miserable, and the way her body felt made her see things different, she was frightened at how little control she had of everything. She could see no good in the ward, the ward where she had been so unbelievably happy days before.

The conversations all began to seem so mean and petty. Over at the far side she heard a woman boast, "Since my husband has been made head of his department things haven't been the same. He hasn't enough time. I often wish he never got it. The money and position are all right but it's not worth it," in a tone that implied that she considered herself head and shoulders above every one else in the ward. She was belittling her position so that they'd be able to feel comfortable in her presence, not for a moment would she dream of insisting on her superiority.

A deadly silence followed before she was given her answer, a voice pretending to make a general statement to the ward, as casual as if it was remarking on the weather.

"It's surprisin' that some people come into the ordinary hospitals at all, it's a great wonder they don't go into the private clinics."

"That's right," an abetting voice joined, "but these places are very expensive and select. They cost money."

They cost money, Elizabeth murmured. How the first poor bitch would be suffering scalds of vanity now. They had her by the heels. They'd drag her down. She had watched grey-hounds once let out of their kennels into a walled yard and they had come excited and roused, biting and shouldering and trying to ride each other, careering round and round on the straw. A brindled dog, weaker than any of the others, suddenly went silly with excitement, made a ridiculous, pawing leap in the air to crash against the wall and fall. The pack were on him almost before he fell. The trainer had to rush in and cane them away or they'd have torn him to bits.

She had never forgotten. She kept her thoughts to herself. Even in the hospital she took good care to buy an evening paper when the man with the trolley came. She never said anything in her conversations that ran counter to the average communal welter. She had her private life and dreams, at least that much joy; she had little belief that people could be really influenced or changed, and she wasn't going to risk her own joy in this useless and doubtful acrimony.

She listened to the first woman try to make a come-back and she hadn't a chance. She must be so stupid, Elizabeth thought, though it seemed too pathetic to pass judgement. One poor person trying to raise herself on the stilts of her husband's promotion and the others busy as hell sawing her down. Of course she was a beautiful and unappreciated person in her own mind, *she had come from fine people*; but if she grew tall as her own estimation she cast a shadow on the others and every one wanted her own share of the sun of recognition. They had to drag her down as she had to seem tall, all tied in the knot of each other, without being able to attain pure love or silence or selfishness or pure anything else. Elizabeth pressed her face to the pillows. She'd have to go under the sickening treatment again tomorrow, though soon she'd be home, away out of this, in only three days, in the last days of June, hay-time. She'd hear the machines and the din of the corn-crakes at night and the wild smell of hay would be all about the barracks, she promised to help herself face another night.

The Council ambulance took her home, it had brought a patient in that morning, and by bringing her back with them they saved Reegan the trouble and expense of a journey. There was plenty of sunshine in the ward as she left and she

138

began to miss the things she'd miss when she was home. Always easy to love something or somebody when you know you don't have to endure them any more, when the goodbyes are being waved, and you can have your dream and choice of them instead of their solid, individual and demanding presence.

Though there was no danger that she'd linger. Outside everything was summery and true and by four she was out of the city, riding in front between the driver and nurse. The windows were down and they could feel the breeze and the driver was in his shirt-sleeves. People were making hay in the roadside meadows and cattle were trying to beat away the flies in the shade. They laughed and talked. Before Edgeworthstown the driver had to pull down the sun-shield, the evening had sunk, and they were driving west into the level glare.

Already she was dreaming of meeting them in the summer evening. Every known name and mark on the road set her nerves shivering. She was going home and it was such a thing to have a home to go to. What did it matter that she'd have to adjust herself bitterly to the lonely reality of it later, for if that reality wasn't there how could she ever know the ecstasy of these hours that burned every boundary down?

5

It was weeks before she was able to take her full place in the house, the shock of homecoming over, the newness and strangeness of things that'd been familiar as the parts of her own body worn away, and gradually she gave up the privileges of her convalescence that she'd come to accept as her right.

The children had got holidays and were dragging the turf out to where the lorries could reach, with borrowed donkeys. Reegan was seldom able to be with them, it was getting too dangerous to neglect his police work as much as he used, for Quirke was watching, and he was tense with worry over the weather. If it rained the small shod hooves of the donkeys, the shod wheels of the carts would tear the skin of the pass to ribbons in an hour. They'd have to drag and struggle through the whole summer if there was rain, trying to patch the pass with rushes and heather and branches of sally, even then the donkeys often sinking to their bellies in the mud and smashing shafts and harness in their panic, men having to come from other banks to loosen the tacklings and goad and lug them up while the frightened and guilty children tried to offer their useless help.

The weather did not break, but as it was Elizabeth saw they weren't able for the strain of this work. She went down to them with hot food some evenings and stayed to help. They were so lonely and silent, these flat acres stretching to the rim of the sky, single men and small family groups working alone on their own banks, their voices carrying clear and far, the tiny purple bloom sprinkled on the dull heather, long acres of sedge as pale as wheat and taller, the stunted sally and birch trees rising bright as green flowers. Always wind, no matter how calm the day, and it grew chill early in the evenings.

She stayed and helped them as much as she was able, she hadn't the strength to be of much use yet, the jagged bits of wood in the turf tore her hands; the dust and mould, hard and sharp as bits of flint, blew blinding and choking. She saw the children endure this and drive and beat the unwilling donkeys out and in without complaint, eager for the prizes Reegan brought, their young hearts hungry for praise: but it wasn't right, she thought; and she protested to him. "Hard work never killed anybody," Reegan argued. "I was doin' almost a man's work at their age and I never saw it do anybody any harm. Laziness and idleness was all I ever saw do harm."

"They're not able to stand it," she said. "They'll not grow natural. Let them have some jobs but they can't stand more than they're able for."

"Turf isn't heavy work," he protested hotly. "If they had to dig or something, it'd be a different story."

"It's too heavy for their age: they're at it from light to dark," their difference almost rose to acrimony.

"They don't mind," he said. "They get oranges and lemonade and stuff. We have this contract and we have to fill it. It'll only be for a little while, soon we'll be gone to hell outa here and it'll be all over."

"That doesn't matter, it's not right, it's not right," she was roused enough to want to say but she didn't say any-anything more. "These children were too young and what was all this mad striving for? What did it amount to or intend to achieve? And the difference a little leisure can make in the lives of people," she thought despairingly to herself.

She was excited with resentment but there was nothing she could say or do. His greed for money to go free out of the police had grown to desperation, there was no use closing her eyes, it'd have to be accepted and lived with, but how it harmed everything, and there was nothing she could do. Now that he saw she wasn't going to say anything more he wanted to justify himself.

141

"They don't mind. I'm goin' to give them a whole day in town when Duffy's circus comes, they know that. And there's no one else to do it. I can't take any more chances with that bastardin' Quirke all the time nosin' about, and they can do as much at that as a man. They'll be finished in not much over another week, if the rain keeps away, and they'll have still the rest of their holidays before them, and I know it'll not do them a pick of harm, Elizabeth."

She nodded agreement and turned and put away the delf. He went. He said he'd be out on patrol and not back till late after ten and he'd try to get to them on the bog for an hour. She saw him fix his trousers with the bicycle clips and she gave him his raincoat folded to put on the carrier and then she waited for the blue bulk and the tyres on the gravel to go by the window.

She finished the washing and drying and sweeping, disturbed and the peace gone out of the day. She was right and he must surely believe he was right and it was all useless and futile. Though it was July still, she said to herself, and she mustn't forget; the blackcurrants were falling with ripeness in the garden and she had yet to pick them, and if she didn't there'd be none left by the birds soon. She could stew some this evening yet and the kitchen would be steaming and full with their scent. Their eyes would light and she'd ladle them some of the jam hot out of the saucepan before she filled the jars. That's what she would do, she'd pick the blackcurrants, she should have picked them days ago; and now she was able to find a gallon and the torn straw sun-hat with new joy. She shut the scullery door and the windows before she went so that the hens wouldn't be able to get in while she was away.

Outside Mullins was scuffling the gravel, and the moment she heard the noise of the hoe she knew she'd have to stand to talk. He was in his shirt-sleeves, no collar on the shirt that was always meant to be hidden under the tunic, the braces hauling the amazing waist of the trousers so tight up on his corporation that it tempted her to laugh. His tunic hung on the back of one of the yellow dayroom chairs that

142

he'd placed in the shade of the wall, a newspaper on its seat, and a spade and little iron rake leaned against the wall beside it. The door and both windows of the dayroom were wide open and inside the open door of the lockup blocked the passage.

"Aw, Elizabeth," he greeted. "I'm doin' a bit of auld scufflin', you can see!"

"It needs it too, I suppose," she said, her eyes following the green scum of weed over the gravel.

"Quirke was complainin' last week," Mullins said. " 'We must take pride in the appearance of our station; if we don't take pride in ourselves no one else will,' he said; and very full the same pride'll fill our bellies I don't think.

"Though this station was the tidiest station in the country when I came here first, it won the prize," he began. "There was a fella by the name of Joyce here then, a quiet sort of strange fella from Galway, and he used keep the place like the bee's britches, just lovely. He was daft about flowers and strange as it may be dirty jokes, and a walkin' encyclopedia on both he was; but you could get him interested in nothin' else, he nearly drove Sergeant Jennings that was here at the time out of his mind before they shifted him to one of the penal stations up in Donegal."

Mullins pointed out with his hoe where the beds of roses used to grow and the gladioli and the flowers he couldn't name, where the lawn was kept mowed between, now wild with scutch grass and buttercups and daisies; and as Elizabeth tried to move towards the gate he continued, "That's twenty-one years ago. I came here twenty-one years ago the 16th September last, twenty-one years too long here, just a month married then!"

"It's strange you were never transferred in that length of time, John," she said, wanting to get away but not wishing to appear too uninterested and silent, it was probably cowardice on her part she thought, for good God, how many versions of this same story had she heard before! She wished she could be alone and picking the blackcurrants.

"They must have forgotten about me up in the Depot,"

Mullins laughed. "I must have got lost in some drawer. Would you believe I was never reprimanded in all that length of time, not to talk of being commended and me name appearin' in the box in the *Review*. Only the pay comes the first of every month, if they forgot about that it'd be the last catastrophe!"

"I better pick some of the blackcurrants, not to let them all go with the birds," she smiled her apology as she moved sideways to the gate, she was growing desperate to get away.

"A fine crop there's there too and I've been watchin' the same birds have the times of Riley," he woke to some sense of her. "You're lookin' powerful yourself, mendin' every day since you came home."

"Thanks," she smiled. "I feel better and it's a lovely day."

"And we're as well make the most of it, while it's in it," he said as she moved away and his hoe went scuffling in the gravel again.

She was through the iron gate at the lavatory, onions spread to dry above on its flat roof, and down the concrete path to the rain-gauge. Every morning the b.o. had to lift the top off its copper casing and take and carefully pour the water that had collected in the bottle since the morning before into the delicate glass measure and note down its reading on the chart on the wall beside the phone. It had to be posted away to the Meteorological Station at the end of the month and a new chart appeared on the wall in its place. On such wastes life goes, it seemed; and at the rain-gauge she had to push her way up a furrow through the matted potato stalks to the blackcurrants, a crowd of sparrows scattering out as she came close, and she tramped down the wild meadow between the bushes before she started to pick.

The over-ripe fruit fell loosely to her fingers, beady black clusters underneath the coarse leaf, some hard and red or green low down in the bushes, where the wild grass had reached. She was shaded by the sycamores along the avenue, the smooth cool fruit touched her finger-tips and the rough leaves brushed the back of her hand and wrist, the saws were screaming through the timber across the lake and there

144

was the muffled hammering of the stone-crusher in the quarry. She was able to lose herself in the slow picking, Mullins's hoe scuffling on the gravel, and then it stopped. There was a clash of tools, the tramp of his heavy boots on concrete, the ponderous door of the lockup being bolted shut. They kept the tools there and the barrel of paraffin and tin of Jeyes Fluid for the lavatory and such stuff. Apart from drunks left to cool at Christmas it had only one prisoner since she came, the manager of a local creamery, a poor wretch who had embezzled the funds over a number of years to feed a passion for whiskey. She'd given him a meal in the kitchen, with Mullins who had several times sponged drink off the man sitting ridiculously by on guard, in an intense silence of embarrassment. Some cruel streak in Reegan must have tempted him to make the man Mullins's prisoner.

The man never looked up as she poured the tea, his shoulders and arms contracted into as small a space as they could find, his head down close to the plate; and, she shivered to remember it in this usual day, the degradation of shame she had suffered for his shame.

The worst was as he went: he said, "God bless you, Mrs Reegan!" and started to cry. She was transfixed with horror where she stood and all she could do was stand and watch him being led away and listen to Mullins's hoarse whispering, "You'll have to pull yourself together, Jim Man. I feel as bad as you at havin' to do this but I have to do it, it's me duty, and there's no use in whingin' Jim Man. Don't you understand that, Jim Man?" She could do nothing or say nothing but only stand and listen and watch him go. They put him in the lockup that night. The barrels and other lumber had been cleared, the floor scrubbed and a mattress and bedclothes fixed on the platform of bare boards four inches above the concrete. He slept for an hour, drugged with whiskey they'd got him from McDermott's, but when he woke he began to beat on the wall. There was no light, the wind from the lake blew in the narrow window that had only a single steel bar in its centre, and the cell must have been damp from the scrubbing. Mullins rose to tell him to go back to sleep like a good man but it was no use, he beat louder, and called and cried. Mullins had to wake Reegan. It was soon clear that they'd have to take him out or listen to him through the night. They took him out and sat handcuffed to him to wait for morning. They had to escort him to Sligo in the morning.

Elizabeth had seen him go, the narrow green ribbon trailing from the silver that fettered his wrist to Mullins's. She had to sign dockets later and Reegan must have got paid for the meals she'd given him. She had managed to avoid learning what happened at the trial and afterwards. She shivered now in the day. Why had she to remember? There was the steel singing of the saws across the lake and the hammering jaws of the stone-crusher in the quarry. Why had she to think, the round red sun was sinking into the west woods, the bright bottom of her gallon was covered with blackcurrants, a springing nettle stung her legs and she rubbed it with a dock leaf. Mullins sat on the yellow chair in front of the open dayroom window so that he'd hear the phone if he nodded to sleep over the newspaper. A cart with ropes on its floor crunched past, it was going for a load of hay to the river meadows that flooded in wet weather. Two men on bicycles passed in excited argument over the price of cattle, a woman with a full shopping-bag slung from the handlebars went by alone. This was the slow village evening: she was no longer in hospital, she could be sure, she was at home at last in what she loved and knew. She could hear the splash of fish, the whipcrack of a roach on water—how blood-red it's fins were and gold the scales and totally unedible the white flesh full of bones—if she stood intent enough. Away towards the meadows and navigation signs at the mouth of the lake the cattle had waded out to where the water washed against their bellies, standing stock still in a daze except for an impatient shake of horns or a tail. A noise of a motor crept near. The square shape of a bread van crossed the bridge and jogged past towards the shops.

"That was a bread van, wasn't it, Elizabeth?" she heard Mullins call.

146

"It was, a bread van," she answered.

"Did you get readin' the name, I just got a glimpse of its tail?"

"No. I never noticed."

"I have the notion I spotted a B: it must be either Broderick's or the Ballyshannon van!"

"It'll be back," she said. "They only do the circle of the village, they don't go this way to Arigna and the pits."

"No, it'll be back," he said. "We'll have to watch this time. That's the worst of dozin' off, you're always missin' something. We'll have to keep our eyes skinned this time."

"We'll want to keep awake so," she said and laughed low to herself as she continued to pick. She heard Mullins's whistle chain ring as he struggled into his tunic, and then she had warning of his feet come on the gravel and out the avenue. He stood to lean against the sycamore nearest to her and lit a cigarette.

"Strange how smokin' soothes the nerves," he said. Before she's time to answer the bread van started up and they had to be silent to listen.

"It's moved from McDermott's to Murphy's," he said. "Believe me that auld dry stick didn't keep them long talkin'. 'Here's yer order and yer money, give me me bread and go in the name of Our Lord and don't disturb me further, me good man,' " he mimicked viciously. "They'll not get away so handy from Murphy's," he continued to comment, "Big Mick'll want to know what happened in every dance-hall in the country. Oh, the big fat lazy bastard! Nothin' troubles him but football and women, hot curiosity and no coolin' experience. The best of rump-steak from the town and nothin' to do but plank his fat arse all day on the counter," and then he paused and said out of a moment's reflection, "Isn't the smell of fresh loaves a powerful smell, Elizabeth?"

"Yes," she spoke out of the same mood. "When I used pass the big bakeries in London or see a van with its doors open outside a shop I used to get sick for home. I'd see a van outside the shop at the Chapel and a bread rake thrown

147

on top of the loaves on the shelves, there's no smell so fresh."

Mullins spoke and after what seemed an age of conversation in the quiet day the van moved again.

"What did I tell you, Elizabeth; they were kept all that length in the shop," Mullins pricked immediately to attention, returning to his former tone. "That lazy auld bollocks has enough information to keep his swamp of a mind employed for another while. Some of the bread-van men and the travellers'd want to be sexual encyclopedias to satisfy some of the people in this village."

"It's never a full-time occupation," Elizabeth said, not able to resist, afraid when she'd said the words that'd tempt him into a monotone of sex for the evening.

"No, that's the good truth anyhow," he laughed, "but when it's confined to talkin' and imaginin' it can be full-time till the final whistle blows."

The van had stopped, it would be for the last time.

"They'll not stay long with that hape of a Glinn bitch with her *Jasus Christ tonight and would you be tellin' me that now* in her man's voice and her legs spread far enough apart to drive a fair-sized tractor through."

"You're very hard on the people, John," Elizabeth accused, though amused to soreness by this time.

"It's easy for you to talk, Elizabeth; you never mix with them; you always keep yourself apart. But if you were fightin' and agreein' with them for more than twenty years, till you can't have any more respect for yourself than you have for them, you might have evidence enough to change your mind," he defended, taking the accusation seriously.

She nodded: the conversation was beginning to disturb and pain her; she wished he'd soon decide to go away.

The bread-van's motor started to life for the last time in the evening and Mullins stiffened as it came in sight to read, "Broderick's—I knew I saw a capital b, B for Bread and B for Broderick's, Broderick's from Athlone: Mullingar, Athlone and Kinnegad as the Geography used to say."

They watched it cross the bridge, dust rising and some

148

loose stones cracking out from the tyres, and Mullins said, "Those loose stones would tear any tyre to pieces. I got two punctures on me back wheel this week. Do you know where I'd like to be now?" he asked when the silence fell.

"Where?" she answered desperately.

"In one of those pubs along the Liffey—the White Horse or the Scotch House—and a nice pint of stout in me fist. Isn't it strange that Dublin's the only place in the country that you can get a nice pint of stout, they say it's the Liffey gives it its flavour!"

" 'Tis strange," she nodded but wished the phone'd call him or he'd take it into his head to go. He was silent now against the sycamore trunk, his heavy red face sunk in reflection as she continued with the picking, the can more than half-full; and she was disturbed by how even his presence grated on her in the silence.

"Do you ever think, Elizabeth, that gettin' married and havin' a steady job takes a lot of the ginger outa life," he soon broke that silence. "There's not the same adventure at all any more! It's all more or less settled and the only information missin' for the auld nameplate is the age!"

She lifted her face: who'd ever think Mullins of the barrack arguments had such dangerous notions running through his head, she thought quickly. She wished she could be honest and giving, that she could strip her own heart bare in answer, for his words were but the cry of a fumbling loneliness, but the only answer she could make was to join his seeking with her own; and she knew she neither could nor would, she'd be deliberately dishonest, smiling and presenting him with the mirage of flattery that'd more than satisfy him. To answer truly could only lead to compassion or the discovery of each other's helplessness and squalor, and the one possible way to go that way was through the door of love, it would probably end the same, but at least it'd be with the heart and not in the cold blood of boredom.

"I don't know," she said. "You'd want to be the two things together to compare them, both married and single at once, and none of us can manage that."

149

"That's perfectly right, Elizabeth," he agreed. "You're the only person anyone can have a real talk with about here. You're the only one who understands anything."

"Don't be foolish!" she laughed.

"That's the God's truth," he said and moved away from the trunk. "And I suppose I'd be better to be gettin' back to base and let you go on with the pickin'."

"It's almost finished, John," she said and watched the back of his blue uniform go, heard his feet stir the gravel when he passed through the gate. She had thought she'd never get rid of him and now that he was gone she felt guilty. She felt such sympathy for people and yet she denied them—but this thinking only made bad worse. She wished she was blind as they.

"Why had he to come to disturb her anyhow?"

She was just out of hospital, it was the summertime, the pain of the clash with Reegan had almost faded when he arrived. Could he not leave her easy to enjoy the garden and the day? The pure shining blackness of the clusters of currants stared at her out of the leaves, the cold grasses touched her legs; the light was making a marvel out of the great rough rhubarb leaves over by the netting-wire, speckled with birds' droppings; the long ridges of potato stalks were all about her, tiny blossoms riding above the leaves and butterflies tossing. Could he not leave her alone to these? She heard him pottering about in the dayroom, then come out again to sit on the yellow chair in the shade, and later she heard him hum over and over to himself:

> *Said the Bishop of old Killaloe,*
> *"I am bored, I have nothing to do."*
> *So he climbed on his steeple*
> *An' pissed on his people,*
> *Singing tooralaye—ooralaye—oo.*

She smiled, she hadn't heard it before, she wondered was the Limerick his own. The singing grew louder and more provocative. She heard the words clearly. Her can was full. She pushed her way through the green stalks to the rain-gauge. He was humming and beating time on the gravel with a stick but as soon as he saw her come he stopped.

"I see you're singin'," she said.

"Takin' to cultivatin' me artistic talents in me auld age," he mocked, his phrases echoing the gossip columns in the newspapers, and then he said fiercely, "Hangin' b.o. about this joint'd drive a man to anything!"

"It'll soon be time for the tea."

"That itself," he muttered but half-grinning.

"Will you leave the door open when the mail car comes?" she inquired.

"I'll give you a knock if Brennan doesn't come to relieve me by then," he said.

"That'll be perfect," she answered.

"The lads are on the bog today?" he made conversation.

"They are," she said, and started to move on the gravel. "I intend makin' some jam before they get home."

"That's what'll be into their barrows," he laughed as she was going, the hens gathering excitedly about, believing she carried feeding in the can.

She didn't think once she was inside and she was happy, absorbed in preparing and washing the fruit, measuring sugar on the balance scales and going to the yellowed cookery book to make sure of the recipe. Soon the kitchen was full of the scent of the steaming jam, she stirred and tasted it to see if it was coming right, and then she had to scald the old jam jars and find rubber bands and cellophane. She'd often pause and smile to herself as she imagined how they'd shout when they'd smell the jam, untackling the donkeys without.

A light evening breeze had risen, blowing the curtains in the window open on the river. The sawmill had stopped, and the stone-crusher. Brennan must have relieved Mullins in the dayroom for he hadn't opened the door and she'd heard the noise of what must have been the mail car go.

She went to the windows where the curtains blew, the light had slanted, making such violence on the water that she'd to shade her eyes to see the reeds along the shore, the red navigation barrels caught in a swaying blaze at the mouth of the lake and the soft rectangles of shadow behind.

In a sort of an awe she put her fingers to the vase of roses on the sill, she'd been given them by Mrs Casey yesterday, and lifted them to her face. How deep and strong the scent at first, and then the longer she held her face close how the scent faded till no fragrance came. She'd want to go away and have other loves and when she'd accidentally return that fragrance would be given back to her fresh as after rain.

That would be the wise way. Things had to be taken in small doses to be enjoyed, she knew; but how that mean of measurement degraded and cheapened all passion for life and for truth, and though it had to go through human hell, a total love was the only way she had of approaching towards the frightful fulfilment of being resonant with her situation, and this was her whole terror and longing. She could love too much, break the vase, cast herself on the ground, and be what she was, powerless and helpless, a broken thing; but her life with these others, their need and her own need, all their fear, drew her back into the activity of the day where they huddled in their frail and human love, together. And she had to watch the blackcurrants till they were stewed and pour the jam steaming into the glass jars that seemed made of light in the evening, and she knew she was waiting for them to come home and when they'd come there would be other things.

July went, the weather breaking at its end, a fine drizzle that spun slowly and endlessly down and wet you to the skin without you noticing. They didn't go to the bog these days, the pass would be soft with rain and Reegan wasn't worried; he had most of the turf sold and what remained on the banks wasn't enough to matter. The borrowed donkeys nodded in the shelter of the sycamore and the hens slept on their feet beneath the heeled-up carts. The children helped Elizabeth inside or played draughts or push-half-penny on the window-sills, where they could watch out at the rain, their knees on the warm rug of the sofa along the

152

wall. Or they got tired of the house, put on old police rain-coats, dug a canister of worms in the garden, and went down the meadows to fish for perch, the eelhook and cork and brown perch line rolled about the rods of hazel they carried on their shoulders.

Reegan sat mostly with the other policemen in the atmosphere of Casey's, chain-smoking in the dayroom, doing whatever clerical work had to be done, and trying to shut his ears to the crazy arguments that went on non-stop. Sometimes, if he thought the children had gone and Eliza-beth was alone, he'd come and they'd have tea together and he'd tell her about the money he'd made out of the turf and his plans for next year. He mentioned nothing about clashes with Quirke or when he hoped to get out of the police; and she suspected that he thought these things might worry her and she was grateful and didn't try to pry beyond his care. She was happy, not since their first days did he show himself so aware of her, and there was something of the hour for the hour's vitality about him that had always excited her. When-ever they kept their talk to the impersonal truck of their lives, not scraping down to the cores of personality, every-thing went smooth and easy, and that was almost always now.

He was specially happy if she found him something to mend on these wet days in the kitchen, a saucepan that wanted soldering or a chair with a broken leg. What he hated most was stillness. He'd complain at first: "These children'll have to learn that they can't be rockin' back on these chairs; that's how the back goes and the legs," but it was complaining for the pleasure of complaining and to throw an extra light of importance on the job he had in hand. She'd watch him as he worked and share it when he'd want something held steady. When she was at peace she loved the kitchen full of the noisy life of his hammering, seeing the metal gleam of the nails between his teeth, and wanting to touch the smoothness of the new wood when it was planed. Sometimes she'd think how lucky she was to have found Reegan, to be married to him and not to Halli-

153

day, where she and he would drive each other crazy with the weight and desperation of their consciousness.

Often he hummed as he worked, the lovely *Danny Boy*, his strange favourite. Then, sensing her about, he'd look up and find her sunk in reflection and call, "A penny for them, Elizabeth!"

"They're not worth that," she'd wake to laugh, but she'd have stirred his anxiety—was she getting ill again? "Do you feel well, Elizabeth," he'd probe.

"Yes. Why? I just get lost in a daze sometimes, start to think, and then find myself drifting into an old dream. It's just a foolish habit."

"Do you not think you're takin' too much on yourself, all the work of the house, so soon out of hospital. Do you not think you'd be better to take it easy for a while? We made good money outa the turf and I was thinkin' if you took a week or two at the seaside, if you went to Strandhill? The Caseys'll be goin' in another week and they'd be company."

She smiled. He had preferred to ignore her explanation. She'd been at Southend and Margate and Brighton. Excursion days, never any place else. To go with the Caseys to Strandhill or any other place would be an absolute impossibility, she knew.

"Would you go yourself?" she asked because she knew he would not.

"What would I be doin' at the seaside?" he laughed, trying to turn it into a joke. "Wouldn't I be a nice cut walkin' round with Casey and me hands in me pockets?"

"What would I be doin' there either?"

"It'd rest you and there'd be the sea air."

"No, it'd be impossible," she laughed, and he joined her.

Casey alone went from the barracks, his love of ease betraying him for once with what was but its shade; for, though he went religiously for his fortnight each year and talked about it for weeks, it had become another barrack joke; they all knew that it was a grim fourteen days, suffering the loss of each of his home comforts, longing for the day that'd allow him home, his burden lightened if he could find another policeman, or someone from Dublin who'd talk about the trams, staying in Mrs O'Dwyer's guest house. The fortnight was a grim duty which he felt in some way that he owed himself. Even to Reegan now the notion of Elizabeth involved in this annual crucifixion was ludicrous.

None of the others ever went on holidays. They spaced out their leave for the turf and potatoes, little jobs in their gardens and house, bringing timber from the woods in the rowboat, and the excursions they made with their wives to town, mostly to buy clothes and shoes.

Elizabeth didn't want to go away. She felt more than ever that she'd never leave this barracks again, here she was meant to end her life, and she grew more sure of that with every new day.

She put turf and some wood on the fire while Reegan hammered, took down the flickering Sacred Heart lamp and filled it with oil, put a cloth and delf on the table and she had most of the jobs done.

There was such deep silence in the kitchen when Reegan would stop hammering to examine his work, the men sent home from the woods and the quarry, the constant drip of rain on the window-sills outside. She was completely alone with Reegan. She thought it might be the only right time she'd ever get to tell him about the money of her own she'd always kept, if she didn't tell it now it'd never be told. It had constantly preyed on her mind ever since she took it out of the locked trunk to bring to hospital. She'd spent hardly any of it there and if she didn't get rid of it soon it'd possess her for the rest of her life.

Fear must have made her gather it the first day. She'd seen scraping all her youth, having to wait for winter boots, till the calf or litter of pigs was born, worry over money gnawing at the happiness of too many evenings in childhood; she'd seen her mother and father bitter over each other's spending, and she never wanted to be under its rule again. She'd saved out of her first wages. But when she'd saved enough to give her few desires some freedom she didn't trouble more. If she had enough to buy some new clothes or go a place or bring something to someone she loved, she was happy. It was not miserliness, there's such fearful unhappiness at the heart of all miserliness, no trust or love, and the passion to live for ever cheapened into the bauble of providing against the wet day, the lunacy of building an outer wall against something that's impregnably entrenched in every nerve and cell of the body.

She hated to either borrow or lend, she'd give money but not lend, she felt any relationship based and bound by money more loathsome than rotten flesh. How her nerves would shiver and creep when a girl out of the hospital would say to her, "I'm not forgettin' about that loan, Elizabeth. I'll be able to pay you back soon."

"No, no, no," she'd want to burst out. "Keep it, do what you like with it, I don't want to see it again," and how hard it was to discipline herself and say the conventional thing that'd be accepted and not cause hatred. So she was never without money, enough to buy her anything she'd want or even indulge sudden whims without having to worry or consider. It left her free, she'd try to reason, but it went far beyond any reasoning. She even kept it to herself when she married. With that money she could be in London in the morning. It was dishonest. They were living together in this barracks, tied in the knot of each other; they had accepted the burden of her, she the burden of them, and they should have at least every exterior thing in common. They had all failed or were afraid to attempt to live alone, could any one of them endure total loneliness or silence or neglect, and enough had to be kept back by people living together without extending it to something as common and mangy with sweat as money. She'd have to put it right, tell Reegan, force him to take the money.

He had finished the chair. His face was flushed and happy and he was hooking the clasp of his tunic at the throat. He showed her the chair for her praise, and she pretended to test it and inspect the joinings.

"It's as good as new," she praised.

156

"Aw, not as good as new, but it'll do a turn. It'll take more than natural abuse to smash it this time," he showed his real pleasure in the diminishment.

"I think it couldn't be better," she said, and they sat together to gaze into the fire and out at the grey, steady rain. It wound down, stirred by no breath of wind, barely fouling the mirror of the calm river.

"It'd put you to sleep, that rain," he said.

"It might be good for the fishing though," she answered.

"It should, it's never bad on a dull, rainy evenin', you always get bites of something."

The silence resumed, the kettle murmuring, the drip-drip of rain on the sills. She stirred the fire with the tongs. She tried to get herself to tell about the money, and then she said awkwardly out of the continuing silence, "There's something I want to tell you that's not easy."

She saw how awful a way it was to break anything, when the words were out: his body went tense, fear came in the eyes. His jerky, "What?" seemed asked more with the muscles than the voice. What could she have to tell him that wasn't easy, it couldn't be pleasant, and he wished he didn't have to hear.

She wished she hadn't to tell, but she was driven. There was no reason to this crying need to speak: what did he matter any more than she mattered; he'd have to die into whatever there was too, and all things were believed to be changed in new light then. It made no sense, this need to speak, she'd be as well to try to get the raindrip from the sycamore leaves outside to understand.

She might as well be honest about why she wanted to speak her truth. It was to ease her own mind. What could it do but disturb his peace or at best leave him indifferent? The Church knew an old trick or two when she said you make your confession to God, and not to the priest in the box, whose understanding or misunderstanding has nothing whatever to do with the Sacrament. But how humanness entered everything. She'd go steeled and prepared to tell the truth to God and end in the squalid drama of trying to get a

157

name printed on a card outside the box, a voice in the darkness, a smell of after-shave lotion to understand.

She could steel herself, make herself cold as death and inhuman to try to bear witness to the truth, but she was so weak that at its first intimation her preparations and disciplines would crumple up, and she'd become only more truly human than before she ever set out. Oh irony of ironies! The road away becomes the road back.

There was no end to thinking and she could even think away the need to think. An age of thought can pass before the mind and be lost in the same flash. What she had to do now was state not reason; state it and suffer it in her human self. She had pondered on it for months up to this moment, reasoned it more than once away, and still the need remained.

Reegan was watching her impatiently, fretting at the wait.

"It's money," she began. "I've some money that I never told you about. I meant to and as time went it got harder to tell. I was afraid you mightn't understand."

She broke down, beginning to sob with shame and squalor. Nothing struck Reegan for a moment. He'd been tensed for something painful, and now that this was all he was taken by surprise. He'd often wondered if she'd spent all she had earned in London but they never seemed close enough for him to be able to ask without fear of offence. She was crying now.

"Don't, Elizabeth," he said. "It doesn't matter. It's your own money and nobody ever asked you to tell. It's your own to tell or not to tell and has nothin' got to do with anybody else."

She heard what he said, it did not matter. She tried to pull herself together, out of this breakdown. She'd have to try and see it through to the end once she'd started.

"No, that's not right. When I didn't want to take money for clothes you used say, 'What's mine is yours. It's there for you to take as much as me'," she said.

"But I married you," he protested. "It's a man's job to keep his wife, she has to keep the home."

"I want to give you that money," she said.

"No. That's your money, not mine. You'll want it to be able to buy things that you'll need yourself. Nobody wants to depend entirely on somebody else. That money has nothing got to do with me."

"I want you to take the money," she didn't try to argue. "I want you to take it now. If I need anything I'll ask you for the money and you'll give it to me."

"You'd get it anyhow. I never refused you for anything, did I? But why?"

"Don't mind the why, take it, for my sake. Of course you never refused me anything!"

"But why?" he puzzled as she left to go quickly upstairs to get the money out of the trunk and hurry down again.

"Why should you . . ." he was beginning an argument he'd thought of while she was away but she pressed him with the money.

"I'll put it in an account for yourself. I'll open a new account for you."

"No, you must put it in your own."

"But why?" he said again.

"No why, except I want you to, that is all."

This useless argument threatened to drag on and on and not till he heard the children did he finally pocket the money.

Water dripped on the concrete from their soaked clothes, but they were excited. They showed proudly the perch they'd caught, hanging on a small branch that'd been passed through their dead gills and mouths, their scarlet tails and bellyfins shining against the grey blackstriped scales, lying against the sally leaves of the branch that were vivid with wet.

Elizabeth gave them dry clothes and when they'd changed they skinned some of the perch for their meal. Roasted brown they were sweet as trout, though full of small bones. Through the meal they talked excitedly of their evening's catch in the rain.

Afterwards the long, dark evening was let rest in the kitchen. The rosary was said. Reegan lit his carbide bicycle lamp, put on cape and pull-ups to go on patrol, more to break the claustrophobia of the day indoors than to do his duty. They played draughts on the sill when he'd gone, and Elizabeth read. She was strangely content and at peace, she felt no guilt nor worry, and sure of this ease until at least this night's sleep.

That broken August crept towards September, the dead sycamore leaves lying on the roof of the lavatory now on calm days, the length disappearing so noticeably out of the evenings that it was all the time in their conversations. Soon the children would be back at school, the summer ended.

There was little change. She had to go one Friday to the clinic in Athlone, as arranged by the Dublin cancer hospital, and there was no deterioration in her condition. It was her heart they feared most now, the strain of the operation and illness proving too much, and they told her to take things easy. She'd have to be careful, they said; but she paid no attention, how could she stay with them in this barracks and not be occupied. She'd go on as she was, as long as ever she was able. She'd no pain, there was no sign of the cancer stirring, and if her heart went she'd probably go out in a flash, without time for terror or thought.

Though often too she'd feel herself trapped on this quiet drift of days and grow a moment desperate. They were all the same, they would not change, the same day would follow the same day and day and day, nothing more would happen. On these days she was being drifted to her destruction, disease had started, and her life was almost ended.

She'd handle objects on the sideboard, lifting them and putting them back in the same place; or go to the window and rest her palms on the sill. The river was out there and the hill and the hedge of whitethorns half-way up; the great sycamore stood inside the netting-wire, a few dead leaves caught in its meshes. All she could do was stay in this kitchen and despair or go some place to break the claustrophobia with distraction. She could wash and comb and dress herself up, these simple acts had saved her many times before; and she could find some of the children and go to the well and shop. One of these evenings was extraordinarily vivid, a lovely evening both green and yellow together, held still between summer and autumn. She'd grown gradually desperate through the day and then made a last effort to live, and when she had washed and dressed herself she began to feel new and better, refreshed, the grime and sweat of the habitual day shed for ever, and desire and eagerness rose in her again.

She was alone in the kitchen and she went out to find Willie on the avenue. He was searching the laurels and talking to himself and she was delighted somehow, it was a habit of her own. He was glad to offer to come with her when she told him she was going to the well. His sisters had gone with Reegan to the woods for timber in the rowboat and he had remained behind because of some sulk or jealousy and probably tiring of his own company by this. He carried the enamel bucket for her, but she kept the shopping-bag, not to have her hands empty.

They turned right at the end of the avenue, away from the bridge, the river and lake gleaming behind till they reached the privet hedge before Glinn's when the block of the barracks and trees about the archway shut it away. Glinn's was a little general grocery place, far out on the road, four fresh shrubs of boxwood on the grass margin the far side, the pride of Mrs Glinn's heart. She'd never trouble to cross the road to water them, but came just to her own doorway, and a basin of dish-water went flying across the road to the terror of every one passing, and there'd been more than a few ludicrous accidents with cyclists even since Elizabeth came.

She'd always an eye on the window or the door open so that no one could go by unnoticed. "A powerful evenin' we have, Mrs Reegan," she greeted Elizabeth from inside.

"It's a lovely evenin', Mrs Glinn," Elizabeth said but didn't stop. "Stuck-up bitch", she thought she read in the old barrel-shaped woman's reaction to her never stopping, but it could be so easily her own apprehensive imagination. Behind the forge the men were at pitch-and-toss, the pennies tossed from pocket-combs, a slight roll and thud when they fell on the tramped earth; she had to pass through and she flinched and tried to smile as they made respectful way and said, 'Good evenin', Mrs Reegan," and she had to force her own quiet reply. The shock of new contact with people was getting more violent than ever, and yet she couldn't stay alone. She saw the boy impatiently ahead of her now, ashamed before the men of this ageing woman who was not even his mother, and the men neither noticing nor caring. Sometimes the smile turned to a shudder, but it was best to go on and not notice, if you could possibly manage, and declare the whole mess a shocking comedy.

She left the shopping-bag and the cloth-bound notebook, in which the monthly accounts were written, at the shop and said she'd call for them on her way from the well.

The well was past the chapel, in the priest's field where the presbytery stood blue and white for the Virgin Mary at the end of the long avenue of limes. Always it amused her, the great whitewashed front and the Virgin Mary door and windows, one man's way of proclaiming a love. "*He turned from grisly saints, and martyrs hairy To the sweet portraits of the Virgin Mary*," she remembered out of Don Juan, and began to laugh. She wondered if the priest could read those lines and still paint the house blue and white; probably he could, it'd only add strength of indignation to the brush. It was Halliday who'd first showed her the lines and given her the Byron.

"What's the joke, Elizabeth?" the boy asked in a neglected tone and she'd quickly to come to earth.

"I was thinking of something. I'm sorry, Willie. We must buy some sweets on our way back. What sort of sweets would you like?"

It drew him away, he answered excitedly. They were on the avenue and then she saw the priest, walking in his soutane at the other end of the limes, reading his breviary. The well was only a little distance, a path between barbed-wire on stakes leading to it from the avenue so that people couldn't tramp indiscriminately over the meadow, and she hurried, she wanted to be away before he'd reach the end of his walk and turn and see her.

162

Soon after she had married he approached her to join the local branch of the Legion of Mary, a kind of legalized gossiping school to the women and a convenient pool of labour that the priests could draw on for catering committees. There was no real work for it to do, all the Catholics of the parish attended to their duties, except a few dangerous eccentrics who would not be coerced.

"No, thank you, father," Elizabeth had politely refused the offer to join.

"Come now, Mrs Reegan," he wouldn't accept the refusal. "All the other policemen's wives are joined. It's one of the most extraordinary and powerful organizations in the world, it's spread to every country under the sun, and it was founded by one of our own countrymen, Frank Duff. Do you know, and I think this miraculous, it was organized on exactly the same pattern as Communism: a presidium at the top and widening circles of leadership all the way down to the bottom; and even in this humble parish of ours we must try to do our bit. Come now, Mrs Reegan! You don't want us to coax you all that much."

"No. I don't wish to join," she said firmly; the half-patronizing, half-bullying tone annoyed her, she'd been too short a time out of London.

"But come now, Mrs Reegan. You must have a reason—why?" he grew hot.

"Because I dislike organizations," she tossed, betrayed by her annoyance.

"So, my dear woman, you dislike the Catholic Church: it happens to be an organization, you know, that's founded on Divine Truth," he countered quickly and she was taken aback; but she saw the roused egotism, the personal fall it'd be if he didn't make her join now. Meaning or words didn't matter, except as instruments in the brute struggle—who was going to overpower whom—and this time she was roused too. She was too angry and involved to slip away and leave the field empty. She wanted to brush the *my dear woman* aside like she would a repulsive arm-clasp or touching of clothes, the assumptions of a familiarity that does not exist.

163

"No, thank you, father. I won't join and I must leave you now," she closed and went, in the succeeding remorse at least she'd escape the pain of brawling. He came to the house several times afterwards but she was prepared and able to thwart him, though one time she'd despaired of him ever giving up. And when he finally did she avoided him as much as was possible in a place as small as this.

She filled the bucket from the well and they managed to be on their way out the avenue before he turned in his slow, reading walk. The gate of the avenue faced the church gate and to the right was the shop and a piece of waste ground hedged with flowering currant where candidates spoke from the roofs of cars at elections. Here she gave the boy money for chocolate and sent him to the shop. She crossed to the church gate and went on the old brown flagstones between the laurels into the church.

It was still as death within, no one entered much this time of day, soon the sacristan would come to close the doors for the night, and the kneeler she let so carefully down frightened her with the way it seemed to crash on the flagstones. Her skin was uncomfortably hot and damp after the blind race to escape the priest.

Pray that you may get well, was her first thought, and then the quietness started to seep into her mind. The long strips of whitewash peeling between the windows, the dark light of blood from the lamp hanging before the tabernacle, late roses and geraniums and tulips in the vases on the altar and no candles burning in the sockets on the gleaming candle-shrines, the wooden communion-rail and pulpit and the Stations of the Cross in their wooden frames, and her mind began to wander dispassionately, an old habit, over the life of Christ. The God made flesh in a woman, preparing thirty years to change the lives of people and being crucified for His trouble after three; the Resurrection and the going away from it all into heaven after declaring it saved; lunatic enough at least to fit the situation it proposed itself to answer. And then odd moments on the way that fascinated her: the absurdity and total humanness of the cry, "Can

164

you not watch one hour with me?" to the apostles asleep in their own lives in the garden, his agony not their drama; and what real good would their watching do, except its little deceit of flattery might obscure for its hour the terror of his loneliness with what he'd have to face anyhow, alone; for even if they did watch they could not take the chalice from his lips, no one can find anybody to suffer their last end for them.

But soon her mind was shifting, not able to stay long on any one thing, her eyes gazing now at the initials cut in the bench where she knelt, some of them covered with so much grime and dust that those who'd carved them there must be long dead, the single letters cut in the wood that lent themselves to so many interpretations having endured longer than the hands that carved them; and a little way from her right hand she noticed the white trade-plate:

> HEARNE & CO.
> CHURCH FURNISHERS
> WATERFORD.

Waterford, a port town in the south, famous for its glass, where there must be a factory that made church furniture. There she woke. Her mind was giving the same attention to this old bench as it had given to the mystery of the world and Christ. There were no answers. All the mind could do was wander and wonder from object to object and find no resting-place, in the end all things were lost in contemplation. That was all, there seemed nothing more, she'd no business to be in the church except she loved it and it was quiet; Willie must be waiting this long while outside, tired to his teeth of her solemn practices.

She found him at the pier, between the bucket and shopping-bag, and she carried the bucket. They went between the churchyard and McDermott's, the pub giving way to the dwelling-house, and then the stables and sheds, where the animals were kept and the drinkers pissed. They had to pass the men tossing at the forge and when she saw the boy stiffen she said, "Don't mind, Willie. They're paying us as

165

much attention as the man in the moon is," but she saw he didn't believe her, resented her touching so close on his secret feelings.

When she got past Glinn's she rested, the weight of water too much for her strength, and the boy coming to himself when she smiled, "We brought the lazyman's load, didn't we, Willie?"

"We'll have to know better next time," he laughed.

"Why does the virginia creeper—you know the stuff on the church, Elizabeth—turn red and the ivy stay green?" he asked with the insatiable eagerness to know that took possession of him sometimes.

"Because it changes, because it dies," she said absently, not really knowing. "That's what I suppose. The ivy doesn't change or die. Oh, I never went to school much; I don't know much, Willie."

"How long did you go to school for?"

"Till I was fourteen."

"You're tired, Elizabeth, aren't you?" he asked and she started.

"I'm sorry, Willie. I'm afraid I'm not better yet, not fully."

She'd not been paying him enough attention. Why could she not keep her mind fixed? Half her attention as they walked had been on the orchard underneath where the Caseys lived, the light coming across the lake, between the great oaks standing in the laurels on the avenue, to fall on the apple trees. The blackbirds flew clacking between the low branches to peck the skin of the honeycombs for the wasps to burrow in, so that they'd fall light as leaves, just shells of red and yellow in the trodden grass of the orchard —and she was beginning to make vague analogies, to think of herself, her mind about to go on its futile wanderings again, when she saw she was neglecting everything else. She was growing too engrossed in herself and no matter what she'd think or where her mind might wander she was still a woman on an earthen road with a boy and a bucket.

"Oh, things get too terrible sometimes, Willie," she blurted suddenly out and when she saw his worried amazement she was sorry. She lifted the bucket. When she'd have dragged as far as the scullery table she'd try to give him all her attention till the others would get home, she promised.

The school holidays ended in early September, the kitchen emptier all the mornings and afternoons, and Mrs Casey began to come practically every day and to stay for hours. She had nothing to do, she complained.

"I didn't mind at all," she said; one morning Elizabeth had praised her for taking care of the house while she was in hospital. "There was great excitement, them all were good and helped, and I felt I was needed—it's when you have nothin' to do and start thinkin' that's the worst.

"I'll go off me rocker some day I'm alone up in that elephant of a house, that's the God's truth," she cried. "If you had a child or something you'd be better able to knuckle down! But when you have nothin', that's the thing! I was at Ned to adopt one out of the Home but he wouldn't hear of it. They'd have bad blood or wild, their father's or mother's blood, he said. What does he care? He's down in the dayroom here or at court or out on patrol most of the time but where am I?"

Elizabeth didn't know what to do, only let her cry. She liked her, but she was afraid the younger woman was beginning to depend too much on her, and she could drag like deadweight. Mullins's wife and Brennan's were hard and vulgarly sure of their positions, always ferociously engaged in some petty rivalry or other, but they were too full of their own things to ever drag. The most they'd want was to make some material use out of you, and it was always easier to deal with them than such as Mrs Casey. You'd only to meet their demands on the one level, and perhaps a person had always to stay on that level to survive as untouched as they were. She'd try and tell Mrs Casey that she was running through a bad time, as every one did, and that it would pass. Though it'd be quite useless as anything else. She'd better make tea. The one thing was that her own situation didn't seem so desperate when it was confronted with such as this.

167

The days grew colder and there came the first biting frosts, the children having to wear their winter stockings and boots, some lovely nights in this weather, a big harvest moon on the lake, and the beating whine of threshing-machines everywhere, working between the corn-ricks by the light of the tractor headlamps. The digging of the potatoes began. And there was great excitement when apples were hung from the barrack ceiling for Hallowe'en and nuts went crack under hammers on the cement through the evening. All Souls' Day they made visits to the church, six Our Fathers and Hail Marys and then outside to linger awhile beneath the bell-rope before entering again on another visit, and for every visit they made a soul escaped out of purgatory.

There had only been one month of peace with Quirke after the day Reegan had been caught spraying, though he had kept it from Elizabeth till it erupted again into the open that November. Quirke had paid an early morning inspection, and afterwards Reegan came up to her in the kitchen in a state of blind fury.

"The bastard! The bastard! I'll settle that bastard one of these days," he started to grind and she saw his hands clench and unclench and touch unconsciously the sharp, red stubble on his face.

"What happened?" she asked when he was quieter.

"He did an inspection this mornin' and after the others had gone he said, 'There's something I want to tell you, Reegan,' and I like a gapin' fool opened me big mouth and said, 'What?' So he stared me straight in the face and said, 'Let me tell you one thing, Reegan: never come down to this dayroom again unshaven while you're a policeman!' and he left me standin' with me mouth open."

She saw he desperately needed to tell some one: to ease the hurt by telling, cheapen and wear out his passion by telling, scatter it out of his mind where it was driving him to the brink of madness. Though she found the tremor of hatred unnerving, his face purple as he shouted, "Never come down to this dayroom unshaven again while you're a

168

policeman, Reegan! Never come down to this dayroom unshaven again while you're a policeman, Reegan!"

"You didn't do anything at all?" she asked.

"Nothin'. It took me off me feet, that tough is a new line from Quirke. Though I'd probably have done nothin' anyhow," he was quieter, he began to brood bitterly now. "I'd not be thirty bastardin' years in uniform if I couldn't stand before barkin' mongrels and not say anything. It's either take them by the throat and get sacked or stop with your mouth shut, and they know they've got you in the palm of their hand. Though they couldn't sack me now, I'm just thirty years in this slave's uniform, they'd have to ask me to resign and give me a pension. You can't victimize an old Volunteer these days!" he began to laugh and then swiftly it turned to rage again. "That bastard! That ignoramus! Never come down to this dayroom again unshaven while you're a policeman, Reegan!" he shouted.

"If you want to get out of the police altogether I don't mind. Don't let me stand in your way. I was afraid of it before but I don't think it makes any difference any more," Elizabeth said.

"You don't mind?" he came close to stare.

"No. You can send in your resignation, whenever you wish."

"And what'll we do then?"

"Whatever you think best, it's not for me," she shuddered from the responsibility. "It won't be my decision, it'll be up to you, though I'd give any help. You know that, it must be your decision."

"I thought after the summer that we'd have enough to buy and stock a fair farm. That's what I was brought up to, Reegans as far as you can go worked a farm, not till 1921 did this bastardin' uniform show itself. With the pension we'd not be worked too much to the bone on a farm, and you'd be your own boss anyhow."

"Whatever you think, that seems good," she nodded, one thing was much the same as the next to her, this game of caring was only something she felt she owed him to play.

"But Jesus there's one thing, Elizabeth," he swore. "There'll be no goin' quiet, that's certain. I'll do for that bastard before I go. Never come down to this dayroom unshaven again while you're a policeman, Reegan! There'll be no goin' quiet, that's the one thing that's sure and certain," he said between clenched teeth and took his greatcoat and cap to go out on another patrol.

The heavy white frost seemed over everything at this time, the drum of boots on the ground hard as concrete in the early mornings, voices and every sound haunting and carrying far over fields of stiff grass in the evenings. The ice had to be broken on the barrels each morning. It was so beautiful when she let up the blinds first thing that, "Jesus Christ", softly was all she was able to articulate as she looked out and up the river to the woods across the lake, black with the leaves fallen except the red rust of the beech trees, the withered reeds standing pale and sharp as bamboo rods at the edges of the water, the fields of the hill always white and the radio aerial that went across from the window to the high branches of the sycamore a pure white line through the air.

And then she'd want to go out and lift her hot face and throat to the morning. But it would be only to find her eyes water and every desire shrivel in the cold. She wasn't able to do that any more, that was the worst to have to realize; and it was driven home like nails one evening she was alone and the first heart attack struck while she was lifting flour out of the bin; she managed to drag herself to the big armchair and was just recovered enough to keep them from knowing when they came home.

Mullins's pig was slaughtered. She heard its screams without any emotion, she'd seen too many pigs stuck when she was a child. She could visualize what was taking place by the varying pitches of the screaming. It'd first start when they tangled it in ropes, rise to its highest when it was caught on the snout-hook for the head to be dragged back and the long knife driven in to the heart between the shoulder-blades, the screaming choke into silence as the knife was pulled out for the blood to beat into the basin that caught it so that they'd be able to make black pudding. Then the carcass would be scalded with boiling water and the white hairs shaved away.

As the screaming died Casey came running up from the dayroom to call, "Did you hear the roars, Elizabeth? It's all over."

He began to smoke and pace nervously about the kitchen.

"Do you know what?" he said heatedly. "He wanted me to give a hand. Some people have a hard neck and there's no mistake. The very thought of it is enough to make me sick! I told him it was a barbarous custom, but that I'd do b.o. and let Brennan go. And he'd the neck to laugh into me face and say that I'd ate a nice bit of pork steak quick enough. It's simple barbarity for savages, that's what it is, Elizabeth," he complained.

A sudden vision of pampered dogs being walked between the plane trees in the parks of London came and went in her mind before she answered, all a London evening held there for a moment.

"It'll be the end of a lot of talk," she said.

"A lot of rubbish," Casey said, "skim milk and did you ever hear the bate of the notion, windfall apples to sweeten the bacon. God, Elizabeth, that pig got more publicity than a Christian."

"You'll have to hear about this morning, won't you?"

"Yes. There'll be a runnin' commentary and nothin' left out," he said with such distaste that she had to laugh in secret.

She felt she was getting weaker; and she grew more afraid that she'd pass out some day and that they'd find her before she had time to recover, and confine her to bed. As they were the days were futile enough, and the whole feeling of them seemed to gather into the late evening in December they came tipsy from the District Court, nothing obviously resolved in the pub or on the bikes home or in the dayroom, and they landed finally in the kitchen, anything that'd prolong the evening so that they'd not have to go home.

"It's a sure prophecy, and with these bombs they have now the end of the world can't be far away. Anything that's ever med grows into use," Mullins was declaiming before they'd taken their chairs, and it was not popular.

"If it'll come it'll come and talkin' won't stop it," Reegan said.

"There was a famous Jesuit once and he was asked if he was playin' cards at five minutes to midnight and the end of the world was announced for midnight what would he do?" Brennan took up, and there was an immediate air of interest, the human and priestly elements together were certain to give reassurance.

"And do your know what he answered? You'd never guess!" so pleased was Brennan with his moment in the limelight that he tried to prolong it.

"No. What did he answer?" Casey was prompting, when Mullins let drop heavily, "He said he'd keep playin'. One act is as good as the next before God, it's the spirit of the thing counts, that's all."

"Where did you hear that?" Brennan asked in chagrin.

"People hear things, in company. They don't spend all their life with ignoramuses," Mullins insulted, he appeared gloomy and surly and more drunken than the others.

"He was a cool man then," Casey tried to obscure the brutality and to ridicule the conversation into shallower and easier waters. "I'd be inclined to jump on me knees and say an *Act of Contrition* or pray for more time. Give me five minutes more in your arms above. Isn't that what you'd be inclined to do, Elizabeth?" he appealed.

"The Jesuits believe in prayer, fasting and alms deeds; not in cushions for chairs and that; and they'd be ready to face their end when it'd come," Mullins was determined to be surly.

"That's not fair, that's hittin' below the belt. I didn't bring personal things in, though I could," he said, the eyes still bright and shallow and gentle.

"Out with it so, be a man, and say it out. There's nothin' worse than hintin'," Mullins attacked furiously.

172

"That's enough, it's nothin' to get hot about it," Reegan said, and in the silence Brennan saw a chance again.

"They're very clever, the Jesuits," he said. "A Jesuit was the only man ever to get 100 per cent in an exam in Oxford. He was asked to describe the miracle of the Marriage Feast of Cana and do you know how he answered it? All he wrote was, *Christ looked at the water and it blushed*, and he was the first man ever to get 100 per cent. Not a word wasted, exactly perfect. *Christ looked at the water and it blushed*."

"Aren't miracles strange?" Casey suddenly pondered. "Plane-loads off to Lourdes every summer and they say the amount of cures there are a terror. And every cure has to be certified, so there can be no hookery."

"There's no cod and it's recognized by Rome," Brennan said.

"Fatima's recognized too and isn't it strange that with all its cures they never recognized Knock."

"A man was cured of paralysis one Sunday I was there," Brennan said, he and Casey the only two left in the conversation. "We were walkin' round and round the church and sayin' the rosary when a sort of gasp went up: there was a cure. A sandy little man, no more than forty; he just got up out of his wheel-chair and walked as if there was never a tap on him."

"Mr Maguire, the solicitor, says that the reason Knock's not recognized is because the Papal Nuncio fellows never got on with the clergy here, and it's for the same reason that we've got not first-class saints. It looks be now as if we'll be prayin' till Doomsday to shift Matt Talbot and Oliver Plunkett past the Blessed mark. If they were Italians or Frenchmen they'd be saints quick enough, Mr Maguire said," Casey droned, the evening sagging into the lifeless ache of a hangover.

"It's a disgrace over about Knock: you never went to Knock yet on an excursion Sunday but they were savin' hay or some other work over in Mayo. A Papal Nuncio'd want to have an ocean of miracles in front of him when he'd land

173

after seein' all that sin on a Sunday before he'd recognize the place," it was Brennan again this time.

"The nearer the church the farther from God," Casey yawned in answer. Reegan followed Elizabeth's slow movements as she washed the delf at the table, his eyes desperate with this vision of futility when she turned to come for hot water to the fire. Is this all? Will they never go away? Will this go on for ever? in his eyes.

Mullins rose, Casey and then Brennan, trying to be before the footlights to the last. "I knew a fella once and he used always say when he was jarred, 'I'll do anything within reason, but home I will not go.' He'd do anything within reason but home he would not go," Brennan laughed.

"Such bullshit," Reegan said when they had gone. "Nothin' short of a miracle would change that crew, and there's no mistake."

She was quiet. Nothing short of a miracle would change any of their lives, their lives and his life and her life without purpose, and it seemed as if it might never come now, she changed his words in her own mind but she did not speak.

6

Christmas was coming and, in spite of everything, the feeling of excitement grew as always. Cards were bought and sent; and returned to deck the sideboard with tinsel and colour, sleighs and reindeer and the coaches with red-liveried footmen arriving before great houses deep in snow. The plum pudding was wrapped in gauze in the sweet can that stood out of reach on top of the press above the flour-bin; the turkey hung plucked and white, its stiff wings spread, on the back of the scullery door, and they'd all join in burning the down away with blazing newspapers Christmas Eve; ivy and berried holly were twined about the hanging cords of the pictures on the wall. When dark fell Christmas Eve they stripped the windows of their curtains, and a single candle was put to burn in each window till the morning. The rosary was said, and the children sent to bed.

Reegan was on edge all this Christmas Eve, the worst evening of the year for the policemen with drunkenness and brawling, the lockup had been cleaned out days before in readiness. Reegan was hardly aware of Elizabeth as he struggled into the cumbersome greatcoat and put on his peaked cap to go out on patrol. He didn't wear the baton in its leather sheath but slipped it naked into his greatcoat pocket, the vicious stick of lead-filled hickory shining yellow before it was hid, only the grooved surface of the handle and the leather thong hanging free.

She watched him get ready to go, her sense of his restlessness starting to gnaw: she could do nothing, and yet she felt she'd failed him somehow, something at some time that she could have done for him that she had failed to do, though she could never know what it might have been and

175

all she was left with was sense of her own failure and guilt and inadequacy. There was nothing she could do or say, only watch him go, listen to him tell her that he wouldn't be back till late. His lips touched her face. His boots faded down the hallway and the dayroom slammed to leave silence in the house. She set about doing the few jobs that were left, and managed to shut all thought of their life together out of her mind. At half-eleven the first bell for midnight Mass rang, ten clear strokes. This would be the first Christmas since she'd come to the village to find her away from that Mass, there was always such a crush of people, and she couldn't trust her strength there any more, far safer to wait for the deserted church in the morning. The cars began to go past. She heard a burst of drunken singing in the village, the last bell rang at midnight, then what seemed the drift of a choir came, and the sense of silence and Christmas began to awe and frighten her as she hurried to get through the few jobs that remained.

The thought of the stable and the birth, the announcement of glad tidings, shepherds, kings, reaching out and down to her in this kitchen drifted into her mind, and it was awesome as she worked to feel it run to this through the dead months and years. She was covering the mug, out of which Reegan drank barley water every night of his life, with a saucer, a narrow blue circle above its handle, the earthenware pale brown; she'd leave it there beside the raked fire in the hope that it'd stay warm till he'd come. To see the first Christmas and to follow it down to his moment, joined in her here and ending in her death, and yet the external reality would run on and on and on as the generations. Perhaps it should be the rhetoric of triumph that it ran so but who was she and what was it? Her thought could begin on anything for object and still it travelled always the same road of pain to the nowhere of herself, it was as far as anything seemed to go.

"Get rid of your mind, Elizabeth: distract it; get away. It is late. You've only to leave the presents into the children's rooms and then you can get to sleep at last," beat at her till

176

she took the football boots and a pair of identical dolls and went. She left them quietly in the rooms, the doors creaked, but the deep breathing of their sleep did not break. An ironical smile rose to her features as she recollected the bitterness of her own disillusionment as a child, the marvellous world of Santa Claus collapsing in a night into this human artifice, and now she was playing the other part of the game. It seemed as a person grew older that the unknowable reality, God, was the one thing you could believe or disbelieve in with safety, it met you with imponderable silence and could never be reduced to the nothingness of certain knowledge. She tried to shut that away as she closed the doors. No blinds or curtains were on the windows tonight, the candle-flame burned and waved in the black shine of the glass like a small yellow leaf, and there was a blaze of light in the village about the church. Out there in the night Reegan was patrolling or at Mass, she knew.

He was with Mullins. At eleven they had started to clear the pubs, meeting hostility and resentment in every house, and in McDermott's at the church a familiar arm was put round Mullins's neck and he was told, "Never mind the auld duty, John. Have a drink on the house, forget it all, it'll taste just as sweet in the uniform." The invitation was greeted by a storm of cheering, Mullins was furious and Reegan had to order him to be still. When the cheering died Reegan said, "I'm givin' every man three minutes to get off these premises. I'll summons every man on these premises in three minutes' time."

He spoke with quiet firmness: a sullen muttering rose but they gulped their drinks and left.

"No respect for anything, just like the bloody animals in the fields," Mullins was muttering as the pub cleared, and he gave full vent to his rage on a man they found pissing in public against the churchyard wall as they came out.

"Get out of it," Mullins roared in a fury of assertion.

"Sugar off home outa that with yourself and mind your own business," the man swayed erect to mutter, certain it was some one trying to joke him out of his position or else

177

a puritan madman he was determined to put in his place. In a flash Mullins was beside him with drawn baton. "Get out of it. Have you no shame, young girls passin' here to Mass, or are you an animal?"

"You wouldn't mind handlin' those fillies closer than ever my pissin'll get to them, you narrow-minded auld bastard," the drunk shouted as he buttoned his fly and a cheer went up from the outhouses.

"What did you say to *me*? What did you say? Do you see *this*?" Mullins thrust the baton before the man's face, gripping him by the shoulder, mad with rage. "Do you know what this is? Would you like a taste of this?"

"No," the man jabbered, the hard wood of the baton against his face, and he saw the silver buttons, the peaked cap: he was dealing with the police. Painfully the drunken brain was made to function in the space of seconds: he'd be up in court; his name would be in the newspapers; he'd be the laughing-stock of the country.

"I'm sorry," he tried to slide. "I'm sorry. I didn't know. I'm sorry."

"You're sorry now! It's never too late to be sorry, is it? You weren't that a minute ago and young girls pass this way to Mass, you know! And what kind of language was that you were usin' to officers of the law? Do you see this? Do you see this, do you? Would you like to get the tannin' you deserve with this and find yourself in court later?" Mullins ground threateningly with the baton, but growing placated, he was master now.

The man watched the baton close to his face, the shock had left him cold sober beneath the depression of alcohol, he was past caring what happened now, he shivered, he hoped it was all a passing nightmare. The cheering had died in the outhouses. Reegan moved close for the first time.

"What's your name?" Reegan demanded.

The name was hopelessly given.

"What do you do?"

"A sawyer."

Reegan knew the man's name, what his work was, but

178

the demanding of the information was an old bullying trick policemen learn and it had become a habit by this.

"Shouldn't you know better than to be at something like that," he began in the official moral tone, but grew disgusted, and with an impatient movement told him to be gone. Mullins had subsided into approving growls, but as the man made good his escape woke to shout, "Get home outa that you disgraceful blaguard and never let me catch you at that in public again." Reegan watched Mullins coldly: the cheeks seemed flushed in the weak light of the candles in the windows.

"Such a disgrace and young girls passin'. Such language. No better than the animals in the fields," Mullins tried to justify himself to Reegan, who only smiled sardonically at the moral indignation, remembering Mullins's gloating stories of the gunshot nights and through blood and sand and shit MacGregory will ride tonight.

A mad surge of strength rose in Reegan, desire to break the whole mess up into its first chaos: there was no order, only the police force. He sent Mullins to the church gate to help Casey direct the traffic, he said he'd do the last round of the village on his own. He felt the naked baton in his own pocket and began to curse as he walked away.

It was later than two in the Christmas morning when they were finished: the last of the cars directed away from the church, the roads patrolled for drunks, the reports filled into the books in the dayroom. No one slept on the iron bed against the wall of the lockup during Christmas. Reegan put a chair against the door so that he'd be able to hear the phone or anyone knocking from his own bedroom. He drank the barley water that Elizabeth had left covered beside the raked fire, believing that it cleansed his blood, something he'd brought with him from his childhood. Then he climbed the stairs in his stockinged feet, carrying the green glass oil-lamp, and placed a boot quietly against the bedroom door to make sure it stayed open. Elizabeth was awake. "Is it late?" she asked.

"Ten to three," he took out his watch, and she heard him

winding. "There's rain and showers of hailstones. It'd skin a monkey outside tonight."

He threw off his clothes and she shivered as his feet touched her getting into bed.

"You didn't sleep?"

"No," and she was quick to change. "Did anything happen?"

"No, except Mullins, the ass, found some one pissin' against the churchyard wall outside McDermott's and a Reverend Mother wouldn't have made more noise about it."

"And was he drunk?"

"Not Mullins; the man was. They considered it a bit of a joke in the pub that Mullins should want to put them out and that drove him wild."

"He had to take it out on something," she supposed quietly.

"He near landed me and the unfortunate he caught in a nice mess, they'd like nothin' better than to laugh themselves sick at a case like that in the town. Man convicted of indecent exposure Christmas Eve.

"There's no law and order, only the police force," he repeated. "And if you were as long with the lunatics that make it up as I am you'd wonder how it lasts together for even an hour."

"It seems to manage to go on, no matter what happens," she said but he was too hot and restless to hear.

"Only Quirke didn't show his rat's face round the place this time and that's some relief," his words flinted on his own shifting thoughts.

"What does it matter about him, even if he did! Better keep them out of your mind, care about the things you want, and ignore Quirke and those things," she spoke out of herself for once.

"But they won't ignore you, that's the trouble," Reegan argued hotly. "And if you have to mix with them, day-in day-out, and put up with them, whether you like it or not, what can you do?"

"Agree with them. Tell them always that they're right, that they're wonderful people. No one will want to disagree with you about that. If you feel that some one expects you to behave well because of their good opinion of you it's always harder to do otherwise: every one gets seduced by the feeling of responsibility."

He didn't understand and didn't want, though most of the words seemed simple enough, but he felt blindly and passionately against.

"No. That's not right," he said. "They're scum and nothin' can change that. They put on a nice face till you turn your back and then it's the knife. They should be all put down and tramped on and the arse-lickers," he had driven his way into inarticulacy, and then she caught his hand.

"It doesn't matter," she said.

He felt the warm flesh of her hand and the frustrated direction of his feelings changed to desire for her, he felt the still smooth flesh of the shoulders with his hands, her thighs: her hair brushed the grain of his throat, he'd lie on her and forget. Mouth pressed on mouth, old words of endearment were panted out of their quick breathing, the loins rose and fell in rhythm, and then died in the fulfilment of the seed beating. The act did not fully end there, the kindness of undesiring hands passing over the flesh remained, stroking, waiting; they'd try to fall apart without noticing much wrench, and lie in the animal warmth and loving kindness of each other against the silence of the room with its door open to the phone or anyone knocking, the wild noises of the midwinter night outside. And they were together here. It didn't have to mean anything more than that, it'd be sufficient for this night. She took his face between her hands, and kissed it softly, in gratitude. She was mindless now of all things, suffused through and through and lost in contentment, and in its gentleness and tiredness they fell into deep sleep together.

Before eight she had to wake to go with the children to first Mass and struggle into the morning. He lay on: he'd stood at the back of the church in his uniform through midnight Mass, officially on duty there, and getting much satisfaction of the fact that he was fulfilling two obligations at the one time. He rose for breakfast when he heard them return, and asked, "Was there anything strange at the Mass?" He listened to her voice, "No. There was only a handful in the church, nearly every one must have gone to midnight Mass. The priest didn't keep us long because of the cold."

"That itself was a piece of luck," he listened to himself inanely remark, and then they had their breakfast, some sausages and bacon, the dinner would be the next meal and late. When they'd eaten he hung idle about the kitchen in Elizabeth's way. He tried to enthuse with the children over their presents, read through the long lists of programmes in the newspaper supplement for Christmas, nothing that he'd walk ten paces to hear, and then he went to the window to watch the grey winter light outside and the withered river grass through the meshes of the netting-wire. How black and silent and purposeful the river flowed, a water-hen close to the far bank, scatters of small brown birds, whose names never interested him, about the whitethorns half-way up the hill beyond, the fields bare and dark with hoof-tracks. His eyes tried to follow the radio aerial from where it left the kitchen at the corner of the window till it disappeared into the sycamore branches, it broke in stormy weather and was often left trail in the earth for days. Tired looking out the window, he went down to the dayroom to search idly through the books, and watched the few people come from last Mass, the sky full of rain or snow. Not even Quirke would come today. All day the doors to the dayroom would remain open. All day they'd have to be alone with each other in the kitchen.

The day passed quickly for Elizabeth, her whole attention absorbed in the cooking of the dinner; she'd forgotten her sickness in looking forward to their enjoyment; the excitement of the children about her, asking her so many questions, telling her so much about their presents.

182

By three it was ready and laid on the bleached white table-cloth and they bowed their heads and, with joined hands, murmured, *Bless us, O Lord, and these thy gifts which of thy bounty we are about to receive through Christ, our Lord. Amen.*

Reegan carved the turkey and handed out the helpings. The children's faces shone throughout and they cried for more and more. The delf was tidied away at the end and they stood to repeat with Reegan, *We give thee thanks, O Almighty God, for all thy benefits, who livest and reignest, world without end. Amen.*

At so many tables over the world, at this moment, the same words of thanksgiving were being uttered, as the Mass in the same way was being celebrated, and it couldn't be all blind habit, a few minds must be astonished by such as *World without end.* Never did the table-cloth appear so bright as on this day, not until this day next year would they have roasted meat, and it was unlikely that they'd sit to a meal for another year at which such marvellous courtesy and ceremony were observed. Even the children said, "Please pass me this and that"; everybody was considered and waited on; there was even a formal exactness in the way they lifted the salt and pepper cruets, and the meal began and ended in the highest form of all human celebration, prayer. It was a mere meal no longer with table and table-cloth and delf and food, it was that perfectly, but it was above and beyond and besides the wondrous act of their reality. All other meals throughout the year might be hurried and disjointed, each one eating because of their animal necessity, but this day and meal were put aside for celebration.

And the day so quickly sank once the meal was over, there had been so much excitement and preparation rising to surges of ecstasy that they could not pace it properly to its end. They'd eaten too much, indulged themselves too much, and now they had to endure the gnawing boredom of these last lifeless hours. Reegan went again to the window after finding a dramatized version of *A Christmas Carol* on the radio. The doors between the kitchen and dayroom were

183

open and they could feel the draughts. All day the doors would be open, none of the policemen would come; everybody stayed in the bosom of their families Christmas Day, it was a rigid custom. A sharp burst of hailstones beat on the window-pane, and Reegan watched the white pellets of hail roll on the sill, interested in any distraction. He fell into a kind of trance watching them beat on the glass and make white the sill and gravel, then jerked himself awake to get the pack of cards from behind the statue of St Therese on the sideboard; he boxed the cards idly for some minutes, standing in the centre of the floor, before he asked, "Would anyone like a game?"

They played before the fire, twenty-one because it would take long to finish, and it was Elizabeth who kept the scores on the margins of the radio supplement. The night began to come as they played, the fire to flame brighter and to glitter on the glass of the pictures, on the shiny leaves of holly twisted with their scarlet berries into the cords. As always close to nightfall, the ghastly red glow from the Sacred Heart lamp grew stronger. Through the windows vague shapes of birds flew towards the wood. There was a pause in the game. The lamp was lit, the blinds drawn, the table laid for the tea, the kettle put to boil. None of them was hungry. They nervously searched each other's faces. The phone did not ring. The doors were open. No one would come.

"It was powerful, Elizabeth—too good—but we'll be all havin' nightmares," Reegan praised the cold turkey and the rich fruit cake she'd made with icing and holly decorations at the end of the last meal of the day.

Afterwards the cards were played, but only for a little time, they'd become tiresome and monotonous. Reegan engaged Willie in a game of draughts, and the others watched the moves till Reegan won. Then he tramped down to the dayroom, Elizabeth took up a book, the children leaned on the edges of the table about the draught-board.

"Two kings and a man against five men now," one of them said.

The evening drew on and on, to its end. No phone rang. No one came. Reegan began to pace restlessly about the house and to search in old boxes and drawers. Eventually it was time to pray and go to bed, the same prayers murmured while their minds wandered and dreamed as on every other evening of their lives, the beads in their fingers, their elbows resting on the chairs drawn close to the fire; Reegan alone kneeling upright at the table, staring at his reflection in the big sideboard mirror, the sideboard that tonight was festive with the Christmas cards.

When it was over he gave the children liquid paraffin out of a bottle he took from the curtained press beside the radio; they grimaced as the thick, sickly liquid went down, the last taste of their day and it wasn't sweet. They went through the ceremony of saying good night and, with their candles in tin holders, their feet passed down the hallway and made a creaking and hollow drum on the timber as they climbed the stairs.

So it was almost over, Elizabeth thought; another Christmas Day, it would take their lives another year to reach it again. She was tired, they had taken no air nor exercise, shut indoors all day with each other. Though she was not disturbed. She'd noticed that she never grew disturbed when Reegan's troubled restlessness was in the house, it prevented her from dwelling on herself, one poison counteracting the other. She'd little more to do: rake the fire, light the green glass oil-lamp, climb the stairs into a hope of sleep.

"It's another Christmas Day over," she said quietly to Reegan.

"Another Christmas," he echoed. "I hate the day. A whole year of waitin' for it and then it goes like a wet week. Whatever people be waitin' for anyhow?"

"Whatever people be waitin' for anyhow," her own mind began to parrot as she did the last chores. "Whatever people be waitin' for anyhow," but it brought neither despair nor desperation, no feeling whatever. She watched Reegan go to bed. Soon she'd follow. "Whatever people be waitin' for anyhow," repeated itself over and over, but it did not affect

185

her, the words remained calm and complete as a landscape that she could gaze dispassionately on for ever.

The next day the policemen trooped back to the barracks and the wren boys, children in old clothes with blacking and red indian daubs of lipstick on their faces, came to make their mouth-organs wail outside the door and pounded their feet in imitation of dance on the gravel while the coins rattled fiendishly in their slotted tin canister. Most houses gave them something. They'd have harmless parties, lemonade and sweets and biscuits, on the proceeds of the day.

New Year's night a few drunken brawlers were hauled to the barracks, and thrown into the lockup to cool—the last gasp of the Christmas spirit, Casey announced. On the sixth of January the ivy and holly were thrown out and the cards swept off the sideboard into one of its drawers. Now the cold months would slowly pass in a sigh for summer. January, February gold of the first daffodils, March that lent itself to dreadful puns, Easter—but that was treading ahead with the names, fast as light compared with the days in which Elizabeth steadily grew worse, little that was haphazard about the decline, it seemed certain and relentless. She was sure the doctor must have noticed, though he said nothing, and she knew she'd refuse if he asked her to stop in bed. She'd stay on her feet this time till she collapsed or changed for the better. And she didn't think she could go on only for the fact that often when she was alone her sense of the collapsing rubble of this actual day faded, and processions of dead days began to return haunting clear, it seemed as compensation. Her childhood and the wild smell of the earth in the evenings after spring rain and the midges swarming out of the trees; streets of London at all hours, groping for the Jewish names on the lintels—Frank, Levine, Lerner, Goldsberg, Botzmans—above the awnings in the little market off Commercial Road, and did the sun still glitter so on the red-stained glass over the little Yiddish Theatre, the left side of the road as you came from Aldgate, *Grand Palais*; and the people in her life crowding into the vividness of the memory, shifting with each sudden change

186

and she there at the heart of everything, alive, laughing and crying and calm. And one fantastic afternoon at the end of January she went, ecstatic with remembrance, to the sideboard and got pen and ink and paper to write to a friend of those days, a nurse with her in The London Hospital, she was still there, for at Christmas they exchanged cards. Their relationship had dwindled to that but it could be renewed. She'd write and invite her here. She'd show her this place, so quiet after London, the church that had celebrated its centenary in its grove of evergreens and tombstones, the presbytery staring blue and white with the priest's love of the Virgin between the rows of old limes and the river flowing out of the lake in the shelter of the hill, Reegan and the children and Mullins and Casey and Brennan.

She'd have to write about herself too: her relationship with Reegan at odd moments now, her heart gone weak, the cancer, the futility of her life and the life about her, her growing indifference. That was the truth she'd have to tell. *Things get worse and worse and more frightening*. But who'd want to come to a house where times got worse and no one was happy? And on the cold page it didn't seem true and she crossed it out and wrote, *Everything gets stranger and more strange*. But what could that mean to the person she was writing to—*stranger and more strange*, sheer inarticulacy with a faint touch of craziness. So she crossed it out too and wrote: *Things get better and better, more beautiful*, and she smiled at the page that was too disfigured with erasions to send to anyone now. Her words had reached praise of something at last, and it didn't appear more false or true than any of the other things she'd written and crossed out. She'd leave it so, it was a ridiculous thing to want to write in the first place, how could she have ever imagined that she'd carry it through. She rose from the table and dropped the sheet of notepaper into the fire, watched the flames crumple it like a hand closing into a fist would, and the charred fragments float in the smoke.

The evening was coming and she had the hens to feed. The

187

feeding was kept in a wooden tub in the scullery, the red and white fowl flocking round as she went with it down to the ovens at the netting-wire. She'd no business playing games of fancy such as the letter, she talked with herself. She wasn't a leisured person, all her life she had to work with her hands, the most of her energy had been absorbed by that, little more than a performing animal; her praying and her thinking and reading just pale little sideshows. A few impassioned months of her life had perhaps risen to such a fever as to blot everything else out, but they were only months or maybe but days in so many years. They'd subsided but the work had to go on, grinding, incessant, remorseless; breaking her down to its own dead impersonality, but never quite, and how often she had half-wished to be broken into the deadness of habit like most of the rest, it was perhaps the only escape.

When the hens were fed she had still much to do inside. They'd be home soon and hungry in this cold weather, if she'd neglected them to think or dream she'd see their resentment rise to such intolerance that she'd not be able to endure watching it: she worked in a burst of energy that must have been close to panic, and all the neglected things were done before they came, the lamp lit, the fire blazing and their food warm on the table. No one could resent or fault her, but afterwards she couldn't stand with tiredness. She thought she had no feeling of the water against her hands as she washed the dishes, nor could she see the real gleam of the white knobs on the yellow press when she returned the dishes to the shelves and hung the cups. She seemed living within the dead husk of herself, as in the weeks before she went to hospital, staring out at life and every sensual contact with it gone, the one desire she had left increasing to overpower her—to sink down within herself to unending sleep and rest.

While this happened the policemen went on as usual in the barracks. The books were kept in order, the b.o. made his bed up each night against the wall of the lock-up and lifted it in the morning, their common sense cut the ridiculous number of patrols demanded of them by the regulations down to bare gestures in this weather of the early year. They did little jobs in their houses—painted or mended utensils or furniture or shoes—played cards in the barrack kitchen, never in the dayroom in case Quirke should surprise them there, and the books brought up for them to write reports on these fictitious patrols.

"Wind from the south-west, sky conditions cloudy, weather showery with bright intervals. I patrolled Knocknarea Road to Woodenbridge and returned via Eslin and Drumgold. I noticed cattle grazing on the Eslin Road and made inquiries, discovered their owner was James Maguire (farmer), and issued due warning. Commencement of patrol 2 p.m. Conclusion of patrol 6.15 p.m. (Signed) Edward M. Casey" they ran.

Elizabeth loved to see them come: there was only the dull silence of the present if they didn't, Reegan, filling pages of foolscap with profit and loss calculations at the table, the amounts of money he hoped to have at the end of the summer, when he'd leave the police. This year he had secured the contract to supply all the fuel to the laundry the Sisters of Mercy ran in the town, the biggest contract he'd ever got, and if it went lucky he'd have enough money to buy a good farm, he'd be his own master, and with his pension he'd not have to slave too hard. So he whiled away most of the winter evenings dreaming on paper over the root facts the figures these contracts provided. He never noticed how drawn and beaten Elizabeth looked: she'd have to collapse before he'd ever notice now.

His enmity with Quirke did not ease. Reegan was decided and waiting. When he'd have provided against his fear of starvation and that Authority would kick his face in if he missed Quirke's throat, he'd act, and savagely. A natural perversity set him on to provoke Quirke within the limits he knew were safe, never going too far, avoiding a decisive clash until his time was ripe.

Many of these small clashes continued to reach Elizabeth, she was too worn to be interested in them for their own sake, she saw them as just the accidental revelations of the same

189

thing seething within Reegan: but what she did notice was their changing tone. The bluster and rhetoric and surges of fierce passion were fast disappearing out of his accounts of the clashes, they became far more quiet, controlled, full of a humour that was both malicious and watching, intensely aware of the ridiculous.

"I ran into Quirke today," he mentioned to her, a wet evening close to the end of February.

" 'It's a powerful job for exercise, the police, sir,' I said. 'I'd be rotten at my age in an office, sittin' down, but this job takes you out into God's clear air and the weather of Ireland. This patrollin' is great for givin' you an appetite, sir.' You should have seen the luk on his face.

" 'It gives you an appetite, does it, Reegan?' he said as if the words were poison. 'The police has a few other functions besides providing its members with an appetite. Seeing that the people obey the law is not one of the least of its functions.' "

" 'It's good for the auld appetite too though, it must be admitted; seein' that the people obey the law isn't of course, as you say, to be forgotten either,' I said.

"If looks could kill I'd be dead, Elizabeth," Reegan roared, laughing on the chair.

" 'It's good for the appetite! Or do you take me for a fool, Reegan,' he hissed like a weasel and drove off as if I stank to the high heavens."

"If you provoke him so much he'll try to get rid of you before you're ready to go, he's bound to get his chance sooner or later, you can't guard against that if you go on like this," she pondered tiredly to him, not seeing any reason why people could want to create a hell for each other in cold blood, surely their world had to be a microscopic place for them to have to resort to that.

"He'll have to get a move on so," Reegan countered. "He has only till September."

"You've made up your mind definitely to resign in September?"

"Yes, the turf contracts'll be done then. They say the

spring's the best time to move but you can't have everything right, and if you keep on waitin' for the right time you'll never do anything, that's what I've learned. You have to make the best of what you have."

He seemed anxious, as if he was afraid she might have changed her mind about the going. "You've decided definitely to go then, in September?" she repeated and that was all.

"Yes. Definitely. You don't mind, do you, Elizabeth?"

"No, no. I'm glad you've decided for certain at last," she said, and closed her eyes as she saw him lift the pages of foolscap that were covered with calculations. He started to explain how much money he had in the bank; the profit he'd make out of the turf; the gratuity he was owed on leaving the police; the little he'd be able to save out of his salary between now and then; what it would all amount to —in September. He was so excited with these plans and calculations that she hadn't even to interject the occasional question to show her continuing attention. All she did was nod and nod her head and fix attention in her eyes and she was certain he would never notice.

September, September, September, it droned in her mind; in September they'd leave this barracks where they'd lived so long. A haunting and beautiful September, the year at its fullness, the summer lingering and the approaching leaf fall, the sway of the year shifting forward towards its death. There'd be reapers and binders, stacks of corn, the hum of the first red threshing mills; apples falling and rotting, the first waste of the orchards; and those blue, blue evenings that always reminded her of the bloom on Victoria plums. March, April, May, June, July, August: it was just over six months away, spring left yet and the whole of summer and all the things that might change before then.

Could she plan till then? It'd be too full of painful joy, and in a few minutes she'd have to make an effort to rise out of this chair. September was too far away, it was unreal, she had only dreamt it in the Septembers she remembered. And she had to live a day at a time, a day between waking

191

and sleeping, not even days, in the passing moments that enclosed her life.

She woke, the gaze that had been directed inwards in rich dream she turned outwards, to wake on the surface of observance, observing Reegan. He too could be excited by September but his September was not hers. Money in the bank, smashing Quirke and going free out of the police to start a new life—that was his September. Starting a new life at fifty, declaring thirty years a stupid waste, and beginning again, at fifty; it had something of greatness, it made rubbish out of the passage of time, it pissed at futility, it took no cognizance of death. It was the spirit of life declaring itself in defiance of everything, and it sent a thrill of excitement to the marrow of her bones, but she wasn't able to rise and affirm it with her own life. She was excited, she marvelled, but she couldn't understand. How do his mind and body work that he is able to be so; how is he able to go so violently on and on and on? She watched his face, the lines of its years and deaths and grey streaks in his hair, the large hands streaked with veins, and the uniform with silver buttons and badges and the three silver stripes on the sleeve that so many had worn and were wearing and would wear, and she wanted to break down and cry. She had loved him, still loved him, and would love him till she died, but how was she to tell him so? She hadn't the beauty and attractions left that can turn the simplest gestures of a young girl into meaning, and she'd no words or her words were not his words. She knew nothing about him, just things she'd observed and what were they; as she'd observed things about herself and still knew nothing, but all grew into the one desire to love and to cause no living thing pain.

"It doesn't matter much whether we go a little before or after September, only the main thing is that we're goin'," Reegan was saying. "And Superintendent John James Quirke is guaranteed one or two exciting days before then or my name's not Reegan. We'll see who'll come out on top. We'll see who'll come out on top then, Elizabeth!"

With an effort she rose out of the chair, swayed for a

moment as if she half expected to be struck, and smiled as she managed to move towards the spool of blue thread on the sewing-machine. Her collapse would come at its own choosing.

She could run now, throw herself on the netting-wire, and call out across the lake to the woods where the saws still sung, "Oh, answer me. Will Something answer me?" and she'd be met with echoes and real sounds of the saws and birds, cloud shadow on corrugations the wind had made on the water, and silence—the silence of the sky and lake and wood and people going about their lives. And if she was heard it could be only by people and what could they do? She'd look silly or gone crazy, she'd have broken the rules. She could only cause painful concern to those involved with her and wring ridicule and laughter from those who were not, the thing that runs counter to the fabricated structure of safe passions must be slaughtered out of its existence.

"We'll see then, we'll see what'll happen then," Reegan's excited words came, able to see past the danger of the living moment and not so far as the moment of his death; absorbed by how the dice would fall; and that was the way to be, that was the way to be safe.

"What does it matter about Quirke? He has his own cares, let him go his own way, what does it matter whether he's right or wrong as long as you can go your own way in peace," she wanted to say but she knew the answer she'd get. "So nothing matters. So everybody's the same. But we're not dead yet bejasus! We're not altogether in that state yet," and he was right in his own way. People didn't want peace but shouting and activity and excitement, that was life; fullness of life for them was not thought, that was to be free and lonely and to die, life was ceaseless activity. Peace was not life, it was death.

"Will you be going to the court tomorrow? It's the District Court day, isn't it?" she asked. "I'll want to get the things ready if you are."

"Aye—I'm goin'; me and Casey, that's all, but don't put yourself to too much bother."

193

She knew the things she had to do: they never varied; and in the morning there'd be the shining of his boots and baton sheath, the scrupulous shining of the silver buttons and badges and whistle chain as on every other court morning.

The year moved forward, cold with frost, the fields firm enough to carry the ploughing tractors. Ash Wednesday, a cold white morning, all the villagers at Mass and the rails, to be signed with the Cross on their lives to be broken, all sinners and needing the grace of God to be saved, the cross thumbed by the priest on their foreheads with the ashes of their mortality. The organ was silent in the organ loft; those who did not get dispensed from the fast could have only one full meal in the day; the yew branches would be blessed Palm Sunday and left in a bath-tub outside the church for the people to take away; and the beautiful, beautiful ceremonies of Holy Week.

On Wednesday and Friday evenings at six they had Lenten Devotions: the rosary and Benediction on Wednesdays; the Stations of the Cross that she loved, on Fridays.

The priest with the small black prayer book, in black soutane and white surplice, the altar-boys in scarlet and white, their breaths blowing like cigarette-smoke in the light of the candles they carried, the candle-flames flickering yellow before their young faces. At every one of the fourteen stations from Pilate to the tomb the priest's voice ringing: *We adore thee, O Christ, and praise thee,* as he genuflects in the stillness, and the self-conscious whispers of the small congregation of villagers scattering from beneath the gallery as their feet shuffle on the flagstones, *Because by Thy holy Cross Thou has redeemed the world.*

Christ on the road to Calvary, she on the same road; both in sorrow and in ecstasy; He to save her in Him, she to save herself in Him—both to be joined for ever in Oneness. She'd gone to these devotions all her life, she'd only once fallen away, some months of bitterness in London. She saw her own life declared in them and made known, the unendurable pettiness and degradation of her own fallings raised to dignity and meaning in Christ's passion; and always the ecstasy of individual memories breaking like a blood-vessel, elevated out of the accidental moment of their happening, and reflected eternally in the mirror of this way. Though, at the fourteenth station, the body was laid in the tomb, it held the seeds and promise of its resurrection, when the door of the tomb would be thrown back and He who was risen would appear in great light, glorious and triumphant. And if the Resurrection and still more the Ascension seemed shadowy and unreal compared to the way to Calvary, it might be because she could not know them with her own life, on the cross of her life she had to achieve her goal, and what came after was shut away from her eyes. She could only smile and Crucifixion and Resurrection ended in this smiling. As a child she'd been given to believe that the sun danced in the sky Easter Sunday morning, and she'd wept the day she saw that it simply shone or was hidden by cloud as on other mornings. The monstrous faiths of childhood got all broken down to the horrible wonder of this smiling.

She was at the end of her tether, she beat off two attacks in the next week, dragging herself to a chair; but the morning came that she failed to rise out of bed. The alarm had torn away the thin veils of her sleep as on other mornings and with the imbedded force of habit she went to reach across the shape of bedclothes that was Reegan to stop its clattering dance on the table, but she fell back without reaching it, as if stricken. Reegan grunted awake, and stopped it with one impatient movement of his arm. He seldom had to stop it and, sensing the break of habit, searched for something wrong. Elizabeth usually stopped the clock without it waking him. She was at his side: could it be that for once she was in heavy sleep, or was something wrong! As if to meet his thoughts he heard her say, "I tried to stop it but I'm not well," between gasps. He raised himself on his elbow; one look was enough to tell him she wasn't well, he thought immediately of the cancer, they had discovered no cure for cancer yet.

She lay quiet there. The weight of bedclothes, the weight of the boards of the ceiling on her eyes, the weights hanging

195

from her body removed any hope she might have that she'd recover in a few minutes and be able to rise. She told Reegan that she must have got a stupid 'flu or something, she didn't feel able to get up. She heard him say he'd ring the doctor, immediately. She didn't care, it didn't concern her. She didn't care what he did. The day was rocking gently in the room, the brass bells at the foot of the bed shone like swinging lamps. She heard Reegan pull on his clothes, and he left the door open as he went.

He woke Brennan, asleep on the iron bed under the phone, who stirred to ask vaguely out of his waking, "Is there something wrong? Is there something wrong, Sergeant?"

"Don't get up, don't move yourself. This woman isn't well and I just want to ring the doctor," and before Brennan could ask more questions Reegan was talking with whoever was on the Exchange. When he was put through to the doctor's house it was the wife who took the call.

The doctor didn't come till ten that day; and late in the evening the priest arrived at the house, for the first time since she had come from hospital.

7

They rose from their knees about the sick-bed, the pairs of beads in their hands, and the children went to Elizabeth to wish her good night, the girls with their lips, a touch of fingers from the boy; and then they went to Reegan, who stayed in the room after they'd gone.

"Do you know what I think, Elizabeth? We should get a nurse, you're four weeks down now, and with a nurse we'd have you on yer feet in no time. What do you think, Elizabeth?" Reegan suggested in fumbling, uneasy tones as the vibrations of their feet descending the stairs shivered through the floor boards and furniture.

"What? How do you mean?" she asked. She jerked out of her drowsiness where the prayers and the touch of fresh lips and fingers lingered in confusion in her mind. The question took her unawares, she had been expecting some remark about the great length that was coming into these April evenings to which she'd add her quiet assent. "What? How do you mean?" she asked and there was panic in the voice.

"I thought it might be better to get a nurse. With a nurse you'd be out of bed far quicker," he said and she was wide awake now. Did he not realize that she was dying? Did they not all realize?

"Is there need?" she answered excitedly. "I don't see any need."

"Of course there's need! There's need for you to get better," he protested.

"There's need for me to get better?"

"Of course there's need! What else is there need for, Elizabeth?"

197

"There's need for me to get better," she puzzled, and it brought such horrible sweet hope.

"It'd cost money, too much money," she said.

"We're not paupers," he answered. "The quicker you get the nurse the quicker you'll be out and about again and the expense will be over quicker, not draggin' on. With the nurse and the good weather comin' you'll be on your feet in no time."

Jesus Christ, she thought; that was rimming it—the good weather! She wanted to laugh hysterically. The good weather, that was rich. All the old tricks were being played back. It was always sunshine and summer for hope, never the lorry loads of salt and sand being shovelled on the slush of the street.

Jesus, how often she herself had comforted the doomed poor bitches in the ward, "No, you're not that bad, Mrs Ashby; and you mustn't let yourself get depressed. Things take time. With the new treatment Dr Granville is getting you and the summer around the corner you'll be home before you know."

She'd see it clutched at, as they clutched at every other floating straw. Even when the bedclothes were lightened, and bodies lay clammy under a single sheet, the reflected glitter from the cars crawling between the stunted plane trees below in Whitechapel Road hurting the eyes at the windows and there could be no more hope in that summer, how their single passion used seek and find other omens to clutch. She'd noticed very little of the irony of understanding in any eyes.

Now it was her turn. She was being played the same tricks back, and she found she wanted to live in the face of all adversity, she found herself wanting to clutch at anything at all, even these old and shabby omens of good and ill. And neither the cancer nor her failing heart, which ever would destroy her the first, knew anything of the change in days or in flowers.

"You know I'll not get better," she tried to reason with Reegan or herself, quietly.

"Not if you go on talkin' like that," he remonstrated,

198

blustery and assertive and surely afraid, as somebody trying to stand on his dignity, trying to stand on anything that doesn't exist unless it's allowed to in the other mind.

"Things take time," he continued. "Miracles don't happen in a day."

She saw he was shaken, his passion of assertion theatrical. He was afraid to face up, as she was. He'd refuse to understand. It was as if he was afraid that if he shared with her the knowledge of her approaching death he'd be forced in some way to share her dying too. No one at all would help her. She'd have to go on as she had lived, alone. She'd have to pretend to believe she was going to get well, whether she did or didn't, and the worst was that it happened to be the one thing in the world she wanted to believe.

"I don't think there's need for a nurse full time. Mrs Lennon might come for a few hours, it'd take the weight of the work off Mrs Casey, I often feel guilty about how much she's doing for us."

"She wants to do it," Reegan said. "When I talked about employin' some one she was insulted."

His face was quiet, she saw. What he said she knew was true, she'd never seen the younger woman so happy before, but it's more often harder to accept than to give.

"I thought we might get some one full time, to stop here in the house with you. Mrs Lennon is only the village nurse. She'd be only able to come for a few hours at a time."

"It'd be enough," she said.

"Are you sure? For you must have whatever's needed to get you on yer feet."

"I'm sure, quite sure," she said. She wanted her own thoughts, even if they'd bring no peace, at least they'd be a change.

"We'll talk to the doctor so tomorrow. We'll see what he says," he decided.

"That'll be best. And open the window a little before you go, the fire all day in the room has it stuffy."

The old pulleys squealed as he lowered the window and the curtains started to sway in the draught of night air.

"Is that enough?" he asked.

"Yes," she said.

"You'll have to get better soon, Elizabeth," he stooped to kiss her. "You can't just go away on us like that. Good night, Elizabeth."

"Good night," she smiled.

"I have to do an auld late patrol. Try to be asleep when I get back," he said as he left, his feet already on the stairs, and she'd see the uniformed shoulders pass down, between the rungs of the stair railing. The door was always open, it was her wish, more than once in the last weeks she believed that open door had saved her from madness. That she could see out on the landing and stairs left her the illusion or sense that she was still connected with the living, and it was something that she couldn't live without.

"Try and be asleep when I get back," murmured in her mind when she was alone, a bitter joke. Perhaps the moon would rise, flood the room with far stronger light than this low night light, the little green glass oil-lamp on the table.

He no longer slept with her in the big bed with the brass bells and ornaments, but over near the fire-place, on one of the official iron beds that he'd taken out of the storeroom. She'd hear him take off his clothes if she kept silent when he came, the creak of springs, and his sigh of relief as he let the day's tiredness sink away from him down into the mattress and springs, soon she'd hear the deep even breathing of his sleep. Perhaps one living moment of tension would enter when he'd whisper, "Are you sleepin' yet. Elizabeth?"

She'd be angry with herself if she spoke: he was too tired, at his turf banks as well as doing the police work, to be kept awake in meaningless talk; but sometimes she had to speak, to try to create some sense of life and movement about her in the night. These words they'd speak or the simple giving and acceptance of a drink or tablet often kept her whole life from breaking into a scream in her mouth.

Such silence and stillness settled over the room and the house, settled over everything except her own feverish mind. With the flickering night light she could follow the boards across the ceiling, then the knots in the boards, dark circles in the waxen varnish; but soon they were lost, the ceiling in as much confusion and emptiness over her eyes as she didn't know what. She lowered her eyes to the plywood wardrobe, the brass handle shining, and there were some rolls of wallpaper on top that she'd bought and never finished putting up. Reegan's bed was in the corner over at the fire-place, iron and black, the piping at the top and bottom curved, same as every official bed in so many barracks all over Ireland. She often felt herself go near madness on these nights. She'd want to cry or call: and only she knew she'd be able to renew some sense of life with Reegan when he'd come late she didn't know how she'd be able to go on. Even when he slept the sound of his breathing kept her mind from worse things, and it was that much contact, her life going out to the dreams of his sleep and the day that had him so dog tired, it didn't seem so blank as the solid ceiling and wardrobe and the brass ornaments between that caught the moonlight. Then the long wait for morning, always breaking with fierce violence since she could no longer join its noise: dark in the room, Reegan's deep breathing, and the first cart would rock on the road, faint and far away but growing nearer, rocking past the end of the avenue with a noise of harness and the crunch of small stones under the iron tyres and fading as it went across the bridge and round to the woods or quarry. More carts on the road, rocking now together, men shouting to the horses or each other. A tractor, smooth and humming after the slow harsh motion of the carts; other carts and tractors and a solitary car or van with men travelling to work. The gleam of the brass on the bed grew brighter. She was almost able to see the figures on the face of the alarm clock clearly, see the shape of Reegan rolled in clothes in the bare policeman's bed. She was hot with thirst and took water from the jug and glass, her feet sticky against the sheets. Outside the morning was clean and cold, men after hot breakfasts were on their way to work. The noises of the morning rose within her to a call of wild excitement. Never had she felt it so when she was rising to let up the blinds in the kitchen and rake out the coals to get their breakfasts, the drag and burden of their lives together was how she'd mostly felt it then, and now it was a wild call to life; life, life and life at any cost.

The light grew clear. She could read the clock, the hands at eight. Perhaps at five or ten or a quarter past the saws would scream and sing in the woods, it might even be later, nothing ran too strictly to time here. The stone-crusher was working in the quarries, the whole morning throbbing with life, calling her out, urging her to rise in passion.

With a bang of doors the children were up, coming into the room to wake Reegan and to wish her good morning. Later, as Reegan put on his clothes, she heard the tongs thud downstairs as they set the fire going.

"Did you sleep well, Elizabeth?" he asked.

"Yes," she lied, though hard to believe from the look in her eyes.

"That's powerful, that's what'll have you on yer feet soon. The doctor will be here on his way from the dispensary and we'll ask how about the nurse."

"That'll be perfect," she said. "You're a little late this morning."

"Aye—half-eight. Always a rush for this cursed nine. Jesus, people get more like clocks these days and they have to."

"Will you go on the bog today?"

"You can be sure. I'll have to see what the men are doin', though I can't risk takin' the day."

"Who have you?"

He named the workmen as he pulled on his tunic, letting it swing open, and then he was gone for his breakfast.

The fire would be blazing, she remembered. He'd shave before the scullery mirror, the eyes blind with soap and the hands groping for the towel; the kitchen clean and lovely, a white cloth on the table. That's where she'd love to be now, in the middle of the life of the morning, and not alone and clammy under these bedclothes.

Mullins was barrack orderly, pounding upstairs to the

storeroom with his mattress and load of blankets, she saw his shoulders and arms clasped about the grey blankets through the open door and between rungs of the wooden railing. She heard his shovel and tongs at the fire. The outside door opened, the gate at the lavatory clanged, he was going down to the ashpit with his bucket of ashes and pisspot. The iron gate shut, there was some minutes' delay while he made his morning visit to the lavatory, and then his feet on the gravel and the scraping of his boots at the door.

"Johnny Aitchinson was thrashin' ashes in Johnny Aitchinson's ash hole," repeated itself in her mind after the door had closed, it brought no smile or grimace to her lips—just, "Johnny Aitchinson was thrashin' ashes in Johnny Aitchinson's ash hole," over and over again.

Close to nine he brought some last thing up to the storeroom and then crossed the landing to Elizabeth's room. Whoever was b.o. came each morning to see her.

"All's finished and ready to go for the auld breakfast now. I'm just lookin' in to see how you are," he stated.

"You're always very good, John," she said.

"Not a bit trouble in the world, for nothin' at all," he said, put ill at ease by the touch of praise or courtesy; it made him overflow with the feeling that he should somehow be better than he was. She saw the effect of her slight politeness, and wished she'd been silent, it wasn't true courtesy if it made Mullins so uneasy, only a silly, affected fashion of manners.

"What kind of night had you?" he asked.

"I slept all right," she said, she must try to divert him away.

"You're lookin' better than ever and there's a powerful feel of the summer comin' and it'd damned near bring a dead man to life, never mind some one foxin', like you."

He'd never accuse her of foxing if it wasn't blatantly untrue: they must have very little real hope that she'd recover, she thought. She must try to divert him quickly.

"Was there rain, was there rain last night?" she asked. "I couldn't hear your boots on the ground this mornin'."

"We can't make many moves anownt of you, can we?"

he bantered. "There was showers, still clouds in the sky, the ground's as soft as putty. Believe me, you're not missin' much not to be out in this weather."

He was returning to her sickness, though she'd easily fence him away now.

"How is the potato settin'?" she asked.

He began to tell her, the hands of the clock were close to nine: the other policeman arrived below, soon he had to leave her.

She heard the bustle of the dayroom and Reegan go down the hallway after he'd gone; the banging of the dayroom door. The roll would be called and she had the sense, as always, from that bang of the door at nine that the morning was over, the day had started.

"I am Elizabeth Reegan and another day of my life is beginning," she said to herself. "I am lying here in bed. I've been five weeks sick in bed, and there is no sign of me getting better. Though there's little pain, which is lucky, and the worst is fear and remorse and often the horrible meaninglessness of it all. Sometimes meaning and peace come but I lose them again, nothing in life is ever resolved once and for all but changes with the changing life, calm had to be fought for through pain, and always when it was given it was both different and the same, every loss had changed it, and she could be sure it never came to stay, because she was still alive.

"The same but different, Elizabeth," that was Halliday and she could only smile and turn.

It was the day, the stale day of this room. The saws were singing, the stone-crusher. She heard a motor, the noise was like the green mail van's, and ten minutes later the postman was at the dayroom door. "Nothing else today," she thought she heard him say. Probably he had no letters except the official brown ones with the black harp, addressed to the Sergeant-in-charge, that no one wanted.

"Jesus! Jesus tonight! Jesus this day," she muttered, hard to know whether it was a curse or prayer, as she heard the postman's feet fade away on the gravel.

The roll call was over, Casey installed as b.o. for the day

204

and night, Reegan coming upstairs to tell her he was going out on patrol.

"To the bog, I suppose?" she managed to smile.

"To the bog," he affirmed, a secret musing on his features that she thought was beautiful.

"Quirke's been quiet these last days?" she asked.

"Aye. A calm before a storm I wouldn't wonder. He'll pester us then for days: some other poor bugger must have distracted him. The gentleman's nature is so busy that if he didn't manage to be all the time on somebody's tail he'd probably have to jump into the river or something."

She laughed: it brought such relief and he was leaving.

"You don't want me to get you anything outa the shops?"

"No. Nothing."

"And if I'm not back when the doctor comes you'll mention to him about the nurse?"

He was gone, nothing but wait for his bicycle to go past beneath the window on the gravel, even now so many distractions to look forward to, far more still to remember if she looked back. She'd probably never have to meet herself alone in the awfulness of the living moment, stranded on a crumbling ridge over the abysses, her life rising to a scream as she fell.

He was gone, the morning of spring light moved alive in the room, she drank water.

Mrs Casey was in the dayroom: she did not stay long there, but came upstairs, leaving the dayroom door open behind her so that Casey could go for his newspapers. She'd have to dash down to call him if the phone rang and there'd be one wild moment of panic but it was unlikely that anything would stir while he was away.

"I'm here at last and Ned is just gone for the papers," she stated, and the same questions were asked, the same answers given, the same encouragements and hopes. The good weather was coming to stay for ever. With relief Elizabeth saw her find a duster and brush, tie a blue scarf over her hair, and she hummed between snatches of talk as she tidied the room.

Casey returned with the newspapers, and roared from the bottom of the stairs that he'd not go up till they'd finished their gossip.

"Go and read your precious paper, you're not wanted here," his wife bantered back.

"It's worse than a harem up there so," he shouted, and Elizabeth wondered how long the little game of sexual titivation would continue.

"Go and read your paper, you and your harems, nice talk in a Christian country," Mrs Casey laughed.

"Oh, why did I ever get married, that's when I met me Waterloo; no man can get the better of a woman," he went grumbling loudly and happily back into the dayroom to smile with general goodwill and well-being out in the direction of the garden and bridge before he fixed the cushion on his chair in front of the fire and opened the newspapers with exaggerated slowness, as if every motion was a beautiful end in itself.

Mrs Casey hummed as she swept and dusted the room, opened fully the window to let out the stale air Elizabeth seldom noticed any more and then left to empty the slops. With her quick young movements and humming she seemed a kind of sunlight to Elizabeth.

"We have it right for the doctor now," she said when she returned. "We'll not be disgraced no matter who comes now."

"It's marvellous, though it's so much trouble for you, you have to do everything for us nowadays," Elizabeth apologized.

"It's no trouble at all. I haven't felt so well for ages. Only yesterday Ned said I never looked so well since I fooled him," she laughed. "It's those four walls in that joint of ours that gets me down. When you've hardly anything to do it's the worst, you start broodin' and then your nerves go. Everything frightens you, that's the worst. I almost think I could sleep on me own tonight if I had to, but it's wonderful then to have Una or somebody." She seemed very happy as she left to get the dinner. She went into the dayroom to

206

Casey on her way to the kitchen, and soon he came upstairs with the newspaper to tap as he always did on the open door before he entered.

"You look powerful today, Elizabeth. You'll be out and about before any time and I brought you the paper," he said and left it beside her hand on the eiderdown.

"Is there anything strange in it today?" she asked to change his conversation away from herself, she couldn't endure much more of it. Why had they all to say the same things, or were all lies one thing as truth was one thing too?

"Nothin' strange," Casey laughed. "Never anything strange but you buy them all the same, don't you? I think the day wouldn't be the same without them, even the handlin' of them and that gives you the feelin' that God's in his heaven and all's right with the world. Jay, Elizabeth, we used to have to fairly sweat to learn the lines out of the auld school-books and you find them all the time, even the ones you forgot, comin' back and back. It's a terror, isn't it?"

"I find the same myself: everybody does I think," she said.

"But they won't admit it," he cried with some excitement.

"No, no," she lingered.

"Only yesterday I was talkin' to Mullins," he was beginning when he heard Mrs Casey come with the cups of tea and he changed, "Well, didn't I manage it well, to be here when the tea landed. It shows you how jealous she was of the two of us talkin' alone and she had to find some excuse," and the eternal game started between them again till Casey said, "Men are the same as women I suppose. They can't be got on without and you can't get on with them, so what are you to do?" and then the doctor's car was heard. Casey rushed to be downstairs in the dayroom. She put a few last tidying touches to the room and met the doctor on her way down with the tray. They exchanged a few polite words before he climbed the stairs to Elizabeth.

"How is the patient today?" he smiled. He put his bag breezily down on the bed, took off his gloves, and shook her hand.

She didn't know how to answer, and she knew it made no difference whether she answered or not.

"How are you today, Doctor?" she asked.

"Wonderful: there's not even the rain to complain about so far today, though it was quite heavy last night. You don't do much complaining yourself, do you?"

"No. There's not much use."

"I don't know," he said. "There's a lot to be said for a few roars too, as most people unfortunately realize. At least they manage to get attention, if it's only for the fuss and nuisance they make.

"How is the pain today?" he asked suddenly. She answered. The examination began. When it was over he gazed at her face; she tried to avoid his eyes; he had little doubt that she suspected the worst.

"It never rains but it pours, that's the way it seems to be in your case, but I'm not worried. A slight bubble of air in the bloodstream can finish the healthiest in a flash, and there's people walking about enjoying themselves who've been miles worse than you. They say that doctors and nurses can't face illness, that they know too much, but I say that if they know one side they know the other side too."

She nodded agreement. She asked him where he hoped to go this year for his holidays.

"To the South of France and if we can manage the money," he said, "probably across and down to Rome. We've had too much of the rain to ever want to see Ireland first, we should get out to the sun when we get the chance. Now it's in a lot of people's reach, and we're losing our inferiority complex about travel and culture and that, the pig-in-the-kitchen days are gone.

"Do you know, when you think, great changes have come over this country in the last years. Now we're reaping the fruits those men that won us our freedom sowed. Do you know, when I was going to University College, people that had plenty of money were awed of putting their foot inside the door of the Shelbourne Hotel because they weren't the so-called gentry. That day is gone or going fast. There's a new class growing up in this country that won't be shamed out of doing things because they haven't come out of big houses. I could walk this day into the Shelbourne Hotel as if I owned it, and I was born with no silver spoon."

Elizabeth nodded: it made her smile to imagine it within her means to go into the Shelbourne Hotel or to the South of France, whatever salvation that could bring to anybody. "Woman, take up your bed and walk to the Shelbourne Hotel", played itself so fantastically in her mind that she nearly laughed purely when he ended, and she had to tell herself that she was becoming cruel and malicious. Her life was in this person's hands, she must remember. He was only conversing pleasantly with her, one of his patients, before he left. Though he seemed to speak with the passion of some deep conviction and she wondered could he really believe in his rubbish, what difference could being able to walk proudly into the Shelbourne Hotel possibly make in any real person's life?

"How do their minds work, Elizabeth? How in the name of Christ do they keep afloat on those lunacies? Can you tell me that one thing, Elizabeth—how do their minds work, how in the name of Christ do they manage to keep going?" she heard Halliday's voice break through her thoughts.

Always she saw people in the light of her own consciousness, and would she be listening quietly to this doctor and seeing nothing if she'd never met Halliday? Would she be better or worse off now if she hadn't met him? Consciousness, awareness, even vision lay within herself, but it was he who had shaken them awake, if she'd never met him they might have slept a lifetime. Or she might have met with some one else but how could she know? All she knew was what she was, what she had become, and neither very clearly. He had changed everything in her life and solved nothing: the first rush of the excitement of discovery, and then the failure of love, contempt changing to self-contempt and final destruction, its futile ashes left in her own hands. If she had never come to vision or awareness she'd be left with some sense of belonging—the dark comfort of the crowd huddled together for warmth in their fear of what must not be named—and how could terror in the dark be worse than this lonely terror of the broad daylight?

The room, the bed, the ceiling, her own sweat and discomforts were still there. The doctor had finished the monologue her words had prompted, she was asking him about the nurse, and he shook her hand before he pulled on his gloves and left. She could hear Mrs Casey moving in the kitchen. Casey was in the dayroom. The newspaper he had brought her lay beside her hand on the eiderdown. Nothing was changed. No matter what happened her life had to continue among such things as these, if it wasn't these it would be some other, and how could accidents make difference now?

Yet she had married Reegan. Why, Oh why in fairness to him had she married him with what she knew? She had loved him, but that was too easy, it had no meaning. Was that love a simple longing for security, could it be so mean as that? Or was it longing for her childhood not far from this barrack and village and river flowing out of the woods into the Shannon lowlands? Was it because of Reegan? He was a strange man, lonely and different, she'd always believed; she'd never understood him much and had lived somewhat near to fear of him. There was such vital passion about him sometimes, and then again he often seemed perverse and stupid. She'd been sick of London at the time, its crazy rush wearing at her nerves, Halliday's cry to her, "I'd come to the end of my own tether and used you to get a short breather. I used you so as not to have to face my own mess. I seduced you because I was seduced myself by my own fucking lust to live," appeared in terms of her own relationship with Reegan. They all lived on each other and devoured each other as they themselves were devoured, who would devour whom the first was the one question. Plainly nothing could be resolved, she had to come to this again and again. Her love might have been all these things and more, welded into the one inscrutable passion. That was how her life happened, nothing more could be said for certain.

210

"Nothing more, Elizabeth! That was how it happened and it was all a balls. The sooner it was over the better," Halliday's words troubled her mind again, but then her vision had never been the same as his, what he had woken in her grew so different that it could barely be recognized as reflections of the same thing. Oh, it was strange and surrounded by only wonder now, she and he reflections of the one thing.

There was such deep joy sometimes, joy itself lost in a passion of wonderment in which she and all things were lost. Nothing could be decided here. She was just passing through. She had come to life out of mystery and would return, it surrounded her life, it safely held it as by hands; she'd return into that which she could not know; she'd be consumed at last in whatever meaning her life had. Here she had none, none but to be, which in acceptance must be surely to love. There'd be no searching for meaning, she must surely grow into meaning as she grew to love, there was that or nothing and she couldn't lose. She could make no statement other than that here, she had no right, she was only waiting and she could not say or know more.

All real seeing grew into smiling and if it moved to speech it must be praise, all else was death, a refusal, a turning back; refusal to admit she knew nothing and was nothing in herself, a creature of swift passage, moving into whatever reality she had, the reality she knew nothing about.

All the apparent futility of her life in this barracks came at last to rest on this sense of mystery. It gave the hours idled away in boredom or remorse as much validity as a blaze of passion, all was under its eternal sway. She felt for a moment pure, without guilt. She'd no desire to clutch for the facts and figures of explanation, only it was there or wasn't there and if there was any relationship they would meet in the moment of her death. She accepted its absolute sway over her life, she had no rights, so how could she have quarrels now! And if the reality is this: we have no life but this one —she could only reflect and smile, it must have been the

211

same before her birth and she doubted if she could have ever desired to be born.

That was the way it must be: but here in this lonely room it ran its course in her cursed life. Mrs Casey was moving downstairs. Why could she not come and break for her the lonely treadmill of this thinking? Was she too busy? She was getting their dinner ready, but couldn't she spare minutes? Could she not come and say, "Is there anything you want, Elizabeth?" It wouldn't take very long to do that much? Or did they care about her? What did they care, they were all right themselves, what did they care about her? She wanted to knock with rage on the floorboards and call, "Can you not come up? Have you forgotten me? Have you no consideration?"

She'd have to think up some lying excuse when they came: how could she say, "I want you to stay with me. Stay with me and don't leave me alone with myself." Mrs Casey would think she was raving. How could she expect her to come when she had to have the children's dinner ready by half-twelve. She heard them come: a door banged; their bare feet pattered on the cement, excited chatter began and the rattle of delf and cutlery. She grew calmer as she imagined them at the table in the kitchen, how many times had she given them that same dinner? Soon they were rushing up the stairs to her, and gone as quickly, to try to snatch a few minutes of the play they hungered for before the bell rang.

Reegan didn't return, he must have risked staying the day on the bog. The Caseys took their meal with her in the bedroom. Her rage and desperation of an hour ago seemed so silly now, they were eating with her when it would have been far more comfortable for them to have their meal downstairs.

"It's very kind of you to come to have your dinner with me here," she said and kept her brimming eyes turned away, afraid and ashamed to let them see the fullness of her gratitude; and then as she watched them eat and listened to their bantering talk she saw with some return of terror that

212

they'd drive her even more quickly crazy if they were booked to sit here for ever than she'd drive herself alone, the one reason their company was exciting was that she knew it'd soon end, she'd not have to tolerate it, she'd lose it, it'd be taken away. A smile began to play suddenly deep in her eyes. What was certain was that her temperament would have to undergo a deep sea change before it was fitted for a life that'd be without end.

The day crawled much as other days into late afternoon. A large black fly with the blue sheen in its wings of oil when it floats on water buzzed so loud and long against the pane that she had to call to have it killed. Though nothing was changed when Mrs Casey finally battered it to death with a newspaper and the silence of the distant saws and stone-crusher had time to settle in the room again. Reegan returned late, tired and hungry from the bog, and as he took his tea another heart attack nearly ended Elizabeth's life.

Afterwards the doctor told Reegan that he didn't expect her to live through the summer. He considered that if it happened soon it'd be almost merciful, she'd get hardly more than the first cancer pains; ventricular failure would cheat the slow drugged agony of that death, he believed.

The green rushes the children had scattered for Our Lady's Eve hadn't been swept and now after the few weeks lay brown and rotting on the doorstep but it was May yet and the bells rang in the evenings for devotions. On the bog, where the white fluffs of cotton tossed, the barrows of turf were fit for handling. The potato leaves pushed their way out of the earth in the garden and Reegan covered them against the frost, but without much care, the turf was his whole care. Night and morning he had the radio on long before news-time to get the weather forecast, and he watched the skies always. If they kept fair he'd be able to go free without fear or worry in September.

The most Elizabeth saw of this spring and early summer was Reegan's tiredness at night, loose clay on the police-men's boots when they came to visit her, a little bunch of primroses Sheila brought. The birds were loud about the

213

house all day, it was their mating-time, and life put even song to use. More flies gathered in the room. They had hung a yellow tape from the ceiling, where they stuck and struggled in its sweetness till they died into another motionless black speck. Mrs Lennon, the village nurse, began to come for a few hours night and morning and she made little difference to anything or any one in the house.

Elizabeth sank steadily, and she didn't care. Sometimes she tried to imagine her own heart and breasts laid bare on the lurid anatomy charts in the Training Hospital; she'd try to imagine what had gone wrong or what could be done but soon that'd fail and she'd be listening to one of the Sister Tutors drone through an hour of words falling like light rain. And when she woke to vital life it was often to hate.

One night a door banged to frighten her to life. She'd been more in a stupor than asleep when the noise rocked through the house, and peeling flakes of whitewash fell from the walls. She woke in a state of panic and saw the children on the landing.

"Who banged that door?" she called as fierce as she was able.

They shifted on their feet and then explained, "We were tuggin' and the door gev."

"Can you give me no peace? Have you no consideration for anybody? Have you nothing else to do?" their explanation only roused her more.

Both Mrs Casey and Reegan came, attracted by the loud bang, and the commotion. "There's nothing but noise and doors slamming. I was nearly frightened out of my senses," she complained.

"Didn't I tell ye not to make noise upstairs?" Mrs Casey reproached and Reegan said, "I thought the blasted house was comin' down about our ears. What did ye think ye were doin'? What was goin' on here?"

"We were playin' and the door gev."

"And have ye to behave like wild animals in the house?"

"We didn't mean."

214

"Ye were warned before, weren't ye? This time you'll have to be taught a lesson, long threatenin' comes at last," and he pushed them before him downstairs.

Her anger drained as she heard them go. She began to curse herself for not holding it in check. She heard their cries, they were being punished, and what was the futile use? Later she was overcome with shame when their tear-stained faces appeared in the doorway.

"Daddy sent us to say that we are sorry."

"It's all right, don't worry. I lost my temper. It was my fault as much as yours."

They stood there.

"It's all right now, isn't it? There's sweets in this bag on the table. Will you take one?"

They smiled and accepted, it was over. No matter how she spoiled them she couldn't take responsibility for causing more pain. Not so many evenings ago she'd flown at one of the girls because her piece of toast was burned black on one side and had a trace of ashes where it must have slipped from the fork. She must be careful. This fiendish resentment was ready to possess her at every petty chance. She'd make a hell for herself and every one about her if she didn't watch. This petty world of hers wasn't the whole world; each person was a world; and there were so many people. None of them had to move to her beck and call, they were all free. They came to her out of their generosity or loneliness; and surely she should try to meet them with some graciousness. That was the way it should be, she was certain. But it was hard to keep that before her mind with this body and room dragging her down till she could hardly tell one thing from another.

Though everything wasn't black, even if it seemed so now, she'd want to affirm. Very late that same night, the house was asleep, Mullins brought down his bed. She had to smile as she heard his feet go downstairs for the second and last time, with the load of green-braided blankets surely, for she remembered how he used always bring the two pillows on top of the awkward mattress first. In spite of her discomfort there was rich enjoyment in her eyes: he'd hardly ever be likely to change that habit now! The dayroom door banged shut. "No concern for anybody, just lorry round the place," Reegan would complain if he was awake. That door would be the last loud noise of the night, she could hear Reegan's heavy breathing from the bed over at the fire-place, there was no sound from the children's room, and then some place at the other end of the house began the quick, pattering race of mice on the boards of the ceiling.

The priest came constantly and soon after she'd been taken bad he gave her Extreme Unction, it seemed awful ordinary, the touching of nostrils and eyes and ears and lips, the hands and feet with the yellow oil, smell of the 65 per cent wax candles burning, the wooden crucifix, the vessels of ordinary water and holy water, the host in the little pyx on the table.

She had prepared patients in the hospitals herself for this same Sacrament. They'd have to wash them beforehand; make the bed so that the clothes at the bottom would be free to fold back from the feet; and when it was over she used burn the cotton-wool that had soaked the holy oil. She'd never been able to envisage herself receiving it, always it was other people.

She flinched as she was touched with the wet wool. The organs of sense, through which sin had entered the soul, were being anointed; and she wanted to declare in the face of the Latin words that sense of truth and justice and beauty and all things else had entered that way too. She felt terribly unreal, frightened of the significance, till her eyes lit on the little bottle of yellow oil the priest had. Surely it was olive oil. Out of the *Cathecism Notes* they used singsong by heart at school,

> *Oil of olives*
> *mixed with balm*
> *and blessed by the bishop*
> *on Holy Thursday.*

That was all, no awe now or intimations or anything, the

priest with the purple stole touching the senses in their turn with the oil and murmuring the prayers and the 65 per cent wax candles burning that had been blessed too and, *Oil of olives/mixed with balm/and blessed by the bishop/on Holy Thursday*, beating in her mind, echoed by a choir of young voices preparing for Confirmation in a lost schoolroom, shutting out the full realism of the Sacrament being administered to her in this room that had grown somehow horrible. They'd got such a careful upbringing in a way, so careful that it was hard now to see what it had all been for, was it just for this? And the terror that brought could be soothed by this chanting in the memory.

> *O oil of olives*
> *mixed with balm*
> *and blessed by the bishop*
> *on Holy Thursday.*

Then it was over, and she'd managed not to realize much, the priest was going away, he'd come again tomorrow.

He was kind, now that she was ill, but she continued to dislike him, their first meeting and clash was deep in her mind and it would never leave it. She had always found her first instinctive reaction to people right, no matter how false somebody's conduct made that first judgement seem for a time it had never been really proved wrong, no matter how successfully she was able to override it with reason or even a late liking.

She tried never to let this priest close. In the confessional she put everything into formula. She didn't let him know any of her thoughts. It was dishonest, though lawfully proper enough. Her thoughts had been with her too long, they had changed themselves too often for her to want to change them now because of another's interpretation of a law big enough to include every positive position of honesty; and if her own truth wasn't within herself she didn't see how it could possibly concern her anyhow. She wanted to be understood, that was the old craving, but was it not an indulgence? How could anyone have time to understand her, they were as

217

full of their own lives as she was of hers; all their lives had to overflow or cripple and die and did it matter where the overflow ran? This priest would have to examine and try to understand what she'd say in the light of his own life, and it could only lead to the wilful agreement of sympathy, or open or silent conflict. He'd want to change her to his view and she'd want to hold her own. The whole of her vital world was in herself, contracting or going outwards to embrace according to the strength and direction of her desire, but it had nothing to do with what some one else thought or felt. She didn't want to struggle and argue, she hadn't blind strength enough for that in years, she wanted to have her own way and be let go it in peace. Now she was losing even that desire.

So few people took on individuality in her mind, and this priest was definitely not one of them. A big tall man in his sixties, as tall as Reegan but not so straight, bloated, a tracery of thread-like purple veins under the red skin of his face. She was detached, she could watch: he was sitting on a chair at the bedside, a priest supposed to be comforting a dying woman; she didn't care. Sometimes the pressure of his talk oppressed her to near craziness, as if she'd been dragged close as inches to the steel singing far away across the lake, and she felt like crying at him for some ease or silence. Mostly she didn't hear what he was saying but agreed with him mechanically as she watched him, his bloated appearance fascinated her most, and she'd think how strange it was how some wore down to skin and bone and others puffed out to burst like a pod in the sun.

The one thing she'd fear if she could care enough was his aggressiveness, when he began to suspect that her total acquiescence wasn't agreement but the evasion it actually was.

"You must pray to Mary, she has the ear of God, she speaks to God for us, we're one of the few nations in the world who understand Her importance. Don't you think we should have great devotion to Mary?" he impressed hotly one evening.

"Yes, of course," she answered wearily.

"There's no of course about it, we should, and that's all," he said.

She went hot with resentment, the instinct to savage him rose and as quickly died. He was simply a person to be avoided if she had a choice in the matter but she didn't care whether she chose or was chosen any more, it was all the same. For a moment a picture of the ridiculous village presbytery, the hideous Virgin Mary blue of doors and windows in the whitewashed walls at the end of the lovely drive of limes, showed itself to her eyes and she wanted to laugh. "Yes. That's quite right," she said. She was able to agree. She'd save herself that much noise.

It was hard enough to accept the reality of her situation; but it was surely the last and hardest thing to accept its interpretations from knaves and active fools and being compelled to live in them as in strait-jackets. To be able to say yes to that intolerant lunacy so as to be able to go your own way without noise or interruption was to accept everything and was hardest of all to do.

A worn and dry craving to see the back of this priest would take possession of her; for Reegan to come from the bog with turf-mould dried in sweat to his face and hands; for them to kneel down about her bed so that she could hear them chant.

> *Mystical Rose,*
> *Pray for us.*
> *Tower of David,*
> *pray for us.*
> *Tower of Ivory,*
> *pray for us.*
> *House of Gold,*
> *pray for us.*
> *Ark of the Covenant,*
> *pray for us.*
> *Gate of Heaven,*
> *pray for us.*
> *Morning Star.*

The rosary had grown into her life: she'd come to love its words, its rhythm, its repetitions, its confident chanting, its eternal mysteries; what it meant didn't matter, whether it meant anything at all or not it gave the last need of her heart release, the need to praise and celebrate, in which everything rejoiced.

She grew worse, she began to sink, though they didn't know when it would end. As she felt herself go she tried to say once to herself, "This is not my life. This is not the way I lived. What's happening now was never part of my life. I have lived in health, not in sickness in death," but suddenly it was too tiring or futile to continue and the resolution was soon lost, as everything was.

Reegan spent most of these May days on the bog, scattering the barrow heaps out into the drying. The weather was dry and hard, white frost at nights, a still low mist white in the morning that couldn't be penetrated as far as the navigation signs at the mouth of the lake from the barrack door; the sun would beat it away before ten and rise into a blazing day, getting quite cold again towards evening. It was the best possible weather for saving turf, and Reegan was on the bog with Sheila and Willie the day she died, Una let stay in the house with Mrs Casey because the illness had reached the stage when some one had to be all the time with her in the bedroom.

She had drowsed through the morning, stirred once to get her dose of drugs, and was breathing heavily when the Angelus rang.

"That was the bell, Willie, wasn't it?" she said to the child.

" 'Twas, Elizabeth," Una answered, and there was noise and smells of Mrs Casey cooking in the kitchen.

"I wasn't sure, all day I seem to hear strange bells ringing in my mind, church bells. It was the bell, wasn't it?"

" 'Twas," the child was growing uneasy.

"Did they come from the bog yet?"

"No, not till evenin', Daddy has a day's monthly leave, they brought bread and bottles of tea in the socks."

"But they were to be back to go to devotions, it grows cold on the bog in the evenings. But that was the first bell, wasn't it?"

"No, 'twas the Angelus, Elizabeth," the child gave a short laugh, though it couldn't be possible that Elizabeth was trying to play tricks with her.

"It's the bell for the Angelus," Elizabeth repeated, obviously trying to understand.

"It's the bell for the Angelus, late no more than usual, twenty past twelve on the clock now," the child said with the faint suggestion of a laugh, the unpunctual ringing of the bells was a local joke.

"But why did you draw the blinds?"

"What blinds?" the child was frightened.

"The blinds of the window."

"No, there's no blinds down, but it'll not be long till it's brighter. The sun'll be round to this side of the house in an hour."

"There's no clouds?"

"No, no," the child said, trying to behave as if everything was usual, but she was stiff with fright. The wide window where she stood was open on the summer, changing corrugations of the breeze on the bright lake and river, glittering points; butterflies, white and rainbow, tossed in the light over the meadows, wild flowers shining out of the green, the sickly rich heaviness of meadowsweet reaching as far as the house.

"No, there's no cloud," the child said, and stood in terror. Elizabeth's head fell slack; the breath began to snore and rattle; her fingers groped at the sheets, the perishing senses trying to find root in something physical; and the child ran calling to Mrs Casey in the kitchen.

After the first shock, the incredulity of the death, the women, as at a wedding, took over: the priest and doctor were sent for, the news broken to Reegan on the bog, the room tidied of its sick litter, a brown habit and whiskey and stout and tobacco and foodstuffs got from the shops at the chapel, the body washed and laid out—the eyes closed with

221

pennies and her brown beads twined through the fingers that were joined on the breast in prayer. Her relatives and the newspapers were notified, and the black mourning diamonds sewn on Reegan's and the children's coats.

Reegan was sent to the town to make the funeral arrangements, and it was the first chance he got to think what had happened since Casey came to the bog with the news. There was such a bustle of activity about the death, and he felt just a puppet in the show. When he got home from the town and undertaker the house was full of people. The wake would last till the rosary was said at midnight; and a few would remain in the room afterwards to keep the early morning vigil, the candles burning close to her dead face while it grew light. All Reegan had to do was stand at the door and shake hands with those offering him their sympathy, answering the customary, "I'm sorry for your trouble, Sergeant," with what grew more and more idiotic to him as the night progressed, "I know that. I know that indeed. Thank you."

The next evening she was coffined and taken to the church where she was received by the priest and left beneath the red sanctuary lamp, surrounded by candles in tall black sticks, till she'd be taken to the graveyard in Eastersnow after High Mass the next day.

Cars crept jerkedly in low gear behind the hearse at the funeral, a few surviving horse-traps that seemed to belong more to museums than the living day followed behind the cars, the bicycles came next, and those who walked were last of all. A funeral's importance was judged by the number of cars behind the hearse and they were counted carefully as they crawled past the shops: Elizabeth had 33 cars at her funeral. The most important funeral ever from the church had 186 cars, it was the record, and labourers hired out for their lives from the religious institutions that reared them to farmers, homeboys, were known to have as few as 5 cars behind their deal coffins, so Elizabeth's funeral with 33 cars was considered neither a disgrace nor a remarkable turnout.

Mullins and Casey rode in the fourth car behind the

hearse, just after the mourning cars, but they had told the driver not to wait for them afterwards, and escaped from the throng about the grave in the first drift-away during the decade of the rosary. They didn't want to face back to the barracks and relatives and last grisly drinks and sighs with Reegan standing silent like a caged animal, they had more than enough of the bustle of death in the last three days.

By the back way, around by the Eastersnow Protestant church, they escaped, this part of the graveyard thinly populated because there were few of any other religions outside Catholicism left in these western districts. Not till the grave scene was shut out of sight by the church did they feel at ease or speak, the way the little whiskey bottle that held the holy water had shivered to pieces on the corner of the bright brown coffin when the priest threw it into the grave and the scraping of the shovel blades against the stones in the clay and the hollow thudding on the coffin boards still too close, and their satisfaction, "It's Elizabeth that's being covered and not me and I'm able to stand in the sun and watch," not able to take the upper hand in their minds till they got the bulk of the stone church between themselves and the grave.

Before the church door was the King-Harman plot, the landowners of the district before the New Ireland had edged them out, the deer parks of their estate split into farms, the great beech walks being gradually cut down, their Nash mansion that once dramatically overlooked the parks and woods on one side and the lake with its islands on the other burned to the ground, and here Casey and Mullins stopped to light cigarettes, Casey's attention attracted by some of the inscriptions on the smaller headstones in a corner of the plot and he read:

Thomas Edward, killed in action in Normandy, 4th August 1944 and was buried in an orchard adjoining the churchyard of Courteil, South of Gaumont.
Capt. Edward Charles, Irish Guards, killed in action 6th

Nov. 1914 at Klein Billebecke near Ypres and has no known grave; greater love hath no man than this that a man lay down his life for his friends.

Chains hanging between low concrete piers girdled the plot, a concrete path ran down its centre to where a pair of great cypress trees rose, one in each corner, and to the right of the path stood the three baronets' headstones, large Celtic crosses in old red sandstone, on each of them two fingers raised from a hand clasping a crown to point skywards with the inscription:

spes tutissima coelis.

"It's easy to see who those gentlemen belonged to," Casey remarked as he read the inscriptions and then he derided as he saw the fingers point to the heavens, "They might get a hell of a land; whoever told them heaven was in that direction anyhow!"

Both of them laughed at the sally, their fear fast going. They gazed a while at the plot, and crossed the stone stile out of the graveyard.

"Though it is up," Mullins said. "They're right in that. It was up Jesus Christ went on Ascension Thursday."

"But how do you know it was that way up?" Casey laughed as he set himself to argue. "The world rotates, it does a full circle every twenty-four hours, in twelve hours it'll be down where Australia is now and it'll be pointin' in the direct opposite direction then."

"It's to Mulloy's we're goin', isn't it?" Mullins halted the argument, but he was not beaten. Mulloy's was a small pub down the Eroona road, out of the way of the mourners who'd return to the village.

"That's where we said, it's a long time since we had a drink on our own, and where there's more than two people you can never get any satisfaction out of talkin'," Casey said.

"To get back where we left off," Mullins said, "in twenty-four hours the earth'll be back where it is now and it'll be still the same direction. I think the Ascension is the important thing."

"But the world rotates round the sun as well," Casey countered and they both squared themselves. It was plainly a problem that'd not allow itself to be solved in a moment, and when they were not putting on a show or face before people they loved few things better than to feel themselves garbed in the seriousness of these philosophical arguments.

When they reached the road they quickened their pace, their speech grew more excited. Away to their right the plains in the summer swept greenly down to the river and village and woods. There was a shimmer of heat in the fields of young oats and the powdery white dust of the road dulled the shine on their boots as they walked, it was the time of year for pints of cider.

8

There's nothing to lose! Nothing to lose! You just go out like a light in the end. And what you've done or didn't do doesn't matter a curse then, wore itself into Reegan's bones in the next months.

He'd won and sold his turf, fulfilled all his contracts, but he hadn't near the money he'd expected to have, the expenses of her last illness and burial eating up most of the profit he had calculated on as well as all her savings, the savings that had meant so much to her now only a pathetic little sum against the flood of bills.

And would he have to knuckle down and grin and bear the police till he died or was forced to retire at sixty, or the children were able to fend for themselves.

"No, no, no," the whisper grew more savage as the autumn wore to winter and the end of another year of his life. "No, no, no! There's nothing to lose! Nothing to lose! You just go out like a light. And what you did or didn't do then doesn't matter a curse, so do what you want, what you want to do, while you've still the time."

It grew and grew as he watched Quirke more. He'd smash him if it was the last thing he did, and he seemed to dog the barracks these days, the other policemen as much as Reegan, with surprise early morning inspections and oral examinations of their knowledge of police duties. It seemed as if he thought he'd hound them into efficiency.

"I can't remember anything I read these days. It just slips through the auld mind, the memory is goin', sir. I had it all off once, sir!" Reegan listened to Mullins near breaking down under examination one early morning.

"But, my good man, haulage vehicles are something that

you should come up against every week," Quirke retorted impatiently. "It shouldn't be even necessary to have a memory, if you had only your eyes open I can't see how you could escape knowing," he said in cold disgust, staring at Mullins's great and sagging corpus. Then, "when have you had your last summons in court?" he asked quietly.

"It's a good while," Mullins tried to bluster. "About a year ago, sir. Nothing ever much happens in this district."

"No, everybody just breaks the law quietly, without any fuss, in broad daylight," Quirke said with heavy sarcasm and then, "Perhaps, you, Sergeant, could illuminate that section of the Road Act for Mr Mullins," he turned to Reegan.

"The Road Traffic Act," Reegan corrected.

"The Road Traffic Act," Quirke said, both of them staring at each other without any veils on their mutual loathing and hatred, and Reegan, who had almost perfect knowledge of duties and regulations, answered in a tone that was calculated to be as blameless on the surface and as insulting as possible in undertone. The examination eventually ended with a scarifying lecture by Quirke, the policemen trooped hotly away to leave Quirke and Reegan alone.

"I've been informed that you've supplied the Convent Laundry and half the town with fuel, Sergeant," Quirke went straight to the attack as soon as they were alone.

"And what if I did?" Reegan stiffened.

"We'll pass that point for the moment. May I ask you this one question, Sergeant? Do you intend to stay long more in the police? Why, Sergeant, are you a policeman anyhow?"

"Is it the regulation answer you want?" Reegan insulted, though well in the grip of the habit of years of discipline that had kept his feelings towards his superiors from erupting into violence.

"Any answer!" Quirke shouted, far the more infuriated.

"To keep from starvin' I suppose," Reegan ground.

"And you don't believe you have a responsibility in the matter? You don't believe you should do a fair job of work

227

for a fair remuneration," Quirke beat with his fist on the patrol book on the table.

"I don't believe anything nor care," Reegan said.

"Well, I'll see that you'll act something at least, I'll see that much, Sergeant."

"You can see what you like!" was Reegan's answer.

Quirke had taken his gloves from the table: he rose and went half-way to the door. He grew quieter to say, "I thought there for a time that you were coming to your senses, and left you alone, but that was no use. Then you had your trouble and I wanted to give you every consideration but that's plainly no use either. Things have passed out of bounds. This station might as well not exist, except as an example in everything that no police station should be. And those men can be led, you're the root——" he was saying when he saw Reegan's eyes look hard as steel, the breath hissing: "You leave my trouble out of this, she's the dead!"

Quirke apologized quickly as he moved towards the door, "Though what I've said stands! I intend to make a serious report. There'll have to be changes."

"There'll have to be changes," Reegan almost bared his teeth to shout as the door closed, and it was to all intents the end of Reegan the policeman. He did no more patrols, rose always late for roll call in the mornings, answered no official letters, and made a complete travesty of the signing in-and-outs, but waiting, not sending in his resignation. The others grew afraid; they had a secret meeting together in the dayroom; and while deciding against reporting him they resolved to attend to their own subordinate duties with blameless care. And they knew that the situation couldn't continue long as it was, soon there would have to be some crash. It was Brennan who was the most indignant of the three, he'd have reported Reegan to make sure of his own safety. "We have a duty to protect ourselves," he said. "The man's gone out of his mind, he doesn't care what happens, and he'll get us the sack as well as himself. We must look out."

"No. I'll not inform on any man," Mullins said.

"No," Casey said too. "We'll just have to see that we do our own jobs properly and then we can't be blamed. No such a thing as reporting though, that'd not be playin' the game, some of us here are a long time under his baton and he reported no man."

"We'll watch our own ends, that's all, but no skunkin'," Mullins said last, and Brennan felt chastised and shamed and angry.

So the next early morning inspection found Mullins and Casey and Brennan lined up the other side of the table before Quirke and their faces and boots and uniform shining clean, but Reegan was still in bed. There was sense of real occasion, and tension; something would have to happen today. It was the children who brought Reegan first news of Quirke's presence.

"Daddy, the Super's car is outside," they had already caught the fear of authority in their voices.

"So he's come," Reegan said, and they were shocked by his casualness; another time the news would have stirred him into some kind of action.

"He's in the dayroom, Daddy!"

"That's all right, don't worry," he said, but there was a shake in the voice; and then Casey pounded upstairs to tap at the bedroom door.

"The Super's down below, Sergeant," he said, the pallid skin as white as ever death would make it. "He wants to know if you're reportin' sick or comin' down."

"Tell him I'm comin' down," Reegan said.

"I'll tell him you're comin' down," Casey wanted it to be confirmed.

"Do."

"Right, Sergeant," Casey shuffled uneasily away as Reegan pulled back the bedclothes and swung his feet out on the floor.

He dressed hurriedly and came downstairs and into the kitchen in his socks, there he laced on his boots, and very quietly got notepaper and envelopes and pen and ink and wrote his resignation. He took much time and when he had

229

the envelope closed, he called Willie and told him to run to post it, now.

"It's finished and done at last," he said to the uncomprehending children, and then went down to the dayroom in a royal state of disorder, unshaven, the hair tousled, the whistle-chain hanging loose, and the tunic wide open on the dirty flannel shirt that was open without collar on the throat.

Both Quirke and the three policemen were in a state of nervous tension when he opened the door; there had been a ridiculous parody of an inspection after Casey's return; their whole minds on Reegan's feet padding downstairs; and what in the name of Christ could he be doing in the kitchen. Quirke was writing when he entered, the three policemen standing in a stupid line the other side of the table, so many red and black inkstains on the bare deal, the official pens and books of foolscap and stampers and pads; seams of dirt in the cracks between the scrubbed boards. Quirke did not look up, he continued writing, as if no one had entered; but Reegan went and leaned against the corner of the table, deliberately jogging it so that Quirke had to take notice before he intended. He surveyed Reegan's appearance and demanded an explanation in as unemotional a tone as he could master. He got none.

"So you have no explanation to offer, Sergeant," he had to say, he'd already lost much of his calm.

All Reegan did was drawl, "No," and lounge more fully on the table.

"Stand to attention, Sergeant!" Quirke shouted, white at the insult, and losing all control.

"Stand yourself," Reegan said in utter contempt.

"I'll have you dismissed! Do you realize that?" Quirke pounded.

"I've resigned, so do you want me to stand to attention, sir," he raised his voice to parody Quirke.

"I'll see you are disciplined. I'll see you get your deserts, you pup," Quirke hardly knew what he said. Reegan moved closer, the mocking mood gone at that last mouthing insult, and the three policemen grew afraid, they knew how dangerous Reegan was.

"No, you can't," and the ring of hatred that came hissing on the voice now even chilled Quirke. "No, you can't. I wore the Sam Browne too, the one time it was dangerous to wear it in this balls of a country. And I wore it to command— men, soldiers, and not to motor round to see if a few harmless poor bastards of policemen would lick me fat arse, while I shit about law and order. And the sight of a belt on somebody else never struck me blind!

"Now get out before I smash you," Reegan ground.

He was dangerous, there could be no doubt, and he'd shocked and overawed the younger officer. Quirke had never been confronted with a situation anything like this: he'd lost sight of whether he should go and report or stand on his authority, and he saw that the line of three across the table would be no use to anyone. He rose with as much dignity as he could keep.

"You're obviously in no condition to listen to reason but you've not heard the last of this, resignation or no resignation," he stumbled.

"I'm tellin' you to get out," Reegan said and crowded him to the door and kicked it shut on his heels.

He was pale as death when he came in to them in the kitchen. They were startled when he spoke but it was only to ask the boy if he had posted the letter. Then he dressed himself properly and went out and round by the window on the high policeman's bicycle and he was away all day, nearly night when he returned to his meal that was spoiled with waiting.

The dayroom door opened as he ate and Mullins ventured up the hallway to tap on the door and wait for Reegan's "Come in."

"I just wandered up," he stated. "A man'd get the willies down in that joint on his own."

He was given a chair at the fire but wasn't easy till he got "Jasus!" out at last. "I never saw the bate of this mornin' in all me life. 'Twas as good as a month's salary. Some of the stations were on the phone already for particulars. Jasus, you have him rightly humped, Sergeant; they'll have to give him an office job in the Depot; this day'll follow him round for the rest of his life."

Reegan was quiet, a sort of bitterness and contempt on the face that leaned towards the fire in the failing light, and then he stared into Mullins's face and said, "It's always easy to make a Cuchulainn outa the other fella, isn't it, John?"

"What? What do you mean, Sergeant?" Mullins ejaculated, either unable or unwilling to understand, a shade of terror on his face.

"No, nothing, don't mind, John," Reegan laughed sharply. "I was only sort of talkin' to meself, you know, jokin'."

The night had come, the scarlets of the religious pictures faded, their glass glittered in the flashes of firelight and there seemed a red scattering of dust from the Sacred Heart lamp before the crib on the mantelpiece. "And is it time to light the lamp yet, Daddy?" the boy's voice ventured.

"Yes," Reegan answered without thought.

He was silent with Mullins, and the silence seemed to absorb itself in the nightly lighting of the paraffin lamp. All the years were over now, and the kitchen was quick and full with movement. The head was unscrewed off the lamp, the charred wicks trimmed, the tin of paraffin and the wide funnel got from the scullery, the smoked globe shone with twisted brown paper, the boy running from the fire to touch the turned-up wicks into flame, and the two girls racing to the windows to drag down the blinds on another night.

"My blind was down the first," they shouted.

"No! My blind was down the first!"

"Wasn't my blind down the first, Guard Mullins?" as the boy adjusted the wicks down to a steady yellow flame and fixed the lamp in its place—one side of the delf on the small white table-cloth.